I0779741

WITHIN THE SHADOWS SERIES
BOOK THREE

POTIONS
AND
PORTALS

AMY NEVILLS

The complete *Within the Shadows* series

Coffee and Fangs

Tooth and Claw

Potions and Portals

CHAPTER ONE

*Arugula, or Hercules semen, gives your spell a boost
or a bite of energy.*

"**M**ove over, you cow." The muffled voice broke through the sleep that felt like it had settled upon Delta just minutes ago. This had to be a joke. A joke or a freaking nightmare.

"What are you talking about, heifer? You have all the pillows and blankets. I had to bring this one in from the sofa." There was no way she was getting out of this bed yet; it was too warm and too soft, even if it was crowded. After the weekend she'd had, she deserved a little peace and quiet. Well, technically the weekend she had a week and a half ago. Had it really been ten days?

Time really does fly when you're having fun.

"Yeah, but you're lying diagonal across the whole bed!" This time, the point was emphasized with a sharp kick to her calf.

Gritting her teeth, Delta fought the urge to kick her sister back. Why in the hell was she still here anyway?

"I thought you were leaving. Aren't house guests like fish or squid or something?"

"I haven't even been here with *you* for three days. I came to spend time with you. Although I didn't know we'd be sharing a bed." Athena punched her head deeper into her pillow, muffling her words, but Delta unfortunately understood what she was saying.

The grating sound of her sister's voice set Delta on edge. Not the way she wanted to start her day and no matter the time, it certainly wasn't time yet to get up. She needed her rest. Or maybe she could swap out her regular tea for coffee. *No one here can tell me I can't have coffee,* Delta thought stubbornly.

"First, you were never invited to visit here, to see me or otherwise. So why would I tell you that there was only one bed available? You happened to be here when I got called out. And apparently, you still happen to be here." Delta needed to nip whatever sisterly plot Athena had in the bud.

To say she was shocked was an understatement when she opened the door and found her sister, as well as a rolling bag, standing on the small porch of Eva Nance's Ohio cottage. As usual, after pushing her way inside despite Delta's objections, Athena seemed to suck the air out of the little home where Delta admittedly was hiding away.

Hands on her hips, Athena shrilly declared the home the cutest place ever. The treacherous house had hummed in approval while Athena explored, running her fingers over the woodwork, laying hands on the walls, and singing her own welcome song to the home.

The call from Sebastian's team, via Oliver, had Delta ready to run out the door without caring what the assignment or the need was. She would have faced a pack of feral vampires if it meant putting some distance between her and any of her relatives—theoretically, of course, since Delta had never laid eyes on a feral vampire and didn't really know the threat level. Still, it was close.

Oliver's request for help couldn't have come at a better time. Although she was his employee, the mission had been, as always, a request, not a demand. Despite his vampire nature, he would never knowingly force someone into danger or a situation they weren't comfortable with. Still, Delta had suspected that it could easily switch to a demand from Sebastian or Oliver if she'd refused to come assist in Ravyn's extraction. The entire event had turned into what Sebastian called a clusterfuck. Delta could handle that, though. She could pivot like no one else. No worries if she was called across the country to help break out vampire royalty and ended up assisting in the capture of a wendigo.

Delta never denied a work request. Either she could handle it, or she would learn from it. Her years with Oliver had taught her to always have a magic bolt bag at the ready, even during a self-imposed sabbatical.

The bag remained filled with the essentials for any magic user, including options for a variety of common spells, healing tonics, blessed candles and gemstones, along with a variety of other herbs and plants she'd found she needed in emergency situations. Once it had been a small, simple pouch, but over the years it had grown into a bag large enough that flying with it as a carry-on item might be questionable. Thankfully, the seriousness of this trip required her to fly private, so there was no need to try to pare down the items to a more flight manageable situation. Her personal hag stone, blessed by her mother, grandmother, and great-grandmother long before her birth, hung around her neck, only to be removed for as long as it took to shower or bathe.

Not quite running out the door—she wasn't that ill-mannered—Delta had instructed Athena to keep the dog snack container filled and the doggie door open until she left. Important enough info that Delta had shot off a text reminder of both items as she boarded the small jet taking her across the country. Athena had officially been promoted from house guest to house sitter. Delta had thought it went without saying that upon her return, Athena could feel free to head on back home.

Delta pulled the blankets covering her face down to look at her sister. Nearly a mirror image of her own face, but simply better. Better. She was the image made from the mold—close, but not quite perfect. Even after a night's sleep, her sister's copper-colored curls hung delicately around her face, not daring to be out of place even after a night of fighting for room in the bed. Without looking, Delta knew that her own curls had frizzed, and she could already feel the rats' nest that had formed on the side of her head while she'd tossed and turned. Athena's porcelain skin had nary a blemish nor freckle, while Delta's held a scatter of freckles across her nose and a hint of sunburn as well from the time in the sun. She'd forgotten to reapply sun protection one time during her time out west. The slight warmth across her forehead made her consider that a hint of red across her nose and cheeks was wistful thinking. Sunburned after going four hours instead of two hours to reapply sunscreen. Damn her pallor.

To this day, Delta found it unbelievable that she was related to her sister at all, or their mother, for that matter. Despite their matching looks, she was the square peg they tried to force into their round hole.

Athena ran a light, cool finger across Delta's cheek, but Delta's sharp look kept her from mentioning the blush of pink, or so she liked to think. "We haven't had a sleepover in years." Athena had dropped the shrill nasal tone she'd adopted sometime in the last few decades. "I've missed this."

"We never had sleepovers," Delta grumbled back. "That was for normal sisters."

"Well, we should have. We should have had sleepovers, done makeovers, and stayed up too late having pillow fights until Mother told us to go to sleep." Athena sounded wistful, as if her being decades older than Delta hadn't stopped this from happening as well.

She wasn't getting into this right now; not ever, in fact. "Mama Hecate wouldn't have been so kind." Delta blinked slowly as she stared into her sister's green eyes, eyes that, of course, matched hers. Only brighter. More expressive.

"What did she do, Sister?" Delta asked softly, half-hoping that her sister would mutter *nothing* and they could move on. Maybe make breakfast together and talk about how much fun it was and how they should do things like this more often.

Then Athena would leave.

Athena sighed deeply, her eyes not giving anything away, but still she pursed her lips. "Nothing more than she ever does, I suppose. Nothing more, nothing less. Except she wants to bring in suitors."

A flash of sadness quickly followed by irritation hit Delta like a fist to the stomach. Athena wasn't supposed to find Mama Hecate unfair or lacking. That was her thing. She roughly pulled her sister's pillow out from under her head. Too surprised to even fight back, Athena let the pillow slip easily free. Nailing her right in the face a bit harder than necessary gave Delta more than a hint of satisfaction. "Here's your pillow fight. You lose. Just ignore her, you're allowed to do that."

Rolling from the bed too quickly for her sister to retaliate, she ordered, "Get dressed, we can make some breakfast." *Before you go…* hung in the air unsaid but hopefully heard by her sister.

Damnation and curse the Mother herself. Delta stared out at the mess in the kitchen. She'd taken a long time in the shower, hopefully using most of the hot water. Not that her sister would complain to her. It really had taken her a long time to comb the snarls free from her hair, even after using the special conditioner she kept at Eva's cottage. Conditioner that was nearly empty, thanks to her sister. How had she managed to use so much in less than two weeks? If Athena wasn't leaving immediately, Delta would need to have a stern talk with her.

The nostalgic little kitchen had been trashed, and Delta knew without a doubt that her sister hadn't done this. It hadn't been pristine when she left, but the newly renovated retro kitchen definitely hadn't looked like *this*.

Chip bags had been ripped open and into pieces. Most of the chips had been eaten, but crumbs littered the floor and counter space. Just before her unexpected departure, Delta had purchased three party-size bags to replace a nearly empty one. *Ugh, regrets.*

A tattered Oreo cookie package mocked her from the center of the floor. Bits of the black-and-white cookies lay strewn across the floor and counters as well. Dammit, she'd been looking forward to munching on those. Apparently, the cookies hadn't been appreciated because it appeared most of the broken pieces would have filled the package back up.

Had the cookies been chewed up and spit out to make the most impact?

The roll of paper towels she kept on the kitchen table had been shredded and left in wet clumps. The amount of dried drool covering the kitchen might have been impressive if Delta didn't have to scrub it up. The chairs were pulled out from the table and one overturned chair, thankfully unbroken, told a story of how the culprit had gotten onto the table. Praise the goddess, he hadn't jumped from the floor; the table might not be unbroken then. The cute ceramic treat bowl that she kept on the counter lay on the floor, smashed into pieces like a disappointed offering, along with the container that held the coffee grounds she didn't even use. The herbs and flowers that she'd hung on a drying board on the counter were ruined, and the board looked broken as well. The remains of the drying plants looked like they'd been chewed up and spit back out. Maybe he'd used the plants as a palate cleanser after tasting the Oreos? Or maybe it was the opposite.

In short, Eva's cute little kitchen that had been remodeled to adorable perfection had been trashed by an angry or bored canine. Delta knew with a sinking feeling that it wouldn't be her sister who cleaned it up. Regardless of where she'd been or what she'd been doing, she was responsible for the place while she squatted in it.

Athena wandered into the kitchen door with a yawn while she scrunched her wet curls into submission. Her eyes grew wide at the mess. "What? This wasn't here last night!" Immediately, her eyes narrowed at Delta. "Did you do this to mess with me?"

"No." Delta closed her eyes, taking a deep breath. Why did her family drive her to want to murder someone? "Remember when I told you multiple times to make sure to fill the treat bowl, and"—she gestured to the now smashed over-sized dog door that had clearly been locked— "keep that door unlocked during the day?"

Exasperated, and more than a bit confused, Athena suspiciously eyed the mess in the kitchen. "I thought you were joking. You don't have a dog. You don't even like dogs, and Eva wouldn't have left a dog with you either. Seriously, you hate dogs."

Any other time, her sister's shocked face would have been amusing, but not today and certainly not for this.

"Hush." Delta waved her sister's words off with sharp frantic motions. "Stop saying that, it's not true," she lied. "Only a monster wouldn't like dogs."

Wrinkling her nose and giving yet another mental sigh, Delta changed gears. "It doesn't matter. It happened, and we need to clean. Maybe we should start with the counters. Make sure to wipe them with bleach. He drools. A lot."

"I thought you were joking! What did this?"

"A hellhound," Delta deadpanned, knowing that blaming the pup was only partially true. Not having treats at the ready and the door open to him when he knew someone was home held the true blame. He couldn't help his nature.

"See this? This is why Mama can't take you seriously. Why no one can! You don't take things seriously and you lie. Fine, whatever, don't tell me."

If Delta rolled her eyes one more time at her sister, they were going to get stuck in the back of her head. Was it worth arguing with Athena to get her to believe her? No, not really. She would be gone soon, and they would all go back to whatever. *Can't believe she's still here anyway*, Delta added savagely, finding it difficult to believe the princess had been set free for this long.

With a deep sigh and a small prayer to the goddess, Delta grabbed a broom and began vigorously, almost angrily, sweeping the debris off the counters and the table right onto the floor. "Grab a trash bag and start dumping it in; this is your mess, and you should help."

Dutifully, Athena began scooping the mess into a bag, while trying to not actually touch anything. Delta noticed with annoyance that her sister seemed to be mostly pushing things around and not helping. "Goddess, grab some gloves from the second drawer over there or we'll be here all day. Scoop it into a dustpan and dump it."

Wordlessly, Athena complied, but Delta knew no one spoke to Athena like that, and she most definitely didn't have to clean up messes—her own or not.

"Delta, why aren't we closer?"

Of course, the silence couldn't last. That was too

much to hope for. But at least her sister had dropped that nasal, high-pitched voice. For whatever reason, she thought it made her sound regal, but really the grating voice made Delta want to knock herself out.

"Athena, you know why. Don't act like you don't know." Hecate had done everything in her power to make her daughters see each other as rivals rather than sisters. If they saw each other as sisters, there might be some compassion. They'd been raised not to see each other as sisters, and pretending like they weren't almost made it true in the eyes of the coven.

Her sister wasn't done yet, of course she wasn't. When you're the heir to the throne, things are only dropped when you want them to be. But Delta wasn't one of her suck-up vassals.

"When you were born, I was so happy. I had the sister I'd always wanted. Everyone had always told me that I'd never have a sister, but I prayed and prayed, and the goddess granted my prayers. You were squalling and crying, and Mother didn't even go check on you. Every time I tried to see you, your nurse would push me out. 'Nothing to see here, girl,' she would tell me. But finally, I made it to you. You were so red in the face from all the crying. Hiccupping and gasping for breath. I laid a single finger on your cheek, a bit afraid that you would destroy me like the other coven members claimed. But you didn't. You stopped crying. So, I touched your head. Hair that matched mine. Still hiccupping, but your screams stopped, and you looked up at me with these big green eyes. It was like you saw me, truly saw me. You grabbed my finger, and you giggled as you shook it. And I loved you; I've loved you from that moment on. Even when the nurse swatted me away and told Mama about it, I still loved you."

With glove-clad hands, Athena worked meticulously, scooping up the mess the annoyed hellhound pup had left behind, not meeting Delta's shocked expression.

"You're using way too many paper towels for that small of a mess." Delta barely recognized her sharp tone as Athena attempted to use too many of the few remaining paper towels to scoop up the broken eggs. What else could she say?

The damn pup hadn't even eaten most or any of the mess. More of a temper tantrum since his favorite treats were in the pantry. Or annoyance at being locked out of the house, although he could easily pop in and out without using the flippin' dog door. It was completely unnecessary to destroy the door.

Ah well, it was a small price to pay for enjoying the use of Eva's cottage and soaking in its generational earth magic. Eva was sitting on a gold mine; witches would pay to stay here and recharge in the little home that hummed with the magic. However, despite her commandeering the cottage in Eva's absence, Delta drew the line at using Eva's bedroom, which was why she'd ended up sharing a bed with her sister. Her sister, who should be gone by now.

Athena continued, as if Delta wasn't purposefully

ignoring her words. "Last night was the first night we shared a bed like sisters. The first time we had a sleepover. Most sisters have sleepovers at some point when they're younger. We never did."

"It won't happen again." Short and to the point. Why was Athena bringing this up now? "Water under the bridge and all that. We're too old to wish things had been different." It seemed fitting to spell out the adage to her sister.

"That's not what I meant. What I meant…" Athena paused. "What I mean to say is that I can force the vote. I think—I know—I have enough votes. I can force Mother to take the role of the Crone. When I ascend to Priestess, you can be the Maiden."

Goddess, this was blasphemy. Did Athena really mean this or was she making up shit as she went along? "It doesn't work that way, Athena, and you know it. Wishing it worked that way doesn't make it true." It hurt to bite the words off to her sister, but this was dangerous thinking. Their mother had drilled into Delta's head since she was old enough to understand that simply by existing, she put her sister in danger. If she held any love for her, she would always and forever keep her distance. Athena's logic wasn't exactly sound either. Yes, each coven needed a Priestess, a Maiden, and a Crone, but the Priestess was also Mother. Mother Hecate wasn't ready to ascend to the roll of Crone, and a Maiden couldn't just be appointed.

Mother, Maiden, and Crone. Denying that also

didn't make it less true. Athena couldn't step into the Priestess role until she embraced all parts of it fully. And Delta? Delta would never be the Maiden. "Maybe check out some of those suitors Mother wants to bring by. Maybe that'll get things rolling." Mentally, Delta snorted at the idea. First, who in the hell had suitors now days, and second, she could only imagine who her mother might decide was ideal.

Athena ignored the suggestions; apparently, even she hadn't sunk to that level of desperation. She continued to smear the eggs around in circles with the paper towels, as she lamely attempted to shift the conversation. "Where did you go so quickly? What does Oliver have you doing? You're safe, aren't you?" Apparently, talking about potential "suitors" was off the table.

"Oh yeah, absolutely safe. I had a call to go to California for a hookup. Some guy I play *Legend and Shields* with challenged me to a sex-off. You know, who can get the other off more times in a twenty-four-hour period?" With a wave of her hand, she added, "You know how it is. Took a couple of rounds, so I was gone longer than I planned. Haha, he won," she lied, "but really, who's the real winner?" Was adding a crude hand gesture too much? "Bone Town, baby."

"Gross, Delta. You're a daughter of a high priestess. You should be better than that."

Yup, the hand gesture was probably too much. But apparently, this was more believable than a hellhound visiting the cottage. "Well, there it is. No surprise, really. It was just a matter of time."

"There what is?" Puzzled, Athena looked at her like she'd grown a third eye, and not the good kind. She really didn't see a problem, did she? Of course, Athena wouldn't.

"Mama Hecate. You sound exactly like her when you talk like that. She would be so proud." Sanctimonious witch, as if she hadn't gone and gotten herself pregnant with a second daughter by some unknown mage during a trip around Europe several decades ago.

It took a long time to finish the cleaning even with the two of them working, perhaps because Delta had to either coach Athena on how to clean correctly or subtly follow behind her and clean it herself. The final act was beating the dog door back into the back door with a meat mallet. There was probably a hammer around somewhere, but this worked as well, if not better, Delta considered with satisfaction. Thankfully, the rambunctious hellhound pup had left the herbs for her tea alone. Three rows of them still hung across the wide window above the sink. Delta had no doubt that if he'd wanted to, he would have ripped them to shreds. He also hadn't disturbed the already prepared spices; he knew how much her tea meant to her. Oreos aside, apparently his tantrum wasn't vindictive as much as it was messy.

Cleaning complete, Athena stood with hands on her hips, overlooking their work in weird, proud satisfaction.

Mentally sighing, Delta opted not to remind her that the mess was her fault to begin with. Pulling out her phone, she tapped out an emergency order to get the salmon and chicken large dog treats delivered. Despite absolutely knowing she'd left a full bag before requesting Athena leave the treats open, she couldn't find a single treat in the house. Clearly, opening pantry doors wasn't beyond the pup's skill set either. Basically, despite his tantrum, he could have magicked himself into the house and gotten the treats without destroying the place. *That hound made a choice.* Perhaps she would start giving him one treat instead of two, if he was going to be so spoiled.

Looping the dog door open, she reminded Athena, "This door is the first thing to open in the morning and the last to close at night. If you're not here, it's fine to leave it open or closed, but if you're here it must be open.

"Nope." Delta held up a hand, determined to cut off any objections her sister would raise. "I don't care what you think, that's the rules. Not that it matters; I'm guessing you need to be getting back soon," she added hopefully. Not too obvious, was it? Who cared.

"Not at all," Athena chirped, incredibly cheerful for someone who had spent a morning cleaning up after a hellhound tantrum. "I'm taking a sabbatical too." She aimed a pretty smile at her sister, and Delta wanted to smack it off her face.

No, no, no, no, no!

"You can't do that. *I'm* taking a sabbatical." Delta could feel her eyebrows reaching toward her forehead. Rubbing her head, she attempted to head off the ache behind her eyes. This couldn't be happening.

"Right, you inspired me. If you can take one, so can I," Athena continued, as if Delta wasn't murdering her with her eyes. "How better than together with my sister?"

"That's not at all how a sabbatical works."

"Says who? You aren't the boss of sabbaticals," Athena shot back, her own perfectly arched eyebrows raised in disbelief. "You left so quickly when I got here. Apparently, for some booty call. Rude."

"It's rude to come into someone's home and start squatting," Delta argued, narrowing her eyes at her sister and ignoring the fact that that was exactly what she'd done. Naturally, it wasn't the same at all.

"I didn't get a chance to tell you, because you left so quickly," Athena repeated, "but Eva is encouraging the use of her cottage. She's back with Oliver in the States for a few weeks. She didn't realize how much the cottage needed magic until Mother explained things."

It was true. The cottage had been built on magic, but it had been more than a decade since a witch had lived here. The home was thriving after having a witch in residence to give and receive magic from. While her sister's offer to add magic to the home might be real, Delta felt more than a little guilt that she herself only wanted to bask in the peaceful magic in the home.

Sure, that meant the house also got to benefit from her magic being present, but she stayed only because of the peace the house brought her. Staying in the home was like dunking in a magical stream.

If Eva said it was fine, then Delta couldn't argue. Well, she could argue but wouldn't; doing so was futile and childish. Maybe it was time for her to move on anyway. On the other hand, she considered suspiciously, if Athena had mentioned the open invite, they most likely wouldn't have shared the bed last night. An open invite meant all the bedrooms and beds were available. Had that witch waited to announce the open door until after they were forced to spend the night together in close quarters? It was official: she hated her sister.

CHAPTER TWO

Black hellebore, the poisonousness Christmas rose, is considered so powerful that its presence can drive evil spirits out of a home.

"It's so cold," the boy mumbled for the third time since they'd begun their walk down the dark road. "Is it always this cold in the north?"

"Aye, but we're not that far north and it's not that cold yet." Malthazar had explained this to his young charge already, but the five-year-old couldn't seem to wrap his mind around the concept that this mild weather wasn't a biting cold. In his short-sleeved, light-weight pajama set, the child admittedly wasn't dressed for this trip, but they seldom were.

"Mama didn't say it would be cold were I was going. She said it was always warm." The boy talked a lot about what his mama said and did, but he didn't ask why she wasn't making this journey with them.

I'll bet she did, Malth though bitterly. *Probably told him he would get stories and tucked in at night as well.* Clearing his throat, he reminded the boy, "Things got changed around, but it won't always be cold." Even though fifty degrees wasn't *that* cold, he fought his body's natural urge to shiver as well. His perception of cold wasn't normal either, but growing up in a sweltering wasteland where the ground could burn through your shoes to blister your feet sort of messed it up. Not quite the same as Julian's experience in his few short years living in Florida. Thank the gods, the boy would never experience true arid scorched earth beneath his feet. For a moment, he could feel the dry heat filling his lungs, drawing all the water from his body at the same time. Fighting against the memory, he focused on what he could see: the boy at his side. What he could feel: the cool night's temperature on his face and hands. What he could hear: an owl hooting, the screech of a small rodent, the sound of their feet lightly striking the pavement.

"We'll be warm enough soon," Malth promised him, once again checking to see if his phone had reconnected to the system. When he traveled through space and dimensions, it took his phone a bit of time to catch up. It would eventually, and as soon as it did, he would order them a car for pickup for the rest of the trek. They were on the right path, and it wouldn't be much longer. "When we get a car, you can rest and be warm. You've done well today, little one."

Not for the first time, he cursed the magic that limited him to a single portal, but at the same time, he was thankful that the jump had taken him at least halfway across the country. He could be mistaken, and he rarely was, but he thought they were somewhere in the Midwest. Not too far north—it wasn't cold enough yet—but for sure somewhere like Indiana or Illinois.

The boy stumbled, his slipper clad feet having little traction as they didn't hug his feet like tennis shoes would. The child didn't have much more in him.

Reaching down, Malth pulled the child up into his arms with a sigh. He didn't like having to get too close to his charges. In past years, he'd learned to harden his heart against them. In truth, it was the only way he'd been able to survive those years. Nowadays, he'd learned it made it that much harder for them to say goodbye. But honestly, the past had taught him that attachments were an entirely new set of problems; easier to avoid them all together. What he did was enough. No need to coddle them as well.

But Julian had begun to stumble more often and drag behind despite their already slow pace. Carrying him was simpler. Within seconds, the boy was dead weight in his arms as he snuggled against Malth, draining him of his body's heat.

Closing his eyes and opening his senses, Malth waited for the pull that told him he was heading in the right direction. Although it had only been a few minutes since he'd last checked and the road before them hadn't changed, habit forced him to continually reevaluate.

The car that picked them up was warm, almost

uncomfortably warm to Malth after the chilled night air. But he didn't suggest to the driver to turn it down. The boy still slept, and the warmth ensured he would remain quiet. No point in offering any suspicion to the placid driver, who kept yawning while his podcast droned on. Despite the heat, Malth readjusted his stocking cap, making sure it was pulled tightly down to his ears. He knew that even if the hat was removed, it was doubtful that the obtuse driver would notice the tiny nubs on his head. But horns had a way of drawing attention to a person, and it was easier to remain less noticeable when he wasn't sporting them. Humans often didn't notice the bits; they saw what they wanted to see. But a particularly observant one or another supernatural creature surely would, and he was trying to cut down on any unnecessary notice as well as conversations.

"This is it, innit?" The driver stopped in front of a cottage at the end of a darkened street. Malth hadn't even noticed they'd come to the far edge of the small town.

"Sure is," Malthazar answered, as he tried to ascertain why this place had been picked as a safe house. But if the magic brought them here, then this unassuming little cottage was their haven for the night.

Knocking on the door on the brightly lit cottage didn't appear to immediately rouse its residents to open to them. Malth carefully tried the handle. Locked. Another sharp knock followed rapidly by another and another. Sliding Julian down to stand on his own two feet allowed Malth to keep both hands at the ready. Here on the porch, he could feel the magic of the place stretch around them, rushing about and over them as if testing their intentions. Not malevolent at all, but curious magic poking and prodding a bit. Still, he felt better having his hands free and fought the urge to pull his stone from his pocket and roll it around in his hand.

"Malth, is anyone home?" the high, sweet voice asked him innocently, the boy once again shivering against the cold now that he was separated from his personal heater.

"Aye, Julian, we're expected." Sort of. The magic talisman hanging around his neck, as well as the feeling deep in his gut, had brought them here. Unfortunately, he'd learned over the years that it didn't necessarily mean that the occupants expected them. But they would be welcome. The magic never steered him wrong; even the most surprised occupants allowed them sanctuary.

After a long moment and still no answer to their knock, Malthazar began wondering if there was anyone inside. The lit-up cottage could be sitting empty but awaiting them. As he raised his fist to knock harder, the door clicked and smoothly slid open.

No one stood on the other side. The cozy-looking living area twinkled with lights while comfortable afghans and pillows lay haphazardly across the extra-long sofa, as if someone had been lying on them and had gotten up for a moment. Another invitingly fuzzy blanket hung across a wide-armed chair, begging to be curled up on.

"Lo?" he called out. Damn, he was bone tired. Things hadn't gone as effortlessly as he'd hoped, and the jumping around had worn him out. In fact, he still wasn't completely sure what state they were in. Opening the car app and inputting the address had been done on autopilot or, technically, a magical connection that overrode his conscience and entered the information with little need for him to actually have the knowledge. Malthazar had learned long ago to accept the magical override and go with it. If he attempted to focus too long on what path the magic took him, it tended to make things fuzzier. Anyway, knowing where the destination was sooner rather than later didn't really affect the outcome of things.

In a better rested state, he might have checked the driver's plates, matching it to the app and gaining a bit of information that way. Long ago, Malth had learned it was better to not ask aloud where he was when he landed. That tended to upset people, especially when one had a child in tow.

"Can we go in?" the boy asked breathlessly, even as he took a step toward the threshold, clearly eager to cross into the warmth.

"Hold up, boy," Malth warned, as he tried to peer deeper into the room. It never hurt to be too cautious. Even if the magic never led him astray, there was a first time for everything. The older home had closed doors across the room as well as a short hallway that led into darkness. No open floor plan for this old beauty. She had doorways with doors that closed and blocked the other rooms as well as their occupants from view.

All was quiet, warm, and welcoming.

However, the moment the two of them stepped into the cozy front room, a door across the way swung open and chaos followed. Flashes of energy, squeals that made Julian cover his ears, followed by laughter that seemed to run up and down his spine wrapped around the room. At first, the women didn't see them in their doorway. Why would they? Most people weren't expecting others to show up and walk into their home, especially if the door had been locked, as he suspected.

Both women were redheads, with bright hair that shone like the sun and wild curls that twisted this way and that way as it fell down their backs. The taller of the two—barely taller—

pushed her way through the doorway first, turning as if listening to something the other had said. Her untamed curls hid her face. Holding an open can of frosting in one hand and a spoon in the other, she seemed to be threatening the other woman. Malth found himself inexplicably curious as to what she might be saying.

The second woman through the door noticed the two of them first. Her laughing face froze, and then her smile dropped as she laid eyes on the two. "Delta…" she warned the first, who turned to see what had startled her.

Malth's stomach dropped, as his heart simultaneously skipped a beat. Clearly the two were sisters, could nearly be twins. But the difference between the two was night and day. Malth could have passed the shorter of the two on the street without even noticing her. But the one called Delta stared at him wide-eyed and open-mouthed, as if she'd cut off her words mid-sentence. Math couldn't catch his breath, but it wasn't the memory of dry heat choking him this time. Looking at the woman was like looking into the sun after a snow-covered night. Her curls were as manic in the front and even from across the room, he could see a perfect spatter of freckles splashed across her otherwise ivory face.

Sticking her spoon defiantly into the frosting while she narrowed her eyes at him, she seemed to consider the two as she glanced up and down. Scooping the spoon deeply into the can, she blinked several times before popping the now full spoon of frosting in her mouth. She grumbled words with her full mouth, "What the fff…"

"Delta, hush, there's a child present," the other chastised.

Not twins, then. That was older sister energy.

"Ma'am," Malth began, but he was interrupted by a small voice exclaiming,

"My mama says you can't eat frosting out of the can like that."

Oh, jeez, kid.

"Well, your mama is a—" This time the elder sister elbowed her. Hard. Still, neither woman moved forward.

"Julian," he said sharply before softening his tone, "we don't take our rules into other homes and impose them."

"What's pose them mean?"

"It means why the fuuuu… are you in my house?" Delta managed to correct her own language that time without a sharp look or word.

The door behind them slammed shut sharply, as if offended by the cold air being let inside. The lock shot into place with a resounding *click*, settling the matter itself. The four of them turned their eyes to look at the door. The house had spoken.

"That's new," the unnamed sister droned, not completely sounding surprised by the event.

Witches. They had to be witches.

Delta sighed. "Welp, guess that means you're supposed to be here, although I don't know why exactly you are."

"I'm assuming since I was brought here, it's safe to talk freely," Malthazar began, with no intention of speaking too freely. He paused, waiting for either woman to interrupt. Surprisingly, they didn't, so he continued, still cautious as he felt out the situation. "My magic brought me here, us here. It marked it as a safe place. Although," he admitted, looking around, "I don't exactly know where *here* is." With as magical as the house felt, he assumed the women were connected

27

to the world he knew. If he was wrong, well, he could call in a favor to the vampire who owed him more than one for a short and sweet memory wipe.

"Ohio," Delta shot out with a wrinkle of her nose and more than a hint of snark, before licking the frosting from her spoon. She eyed him suspiciously. "Oddly enough, it does, in fact, exist."

Malth wasn't sure how he was expected to respond to that. Of course, Ohio existed, although he didn't think he'd been there or here before. Nodding, he said, "Yes, of course."

The older sister peeked around, eyeing them curiously but not fearfully. Malth realized in that moment that Delta had subtly maneuvered to put herself more in front of her sister and between the two of them. Interesting.

"Where are you from, if you don't know where you are?" the unnamed, protected sister asked in a nasally, high-pitched voice. Strange how the few words she'd spoken before didn't seem to grate on him as much as her voice did now.

Julian took this moment to remember his manners. "Mama says I'm from hell and that the devil's my daddy and he's going to take me home soon."

The women's mouths simultaneously dropped open and Malth mentally groaned. Couldn't the boy stick with critiquing their eating habits? Then, at the same time, their eyes shot to him with a shocked, fiery look.

"No, no, no." He waved his hands between

himself and Julian. "I am NOT his daddy, his father. I'm here for completely the opposite reason." He didn't want all that anger directed at him.

Pulling her spoon out of her mouth once again, Delta began talking around a mouthful of frosting. "What the…"

Could she swallow between bites or maybe stop eating while they got things settled? Thanks to Julian, it appeared he may have to explain a hint more than he'd originally planned. Generally, the less people knew the better, plus that meant less talking for him.

"Whoa, enough of that." Pushing around her little sister, the bossy one gestured invitingly toward Julian. "Come here. Clearly the house invited you in, and you look like you could eat. I'm sure this one"—she gestured with a thumb toward Delta and scoffed in her shrill voice—"has some pizza rolls and chips. Probably even soda. I'll bet you both like a lot of the same food." She held out a hand, even as her sister stuck an arm out to keep her from moving too close.

"There. Are. No. Chips. Remember?" Delta bit off the words, oddly angry, it appeared, at not having some of the bagged snack potatoes.

Julian seemed to consider the offer and looked between the three of them before nodding in agreement and softly admitting, "Sure, I could eat, and it's okay if you don't have chips. Don't wanna be no trouble," he added politely as he stepped farther into the room.

"Julian, shoes." Malth didn't want to frighten or

embarrass the boy, so he kept his voice low and quiet. Julian walked out of his slippers without missing a step toward the offer of food. Thankfully, the precocious child hadn't argued shoes versus slippers versus inside and outside. "And no soda for the boy, please." Who would give a child soda, especially this late at night?

Once the two cleared the door that led to the kitchen, he began trying to explain his presence a bit better.

"Delta…" Malth dropped his voice to the same tone he used when approaching skittish animals and kids, determined not to set the already untrusting female over the edge.

"Wait, how do you know my name?" she shot out dubiously.

Mentally, he groaned; already a misstep. Delta clearly wasn't going to make this easy, but he suspected nothing about the woman would ever be called easy.

"Your sister said it," he stated, pausing to wait before he attempted to move on, letting his answer settle in. Even as unbelieving as she was, he knew that his answer made sense. Delta just needed to see that.

"How…"

Malth knew the look he shot at her was exasperated, but seriously. Generally, his charges took him at his word. Explaining his every move was going to get old quickly, no matter how much he wanted to spend time near the redhead.

"Oh yeah, of course." She muttered with a bit of chagrin pointing to her hair, "Yeah, all this is kind of a giveaway."

"My young charge is Julian."

"Charge? Are you, like, his guardian or babysitter?" Delta's eyes narrowed suspiciously, as if she hadn't been the one to interrupt his introductions and explanations. Distrusting might be her default setting; if so, this was going to take a long time.

Rubbing his eyes, trying to relieve some tension, did little. Damn, he needed sleep.

"I'm Malthazar," he continued. Maybe he should suggest she save all questions for the end.

"Oh wait, shit! You're Malthazar? Malth?" At his words, her entire demeanor changed as her face lit up and her eyes widened in some sort of excitement. Pointing to herself, she blurted, "I'm Delta." She followed up with nodding eagerly, as if they hadn't already covered her part of the introduction.

Confused, Malth scrunched his face up as he considered her words. Before he could respond, the tiny redheaded ball of energy crossed the space between them, grabbing his hand and shaking it vigorously in greeting. She excitedly continued the exaggerated greeting as she backed up, pulling him deeper into the room with each step.

"Sit, sit," she invited him, gesturing toward either the long sofa or the wide armchair. "I'm Delta." She pointed at herself repeatedly, somehow expecting this to mean something to him.

"Well, yes, but I still don't—"

"I work for Oliver. Oliver Patrick. You're partners or work together or something. To be honest, I've never been sure what your relationship is." She continued speaking so fast her words nearly ran together. "Oliver isn't always exactly forthcoming, and I haven't found..." She paused as she considered her next words.

Hmmm, Delta seemed to be a little snoop, and if she admitted that, well... "Wait, Delta? Oliver's witch Delta?" Things began to turn and finally clicked into place.

"Yes, yes, not exactly his, but you know..." Her head bobbed up and down as she beamed at him. "We've spoken on the phone, and I know you helped with Eva's rescue. I was there too, but somewhere else." With another wild gesture, she waved all of it off. "Of course, Eva has opened her home for visitors. That must have included you, or your magic must have known the invitation." Delta pushed the nest of blankets and pillows off the sofa, then knocked them aside with her foot, before gesturing toward it.

"Yes." Malth nodded in agreement, as he took the offered seat, nearly afraid to do otherwise. "She's my sister. If she opened it up, it would include me." His magic had brought him to a new safe place. As always, it hadn't done him wrong. For whatever reason, this was where he and Julian were meant to be for at least the night up to a few days.

"Sister? I did hear something about that. I guess,

how are you?" Delta blushed softly, the color running prettily up her neck into her cheeks. "I'm so sorry, sometimes I don't stop. My mother says it's one of my worst traits."

"Yes, sister," Malth offered gruffly, lowering his voice and knowing he should explain, but not sure how. "Not as though we share the same father, but our father or grandfather could be of the same lineage. We're siblings under the demon hood that spawned us." He hated explaining that he was a half- demon. Even though the other half was witch, the witches looked at him suspiciously. His demon brethren would most likely kill him on sight before recognizing any sort of equal relationship. Family reunions clearly were impossible.

"Oh, of course, of course. I'm so sorry for being blunt. I'm afraid I don't have any excuse. I'm terrible about shutting my mouth, but truly, I'm working on it." Delta topped off the admission with a sincere smile.

She was working on no such thing, Malth suspected, and if his memory served him correctly, she didn't apologize for words or actions. Assuming, of course, that Oliver's version of Delta was truthful. Oliver had little patience for such things, and he'd often referred to Delta as a child. There was absolutely nothing childlike about the woman who sat before him, bubbling out words that would usually drown him. Curiously, he didn't want her to stop talking.

"She is not!" her sister shouted from the other

room, confirming what he'd already determined. Obviously, caring for Julian wasn't taking up the sister's full attention. "She doesn't give a craaa-damn." Interesting, the shrill tone was gone while she tattled on her sister.

Delta looked up at the ceiling before turning her focus back to Malth. Pressing her lips together, she lowered her voice. "Please ignore my sister. She's feeling unwell today." She followed this up with a smile so sweet that Malthazar found himself nodding along in agreement.

Unable to look away from her pert mouth and without thinking, he returned the smile. Smiling? Since when did he smile at witches? Unless it was a sardonic smile followed by the promise of a quick death for their deeds. This entire situation should be making him feel uncomfortable, but Malth found he wanted to lean in closer to Delta, wrap her hair in his fingers as he untwisted a curl.

Were those lips as soft as they looked? If he kissed her, would she stop talking or attempt to keep a conversation going? He dropped his smile as quickly as he'd given it. What game was he playing at? Or was this all her? Could this woman, who claimed to be Delta, bewitch him so easily? Was this a game she played?

There shouldn't even be a game; he was on a mission. It had been too long since he'd been with a woman, and he shouldn't be smiling at this one. His body didn't seem to care that the woman across from him should clearly be off-limits due to her connection to Oliver and, well, she was a witch, obviously. Being with a witch would bring nothing but trouble. Hooking up with her, even for a night, could be catastrophic even if their paths never crossed again.

"I'm sorry," Malth told her. "I missed your sister's name," he added politely. There had been no introduction, but he wanted to quit thinking of her as "the other redhead."

"Oh yes, of course." With an eye roll, glorious green eyes he could get lost in, she said, "My elder sister Athena, Maiden of the Midwest and Greater Northern Regions, Heir of the High Priestess Hecate."

"He doesn't care about all that; he's not a witch," Athena called from the kitchen. "Just call me Athena."

Malth considered how she could hear everything so clearly from the kitchen, when neither woman had heard him pound on the door. As for his heritage, he wasn't about to get into that history with someone he'd just met.

Delta took another vigorous bite of frosting and rolled her eyes toward the doorway.

"I wasn't done yet," she retorted with an edge that didn't quite seem to be still all in fun. "I know how important labels are to you and Mother." Turning her focus back on the frosting in hand, she stirred it vigorously, appearing angry at the sweet treat.

"Malth… Can I call you Malth?" she asked between bites of frosting. Delta now had a creamy chunk of pink frosting sitting at the edge of her lips.

"Sure," he agreed. Honestly, he didn't care. As soon as the magic led him, he and Julian would be out of the house. He wished he'd chosen to sit in the armchair. Sitting on the sofa had been an invitation for her to set next to him, and that didn't seem wise tonight. Like Julian, he was exhausted and couldn't trust his own judgment in his current state. That state? Apparently horny. Exhausted and horny. Not a good combination to have when temptation dangled so close.

"Wonderful, Malth." She beamed like he'd done something wonderful. "After all, we are co-workers, of sorts."

Oh yes, because she thought he worked for Oliver. He didn't. Oliver assisted him with his quest, and they'd become friends over the years. Or had they been friends first and then Oliver began helping? Strange how he couldn't remember which happened first now, he mused. But yes, co-workers. Co-workers couldn't fuck, could they? Damn, they weren't really co-workers. Wait, Oliver. They were talking about Oliver, or should he be thinking about Oliver?

Athena stuck her head out the kitchen door, hissing, "Did you even feed this child? He's starving, and I don't think we have any more pizza rolls."

"Of course I did," Malth lied, indignant. They'd been on the run, and he'd offered beef jerky to the kid, who had, in fact, turned up his nose at it. Saving the boy from a lifetime of pain and suffering seemed a bit more important than food. "That's what kids do—they eat." Someone had told him that once, but he couldn't remember who.

Malthazar's job was to pick up the kid, run and hide with the kid, and then stash him in a safe place until he could be picked up by someone else. Sometimes, he took his charges to their final destination, but ultimately, he was a pickup and delivery guy. Basically. His time with any child would be short and to the point, no time to trade favorite snack information. He fixed food when he could, and they would either eat it or not eat it. None were very picky, but all were scared, so it could be a crap shoot if they ate before their final destination. Food had never been the priority.

"There's more in the freezer on the porch," Delta called back, scraping the side of the frosting can with her spoon, the wayward bit of frosting still on her face. She took another bite before asking innocently, "Should we contact the boy's mother? She must be worried about him."

"No!" Malth shouted, making Delta startle with a spoonful of frosting mid-air. Lowering his voice, he explained, "Please, no. I would appreciate it if you didn't tell *anyone* the boy or I are here, or were here when we leave."

Delta's forehead wrinkled up in suspicion, her eyes narrowing as she considered his answer. Was she kidding? He'd rescued this child from his mother. No way in hell—pun intended—was he going to let her know where Julian was. Not that she was in any position to come get him. Another thing he didn't want to exactly spell out. It was so much simpler when the safe houses were stocked, but empty of people.

"Oh, you're not leaving tonight, are you? You two look exhausted. You need to at least stay the night. Please."

Damnation, he wished she'd made the invitation in a different way, but the look on her face didn't seem like she was inviting him to sleep with her. Fisting his hands on his thighs, he swore to himself that after this drop-off was done, he was going to go looking for a fight and a fuck. Maybe multiple fights and fucks, if time allowed.

His internal magic compass stayed quiet. The little voice that demanded things of him like "go" and "run now" had nothing to say either. They were definitely staying the night, and what a long night it would be.

CHAPTER THREE

Caraway fed to animals keeps them from straying, and perhaps the same could be done for a faithless husband.

*H*oly goddess, Malth was gorgeous. Thank the goddess that Athena had volunteered to feed the boy. Clearly, he needed it, but then Delta wouldn't be sitting across from this honey-colored beast of a man. Laying eyes on him coming through the door should have scared her, but all she could do was marvel at the height and size of the man. So, this was Malthazar?

Oliver had been holding out on her. Clearly, she needed to talk to him about keeping his tall, gorgeous friends hidden away from her. On the other hand, Delta was acutely aware that Oliver kept everyone he knew away from her. Mostly anyway. It was only need that had connected her with Eva, and she was certain Oliver had regretted that decision a time or two.

Delta continued scooping frosting into her mouth, aware that she looked like a crazed crone, but she simply couldn't stop or she might blurt out the worst of things. Things like, *Can I touch you? Every part of you? Spend the night? In my room… if I can get my sister to leave the bed.*

Athena walked back out with the now smiling but still sleepy boy. Julian, Malth had called him.

"You're out of pizza rolls now, sorry," Athena dryly told her, not sounding sorry at all. "Tomorrow, we can feed you something better." She patted Julian, whose eyes were growing heavy after the food and his adventures—whatever those adventures had been.

That bitch wasn't sorry. Since she'd been here, all she'd done was complain about the food Delta ate and how there wasn't anything worth eating in the house. Seemingly, Athena had forgotten that she'd happily been eating Delta's groceries the entire time she was gone. Any of the food the cow hadn't eaten, the hellhound had destroyed. Sure, Delta mourned the chips, but damnation, she'd gotten the fixings for one hell of a salad.

Athena complained a lot for a girl who hadn't been invited nor done anything like grocery shop. On the other hand, had Athena eaten all of Delta's groceries or had the hellhound really destroyed them all? Ungrateful witch! Delta had to arrange another grocery order to be delivered, and she ignored anything Athena suggested and even opted out of her own usual order of partially healthy items if Athena suggested it. She wanted a piece of fruit so badly she would kill for it, but she also didn't want to have anything in the house that might encourage Athena to stay. Although to be honest, it hadn't been too horrible. Not that she would admit that even under torture.

It had taken the past two days to get Athena to grab a spoon and share the frosting tub with her. Delta had teased and provoked her sister until Athena finally agreed they could share the snack. Guiltily, Delta looked down at the now empty tub. *Maybe next time.*

"You're spending the night." Athena didn't ask, she informed—exactly the way she always did. This time, it didn't bother Delta as much as it usually did as she looked hopefully at the monster of a man sitting uncomfortably on the edge of the sofa. Maybe she shouldn't have forced him into the seat, and maybe, just maybe, she should have left more room between them.

Closing his eyes for a moment, he appeared to be listening to some inner voice. Whatever it told him seemed in agreement, though, because when Malth opened his eyes, he nodded reluctantly with a frown. "Yes, it appears we are."

Delta wasn't going to let his non-excitement ruin the mood. Anyone in the house was better than being alone with her sister, and bonus points for being some extra hot eye candy.

"Delta, please take the man's coat. I'll get this little guy ready for bed. He should probably sleep on the chaise lounge in Eva's room. Malthazar can take her bed." Pausing, her sister looked the specimen up and down.

Delta refrained from scratching her eyes out.

"It's most likely the only place he could sleep comfortably. If Eva's put the word out that her home is open, then she certainly won't begrudge someone using her bed." Of course, her sister would immediately decide to start barking orders. It rankled Delta even if what she was saying was exactly what needed to happen, but for goddess's sake couldn't she do it without treating everyone like children? No wonder Athena seemed to like Julian so much; she could order him about easily enough.

Sulking, Delta couldn't decide if it might be a better option for him to share her bed while her sister slept on the sofa or, better yet, went home. *Down, girl,* she mentally chastised her libido. Despite the lie she'd told Athena; it had been too long. If only she'd been able to have some escapades while in California; all work and no play, that sort of thing. For that matter, when was the last time her sister got laid? Maybe Athena wouldn't be so damn irritating if she was getting some something-something. Again, why was this witch bossing everyone around?

"Come," Athena told the boy, clearly used to being listened to immediately, but instead Julian shot forward to wrap his little arms around a surprised Malth.

"Tanks for taking me, Malth," his face buried against the now stiff man who awkwardly patted the child's back after a hesitation. "I don't wanna be taken to hell."

Delta's ovaries screamed at the vision, and she didn't even know if she liked children. But why did this child think he was being taken to hell? What a strange thing to believe. The quiver in his voice clearly meant he was happy to be with Malth rather than remain where he was. What had started off as an evening in pajamas and overindulging in junk food had taken a strange turn. Her sabbatical hadn't been quite as restful as she'd planned. But on the other hand, outside of her trip to California to subdue and destroy the wendigo, her sabbatical had gotten a little bit boring.

"Off to bed, little man," Athena repeated with a softer tone, unraveling the boy from the man. Who knew she had such a way with children? This might be a side of her sister Delta had never seen before.

She stared at the enigma before her. Had she hit her head and entered a vivid conscious dream state? This man had dropped out of nowhere. *Sex on a stick*, came to mind. He had her thinking of things she absolutely shouldn't be thinking. Her sister appeared to be kind, almost motherly. None of it could be real.

Malth leaned forward, propping his elbows up on his knees, and clasped his hands together, laying his forehead in them. Despite him not looking at her, she could see the waves of exhaustion floating off him. Rousing herself with a small shake, she offered, "Let me take your coat and cap. It sounds like you'll be staying a bit. Might as well get comfortable."

Standing up with a deep exhale, he seemed to

reluctantly pull off his jacket, as if he felt more comfortable remaining wrapped up in it. Like any good Midwest guest, he'd removed his shoes at the door, so obviously he wasn't worried about making a speedy exit. Setting aside her spoon and empty tub, she stood to take it to hang up like a good Midwest hostess should.

Mother Goddess, he was tall—tall and breathtaking. His height had her craning her neck to look up at him. Malthazar was even taller than Oliver. Was it possible for a man to be seven foot tall? He wasn't, but he towered over her. His worn brown duster hid a plethora of muscles under it, or so her quick glance up and down his body told her. His long-sleeved, dark brown henley did no such thing, clinging to him before tucking away inside his jeans. Delta kept her eyes on his face, refusing to vulgarly examine his body, although she did dare another quick peek up and down. Taking his coat in hand, she fought the urge to bring it to her nose and smell it. She could only imagine the pheromones that soaked it. Maybe when she hung it up, she could lean in closer and give it a sniff? A test, perhaps? Things didn't smell in dreams, did they?

He slowly raised his hand to his black stocking cap that was pulled low on his head, only allowing a few soft brown curls to escape under it. Wiggling her fingers, she wordlessly demanded it. Taking a deep breath and letting it out, he seemed to make a painful decision. Tilting his head down, he removed the knit cap before folding it in half and handing it to her.

Reaching for it, she glanced up, realizing he'd never straightened himself back up. Instead, the top of his head continued tilting downward, toward her. Delta looked up at the array of light brown curls wildly dancing around his head. It was on the tip of her tongue to comment on his curls, but his strange hesitation had her watching him, confused.

Delta stopped her perusal and felt her eyes go wide before he drew his head back up. Meeting his golden-brown eyes, she understood; he wanted to get this over with. This was why he'd seemed reluctant to shed his cap, but at the same time ripped the bandage clean off. Unsmiling, with raised eyebrows, he stood before her for a split second before tipping his head down, his intent clear, as if waiting for her reaction. Getting the inevitable out of the way, Delta presumed.

From the top of his curls, two small nubs, a few shades of brown darker than the light brown hair, poked out several inches. Most likely, he kept his hair this style to camouflage them. Delta assumed the hat kept people from looking twice and even if it were removed, humans might not immediately notice the protrusions. They tended to see exactly what they expected to see. They certainly wouldn't expect to see a tall, handsome man sporting tiny, bony horns.

Malthazar could almost pass for human, but the horns would be a dead giveaway that he was something other. Staring at a blank spot well above her head, he waited for her reaction. Clearly, he expected one and wanted to get it out of the way. Perhaps Malth even questioned if his invitation given in haste would be revoked at the sight of his half-demon heritage.

"Let me put these in a closet over here." For once in her life, Delta hadn't blurted out the first thought that came to her head. Malth was certainly used to surprise or downright rejection over the clear implication that he was at least half demon. Belatedly, she wondered if that was why he was so large? She'd heard whispers from witches about the size of demon lovers and their skill. Was that a trait passed on to their half-human offspring? None of the witches she'd known had ever admitted to taking a demon lover. Her lower body tingled as the thoughts flashed through her mind. *What in all the holy goddesses is wrong with me? Thinking about things like* that *when they obviously need help.*

"While Athena puts the little guy down, can I scrounge you up something to eat? I hope you didn't have your heart set on pizza rolls. It sounds like your friend ate all of them." Despite her rapidly beating heart, she was sort of proud of how calm she kept her voice. Even Mama Hecate would be proud to know that finally her lectures and lessons on manners in polite society had come to fruition.

Growing up hearing about demons had left no doubt in her mind that they would kill you as soon as look at you. Unless you summoned them to make a deal; then it was fifty/fifty on survival rates. Cunning and lustful, they could seduce you and then suck the marrow from your bones within the same hour. But her friend Eva was a result of such an event, and she wasn't a terrible demon at all. In fact, she was one of the nicest people Delta had ever met. She just happened to be part demon; succubus, to be exact.

If Oliver trusted Malth and considered him a friend, he couldn't be so bad. Plus, the house had welcomed him in, nearly insisting he stay. Being a half-demon wasn't a choice; it had been so easy to forget he was one until the proof popped right out of his head.

"I can stay outside," Malth announced softly after a long pause.

"No, no," Delta repeated. "That's not necessary at all. It took me by surprise."

Emboldened, she craned her neck to look way up at the top of his curly head. Once again, he tilted his head down for her to gain a better view. The horns curved back gently and were just long enough that his curls couldn't quite hide them completely.

"In fact, now that I look, I think they're sort of cute." How would they feel if she ran her fingers over them, exploring their curve and ridges? Would he feel her touch? Definitely too soon to ask that sort of question, she thought, even though as she squashed the idea, her fingers itched for exploration.

Sitting across from him at the small kitchen table emphasized how large Malth was and how small everything else suddenly seemed. Holding the bowl of soup she'd heated for him in one hand, he spooned it into his mouth, shifting carefully on Eva's retro kitchen chair as if one wrong move might topple it. Delta refrained from sharing that it had held a hellhound intent on jumping on the table, so it would surely hold him safely.

Malth chose the seat with the wall to his back, and he had to scoot the table out before he could slip into the chair. Despite his size, he moved smoothly and silently, barely making a noise as he'd walked through the old house.

Having a guest suddenly made Delta's childish, meager grocery order look even more pathetic. They'd been pretty much living on sandwiches and chips the last few days, and all that remained was some cheese and a few slices of bread. Using the last of her bread, Delta made four generously buttered grilled cheese sandwiches, two for him and one each for her sister and her, adding extra cheese to his two. It appeared they might need some carbs on top of their sugar to prepare for the night. A quick search of the cabinet had unearthed a few cans of tomato soup. Not ideal, but easy enough to doctor up with some of the herbs on hand. Adding an extra pinch of finely chopped basil, Delta gave the mixture another stir. An extra dose of protection for those who partook of the soup couldn't hurt anyone, plus the fresh basil almost made it taste homemade.

Malthazar ate his sandwiches quickly, as if he hadn't eaten in days. Delta quietly topped off his bowl with the remaining soup. He needed it more than she or Athena did. With a mental sigh, she passed another sandwich toward him as well and cut the last one in half to share with Athena. They were out of bread now too.

Naturally, Athena hadn't taken the time to replace anything she'd eaten while Delta traveled, and a pissed off Delta ordered as little as possible, as if to punish her sister in some weird way. Clearly that plan had backfired, and her sister still hadn't left. Nothing seemed to work in her favor as of late.

Athena slipped back into the kitchen, announcing, "He's asleep. I had to promise three stories, but he passed out during the first one." Taking a dainty nibble of her half of the grilled cheese, she continued in her shrill voice. Delta hated it when she spoke like this; it grated on every nerve in her body and made her want to gouge out her eardrums. When she'd questioned Athena about the change in her voice, her sister appeared to be unaware of it. Delta suspected it once had been a useful tool to deter witches she didn't want to socialize with and somehow it had evolved to being used all the damn time.

It took a moment for Athena to look straight at Malth. Delta knew immediately when Athena's eyes settled on the man's small horns. Her gasp was silent, thanks to their mother's training, and her eyes grew large and round while she struggled to determine what she would say. Thankfully, Malth's head was down, looking at his bowl, while he used the last bits of his sandwich to wipe it clean.

This time, it was Delta who sharply kicked her sister under the table, before fixing her narrowed eyes on Athena in a threat if she offended the man.

Still, Athena felt the need to butt into the situation. "Why does that child think he's being dragged off to hell?" she asked Malthazar almost angrily. She refused to look at his face, instead focusing on picking at the half sandwich in front of her. "I had to pinkie promise him, whatever that is, that he wasn't going to hell tonight."

Malth looked up from his now empty bowl at the two of them. Delta hoped his glance had lingered on her rather than her sister, despite her asking the question.

"Because he was," he responded dryly with a slight shrug, as if it were obvious. "And a pinkie promise is the most important of all promises you can make to a child. Breaking it is akin to death."

It wasn't obvious to Delta or her sister if the steam rolling off Athena was anything to go by. Her sister was going to blow, and as rare as that was, Delta needed to head that off. Only one of them was allowed to be the emotional one at a time. "Wait, what? Malth, surely you're not taking that child to hell? I mean, can you even do that?" Delta couldn't believe he would be that cruel, and Oliver trusted him.

Malth expanded his words. "It's his destiny, but *I'm* not taking him. I'm doing everything I can to not allow that to happen. It will not happen." He bit the last words off, ensuring the finality was understood.

As handsome as he was, his good looks weren't going to get him out of actually answering their questions. Delta put a calming hand on Athena as she looked ready to boil over. How the tables had turned; usually it was Delta's emotions at the ready, barely controllable or tolerable, her mother told her.

"Malthazar…" Delta strove to keep her voice calm. "You have shown up at our doorstep. Eva's doorstep," she amended quickly, "while we're in residence, with a child who is not your own. One who at his age should be with his mother. Who apparently is destined for hell and, well, you're a demon."

"Half-demon." Malthazar bit the words out as if they pained him. Glancing between the two, he added, "Half-witch, same as the boy."

"Right, right." Delta wasn't going to argue semantics with the demon. Half-demon. Whatever. "We're asking you to tell us what is going on. Is that child in danger? Are we in danger?"

"His mother is the reason he's destined for hell." Malth pushed the empty bowl back as he examined the two, his eyes devoid of emotion, as if determining how much to tell them.

Patiently, Delta continued holding onto Athena's arm; he would tell them, she mentally promised her sister. Usually, her sister was the first to calmly and rationally approach any situation, but this situation, this boy, had her out of sorts.

"His mother is the reason he's in this mess to begin with," Malth began. Apparently, he'd made a decision of sorts. Who knew how much he would truthfully share with them, though?

"Over five years ago, his mother"—he spat the word "mother" with near hatred—"made a deal with a demon. Not a low-level one, but mid or higher, for sure. As these deals tend to go, she agreed to… breed with the demon in exchange for magic and power. The witches carry the child and care for them until they reach the age of acceptance and their *father* or someone acting in their interest comes to collect them. Care loosely meaning, keep them alive. Julian is days away from that age, and when it comes, someone will get him and take him to hell. Well, that sweet boy would be gone."

"What, a witch? A witch wouldn't make an agreement like that!" Athena argued. She hadn't seen the same sort of things in her sheltered existence that Delta had. Mother's choice had been to shelter her elder daughter who now, despite her remarkable age, was also very unaware of the world outside of the coven.

"Occasionally, a black magic user of sorts, surely, but nothing on the level you're speaking of. You make it sound like it's some sort of planned event or that it happens on the regular."

"Thena," she began gently, as Athena pulled her arm away, looking at her in shock.

"You believe this, this blasphemy? Clearly there is some sort of mistake or he's lying."

"Yes," Delta affirmed softly, "I do believe it.

Mother has kept you… in a bubble of sorts. Not wanting you damaged by the outside world, but witches aren't all good. Like in any species, there are good ones and bad ones. To say all witches worship the goddess and nature is naive. Gravely so. Some crave things they shouldn't and clearly make deals that are deadly."

It went without saying that something of this sort had happened with Malthazar, to Malthazar. He seemed too knowledgeable for it to be otherwise, and Delta found she didn't want to look at him and see pain from such memories in his eyes. One didn't tend to stumble easily upon a mission like this; this type of thing was personal.

CHAPTER FOUR

Devil's dung may be called that due to the odor or the resulting gastronomic effect of consuming too much asafoetida.

The sweet smell of the kitchen had lulled him, for a moment, into believing that he could sit down and relax. Release the tension of the last few days; hell, the last few years. It was almost as if the dried herbs had been put together to have such an effect, but the array of scents were really a mishmash of healing, protection, calming, and more. He could pick out the peppermint as it simultaneously cleared his mind and made him breathe easier. Cinnamon and cloves brought him relaxation, comfort, and even a small smile. The warm, comforting scent unlocked the memory of a pumpkin pie he'd once tasted long ago on a whim.

One fall afternoon, when he sat in a diner, exhausted, unsure what to order, an overworked waitress had snappily asked, "Wadda ya want?" Too damn hungry to even think about what he wanted, and in a lapse of judgment, he admitted he'd never eaten pie. The shocked matronly waitress's tone turned sympathetic as she suggested the pumpkin with loads of whipped cream. He nearly licked the damn plate clean and even considered ordering another piece. Instead, Malth had drunk his hot, black coffee, staring at the plate in amazement and resisting the urge to rub his stomach. Who knew a pumpkin could be made into a pie? Humans were amazing when it came to food; they could create and create and create. Why was there war when there was pie? He couldn't remember what else he'd eaten that day, surely something simple, but he never forgot the pie.

As the tension eased out of him, Malth realized with a start that the house was lulling him into this feeling of serenity. Oliver had spoken of Eva's house in whispered tones, the generational magic that had built it and seeped into it year after year, generation after generation. How many deaths had bonded the witch's magic to the structure? He knew Eva's adopted grandmother had died on the land, and he suspected she wasn't the only one who had timed her death to tie her to the house and land. This house was a gold mine—or a land mine, depending on how you felt about witches.

Goosebumps ran across his skin, as he fought the house lulling him into comfort. It could be as simple as the house wanting him to rest and be comfortable, or it could be a trap. Was it embracing the witch half of him or trapping the demon side? Ever so briefly,

Malth mentally warred with himself; his magic had never intentionally led him into danger, and he always assumed that if he was led there, he was avoiding an even greater threat elsewhere.

Trust. Trust. Trust, he silently chanted, trying to let his guard back down. Oliver and Eva wouldn't have allowed him to venture into a trap knowingly. If his sister had found safety here for decades, then surely the house meant him no harm overnight. But it was hard. Trust was hard. He offered a silent but heartfelt thank you to the house for its hospitality. He received no response, but that didn't mean it hadn't heard or felt the intentions.

Silently, Malth watched the two sisters as they argued in low tones, as if he wasn't sitting right in front of them hearing their whispered shouts, so similar to the children he saved. He hadn't been unaware of what passed when Athena sat down across from him. The moment she'd noticed his demon horns, the air around them had snapped with her fear. Both sisters wore their emotions in different ways. Malth knew his horns weren't as noticeable as a full demon's would be. Hell, even some of his brothers had horns out the sides of their head that grew thick and curved around their ears. No amount of curls could hide those protrusions.

Delta's vicious kick to her sister's shin made him wince in sympathy and nearly had him feeling sorry for the older sister. The looks, the fear, and the devil signs were what he expected when people truly saw him; it hadn't bothered him in years. But Delta's attempt to defend his differences made him feel warm in a way he never remembered feeling before. Oliver had accepted him from the moment they met, but for some reason it felt different with Delta. Better.

The women looked so much the same, but at the same time were so different. Each had vivid green eyes, but Delta's eyes sparkled with gold flecks that seemed to dance around if he looked at them for too long. And he'd been furtively looking every chance he could when he felt like she wasn't looking at him. Both had curly red hair, but Delta's wild and vivacious curls called to him to wrap his hands up in them. The scatter of freckles across her pale cheeks and nose looked like the sun had kissed her beauty, or perhaps a hint of the cinnamon had been powdered across her nose.

The words were hard to form. He understood it was hard for some to imagine that a mother could carry a baby, raise and care for it, and then hand it off to hell without a second thought. But Malthazar had seen it far too often; hell, he'd lived it. A mother could hug her child, offer a kiss, and promise to see him soon. All the while, the cold bitch would be holding her newfound power to her teat in place of the child.

"It's happened for as long as man has walked the earth. Demons come to earth to lie with women, willing or not. Then in the child's fifth or sixth year, they or one of their servants usually return to collect them. They're taken to hell, where they serve as amusement to their creators. Calling it a father isn't quite accurate. They definitely don't see it as you might see a child."

"Is that what happened with Eva?" Delta half whispered, as if such questions might conjure a demon into their midst. "Is she truly half or is the demon blood more diluted?"

"Yes. Well, to be honest, I'm not sure about her creation. She's the only half-demon female spawn I've seen," Malth admitted. As soon as he laid eyes on her in Oliver's arms, he'd known her to be a sister. At that moment, Eva had been the most beautiful thing he'd ever seen. Obviously, he didn't look at her as Oliver did, but differently, even if he couldn't explain the fascination.

He paused a heartbeat to consider how that had changed within the last few hours. Eva had been replaced by a sassy redhead as the most beautiful creature he'd seen.

However, even beaten and magically abused, Eva's demoness part, her strength, still showed through, exactly as it had for every brother he met. Truth be told, he hadn't even known that females could come from such close demon interactions. Whoever had sired her clearly hadn't returned to find her, or her mother and grandmother had done a perfect job of hiding her. Although as the house closed in around him, he had to admit, it probably did the job itself. Its immense power nearly breathed in and out as the magic flowed through its walls, strong protection magic that had hidden a few generations between its walls. The house had decided that Eva was worthy of all the protections it could muster. Powerful enough, it could protect anyone within its walls. Julian was as safe here as he could be. The house would ensure that.

"Somehow, her existence went unnoticed." More than likely, her demon sire had come to earth for a little fun and debauchery, not planning on creating any offspring, especially if the mother was human. Witch hybrids were much more sought after, but human hybrids could still fill in the ranks. Being forgotten was a much better option than the alternative. It was the magical offspring that kept the demons coming back. Despite the fact that Eva's mother or maternal grandmother didn't appear to have magic, Eva had evolved due to the vampire blood entering her system when Ravyn saved her life. Her demon DNA had grabbed a hold of the blood, mutated, and made her into something new. Something different.

"You have to help that child," Athena demanded in her nasal voice, her eyes flashing at Malth as if he were personally responsible for what Julian faced. Was this witch not listening to him?

"I am," Malth asserted firmly, clenching his jaw to shut off the barrage of responses that filled his mouth. Gods, he was tired and his head ached. He couldn't begin to count the number of offspring he'd collected over the years. The demon world was vast, and the creatures didn't seem to be able to keep their dick in their pants, so to speak. If the older sister didn't have the child's best interest in mind, he might have snapped her neck for speaking to him that way. She demanded things of him but couldn't even police the witches who made these deals. To hell with her title and whatever title she was set to inherit. Snap and he could be gone before she hit the floor. He felt his lips move up slightly at the thought and then dropped the half smile. Surely that would upset Delta, and he didn't want to see those beautiful green eyes staring angry daggers at him. On the other hand, he considered, the sisters didn't seem to get along all that well.

"Athena, quit hounding the man. Clearly, he came here with the boy for sanctuary. And he's as tired as the child. Surely all this"—Delta waved her hand sharply as she narrowed her eyes toward her sister in warning—"can wait until morning."

A bed. Yes, a bed to sleep the night away in sounded like heaven, if such a place existed. Malthazar had only seen proof of hell, and if heaven existed, wouldn't he know about it as well? For now, he would rest and rest well, knowing that the house would keep them safe and hide them away, at least until morning. More tension released as he made the decision. It was right; this was right.

Athena's phone began buzzing from her pocket, causing the two sisters to jolt in surprise.

A second later, Malthazar's vibrated as well from his pants. As always it was silent, his life often depending on the silence. Still, it was surprising that it buzzed; few knew the number and fewer reached out to him. Reaching down, he pulled it free from his front pocket, seeing Oliver's name flash on the screen along with a text. His one consistent contact; the one person who had never given up on him no matter how much he ignored the vampire or pushed him away. The only time Oliver seemed impatient was when he repeated his texts or calls until Malth could or would answer.

"Delta, did you block Mother again? She's been trying to reach you." Again, that sharp, nasal tone cut through the air. Perhaps it was a good thing not to have had a sister growing up.

"What? No, not again." Delta picked up her phone that had been face down on the table. "Nothing from her. Does she have the right number?" The faux innocent tone had Malthazar considering the lie. She hadn't blocked her again. Delta had never unblocked her mother for whatever reason. Families were weird. However, for as many brothers as he had, none of their relationships sat quite like this.

"Well, please call her, immediately."

If her sister was any indication, Malth could see why she had the mother blocked. And after reading Oliver's message, he suspected they were receiving similar messages. Oliver stated that as soon as his witch could be contacted, they would be connected. Surprising that Oliver didn't have the little house monitored—or maybe the magic did a better job than any of Oliver's gadgets could.

"Mother—" A barrage of unidentifiable chatter cut

her off. Pursing her lips, she rolled her eyes at Malthazar as she took the brunt of her mother's anger. "Of course, High Priestess. Yes, yes, of course."

Oliver had requested Malth's assistance in tracking down a rogue magic user. He would be partnered with a witch named Delta. *What a coincidence. What a strange coincidence*, he thought with irony. Apparently, the magic hadn't just brought him here for sanctuary overnight.

"Why didn't Oliver… Yes, High Priestess. Of course I can reach him, if we're meant to work together."

Sighing, she ended the call and eyed Malth suspiciously. "I suppose you got a text from Oliver? Apparently, we're working together? But unlike you, I'm working this job for the coven." Her tone bit down on the word "coven." There was history here, but Malth wasn't going to ask.

Working for the coven irritated her for some reason, perhaps more family issues. He knew Delta worked for Oliver and was considered an important part of his operation, but why was it so disappointing for her to work through her own coven? Staying within the coven seemed preferable, but Malth wasn't about to untangle the familial relationship that had been laid out in front of him.

Athena looked between the two of them, thankfully staying quiet. As much as Malthazar hated talking to people, speaking up might keep her irritating voice quiet. It might be the dumbest reason ever to speak, but perhaps this once, it was better than the alternative.

"We are to track a magic user." Odd that Oliver hadn't said a witch, but a magic user. "Your High Priestess. Your mother?" he verified. "Asked for Oliver's assistance, but her coven still needs to be the responsible party."

Tight lipped, Delta closed her eyes briefly and nodded shortly. He wasn't a reader of people, especially women, but she was angry. Angry and hurt. Those two emotions were fueling the mad swirls in her eyes.

Usually, Malth worked alone. Always, really. Oliver knew this, so why was he saddling him with this… this… witch? And over the years, Oliver had complained enough about her that Malth hesitated to work with her.

"I can go alone, leave tonight," he offered what he considered a reasonable suggestion. "Then you can join me for the return and surrender the prisoner. No one would know the difference."

"No, and no. No one is leaving tonight; we've got forty-eight hours before we need to go. We all need a good night's rest, probably even more than that," Delta replied sharply, before rubbing her eyes. With a gentler tone, she repeated, "And no to doing this alone. Apparently, this is witch business, but her witches lost the trail. It's our responsibility, but she's *allowing* Oliver's help. The old Crone can't admit when things are out of her control. So she's paying me for this job, instead of Oliver. It's all semantics, really."

Athena hissed at Delta's words but wisely didn't reprimand her. Calling out the head whatever, even if she was your mother, was apparently frowned upon.

The long pause hung over the table. Even Athena stayed quiet, looking guiltily at the remnants of her half a sandwich on her plate. Malth studied Delta, trying to determine why she seemed upset to be working simultaneously for her mother and with him.

Athena finally pushed herself back from the table, still attempting to process what she'd learned, or head spinning from the mission that had been sent Delta's way. "It's past the time for me to rest. I have lots to prepare for tomorrow."

Turning toward Malth, she offered almost formally, holding her emotions in check, "Do you need anything to help you sleep? I can offer…"

Malth shook his head. He was tired enough to not need a boost of either magic or herb to sleep. Falling asleep was never a problem for him.

Alone now with the witch who had bewitched him from the moment he'd entered the house, Malth waited for her to excuse herself. When she didn't seem to be in a hurry to go to bed, he asked her, "Were you there when they defeated the wendigo and discovered the… witch?"

Nodding, Delta focused on her tea for a moment before responding aloud. "Yes, I arrived in the midst of things. I didn't see the witch, but her magic was everywhere, in everything. I have a good feel for it now. We were fortunate that it all worked out even if we couldn't stop her then. I don't know if we could have at that moment, so much was happening. When Ravyn came out of the compound, it was one of the top worse things I'd ever seen. The closest I've been to a feral vampire or close to feral. That's some terrifying crap."

Malth nodded in agreement; at one point, he'd hunted such ferals alongside Oliver. Sadly, the ones they came across were beyond reason, and it was a miracle Ravyn had the fortitude to recover. Once they turned, shutting off their oftentimes tentative grasp on their humanity, they couldn't seem to reconnect to it.

Staring at her cuticles, Delta continued, "Ravyn didn't seem like Ravyn at all. I didn't know what to do. Everyone acted like she was going to slaughter us if we breathed the wrong way. But Sebastian calmed her down, brought her back to herself. It was the most amazing thing I've seen. I knew then that he loved her, even if he didn't know it yet." Delta grinned at the thought of the two unlikely lovers.

"The spells, the trapping of the wendigo, it took a lot out of me. I don't know how anyone who was there could walk out on their own two feet." Delta considered her next words. "But dammit, I couldn't let anyone see how badly it drained me. Now that I'm familiar with this magical creature, I'm more prepared. I know a bit of what we're up against. You don't need to worry about me being dead weight." Her words were disjointed, as if her thoughts were being tossed out without organization, but Malth understood what she was saying, as well as what she wasn't.

Malth hadn't considered that his curiosity would come off like he was questioning her ability to handle herself. Perhaps she thought he'd heard something of the mission, but this was the most he knew of it other than it had occurred. Shaking his head, he said, "I know you're good." Oliver wouldn't have suggested they team up otherwise, no matter how important this Hecate was. "Did your family help your recovery?"

Delta snorted at that, but at least she'd visibly relaxed from his questioning. "Hell no. I have an online friend I game with, one who knows nothing of this world, and I crashed at his place a few nights."

Malth found himself bristling, feeling strangely uneasy upon hearing of this unnamed man who had taken care of her when she needed it. "This man…" he began, knowing he had a tone that would rub her the wrong way, but he couldn't stop himself as the tightness in his chest built up into his throat.

Misunderstanding, Delta waved off his concern. "I didn't give anything away and he had nothing to do with the mission at all. But yeah, I spent several nights on the sofa. His boyfriend wasn't generous enough to offer up their bed to basically a stranger. After about twenty hours of sleep, I was able to visit a few of the sights out there, enough to say I'd seen California. Then I spent a mind-numbing amount of time playing video games with the guys. They're good guys. Too bad I'll never get to see them again."

Malth knew the feeling too well. Friendships were a weakness to be exploited, and if someone wasn't enmeshed in the paranormal world, such friendships could be dangerous. Sometimes you had to take what you could get for a few hours or a few days and then slink off at the first chance.

CHAPTER FIVE

Eyebright can be used as an eyewash or ingested to help see the bright side of things or reveal truths.

The adventurous duo slept for twenty hours.

Athena and Delta had even slept in a bit, waking up after the sun had worked its way a quarter of the way through the sky. They didn't speak of their visitors or what they'd learned the night before.

Having no qualms about raiding Eva's closet—after all, she'd shared her own wardrobe with Eva when she needed it—Delta dug around until she found clothes that might be warm enough for the day. When she arrived mid-summer, she hadn't packed or planned for anything beyond the warm weather. Yet here she still was, hiding out in Ohio, of all places.

Wrapped in a thick, olive green, slightly itchy, oversized sweater that had most likely belonged to Eva's Gram, Delta flitted in and out of the yard, gathering plants and comparing them to the ones in her bug out bag. Switching them out regularly ensured the best results when they were used. Delta hadn't needed to use the potions and herbs often, but better to always be prepared than caught short in a battle because the sage had crumbled or the damage potion had turned sour. Although she'd done this the first day she'd returned from California, out of habit she went through them all twice. She refused to be caught without the freshest of ingredients for any need.

Athena wandered about as if she might be cleaning, but didn't because, well, she couldn't. She settled on the sofa with a book but kept looking down the hallway as if waiting for the two guests to waken. It had crossed Delta's mind that perhaps Malth had crept out with Julian under the cover of darkness, but their shoes and slippers remained by the front door. Leaving without those essentials in any sort of weather wouldn't be wise, and Malth struck her as generally acting rationally. Besides, he said they would stay the two nights her mother had requested before they started their search. Delta suspected her mother's own witches had mucked up the trail, and she wanted time to erase their ineptness. The thought brought her little joy. She hated the idea that she was working for the coven or her mother. She liked to imagine she was on loan from Oliver for the duration, and that she still answered to her employer—definitely not her mother. A few times, Athena had opened her mouth as if to ask Delta a question, and Delta had rushed about finding a reason to leave the space her sister occupied. Now wasn't the time to try and hash out a relationship, and if Athena wanted to question the validity of Malth's story, Delta might be tempted to put a hex on her.

Thank the gods and goddesses, Malth finally came out of the room after she'd packed and unpacked her bag several times, deadheaded a few flowers, pruned some bushes, and pulled the two or three remaining weeds that had crept past Athena's watch. The sun, already low in the sky, signaled either food or enough sleep would wake the two males. Starting to fear she would need to make small talk with her sister, Delta pretty much shouted her greeting when Malth wandered down the hallway with wet hair that had been combed firmly against his head, not hiding his horns at all.

"Tea or coffee?" Delta kept her voice chipper, despite her sleepless night of tossing and turning and the day spent running from her sister. She was ready to go back to bed, if only her sole option wasn't with her damned sister. Itching to get on the road and knowing that another night needed to pass had her ready to sleep the remaining time away as well. She would like to blame her lack of sleep on her sister. In truth, it was much more than that. Malthazar and his soft curls had kept her awake. Something about him spoke of loss and sorrow, clinging to him and then nailed into place with regret. That and her mother, but if asked, she would adamantly deny that anything her mother could do would cause her to lose sleep.

"Tea." He spoke gruffly and shortly, as if the words got caught in his throat. Clearing his throat, he added, "Please. Tea please."

Delta smiled to herself. Somehow, by picking tea it had cemented in her mind that there was something special about him. But tea instead of coffee? How silly of her, trying to find connections that didn't exist.

"I slept well enough to not need coffee," Malth added with an awkward half smile that had Delta wondering if small talk didn't come easy to him.

"That's wonderful to hear." She channeled what she called her inner Athena and turned up the chipper in her voice while pretending not to notice that he also looked surprised that he was volunteering information. It was clearly something he didn't do easily or often.

Mixing his tea, she added cinnamon first, breaking the stick in half for each of their cups. A few whole cloves and more for her went next. Despite how rested he was, intuition told her Malth might need the boost of power from the spices. Keeping your body strong, healthy, and focused was a necessity for anyone who worked with Oliver. If he were trying to stay ahead of the demons that might currently be hunting the child, Malth could use all the extra boost she could give him. Laying a hand over his cup, Delta closed her eyes and offered a silent prayer of protection and strength. The cup hissed as her power took hold and the spell settled into it.

Standing in the kitchen, they silently waited for the tea to steep, its aromatic scent already helping Delta to center herself. She'd lost count somewhere after her fourth cup of tea, but she couldn't seem to make it without pouring herself a cup.

Silently, she passed him his mug, refusing to be the first to break the peace and calm unless he wanted to. Difficult as it was for her, she managed to keep from bombarding him with the questions that had been building up all day.

Julian still slept, making her wonder how long it had been since the boy had felt relaxed enough to sleep. How long had it been since the half-demon seated in front of her had relaxed? Malth nodded a thanks to her and settled his body back into the chair at the table against the wall. Holding his mug in both hands, he took a careful sip, closing his eyes as Delta hoped he savored the flavors.

"Morning, or should I say good evening." Despite Athena's gliding into the kitchen with little fanfare, she still managed to make their need for sleep an accusation. Of course, she said the words so sweetly while looking immaculately put together that one might doubt she had any double meaning at all.

Delta narrowed her eyes in warning at her sister, still angry that she'd claimed to have slept so well while Delta had remained sleepless and fussy all night. Athena fell asleep almost immediately, with slow, deep breaths. No chance a snore would dare to escape from her. Now her sister's smooth coif made Delta acutely aware of her own unruly mess of curls. Suddenly aware of the difference in their appearances, she reached up to smooth down her hair. Her fingers caught on a knot with something attached. Casually, she attempted to detangle the now crumbling leaf without frizzing her hair too much. Why did she bother? They were as different as night and day; comparing herself to Athena was like comparing the moon to the sun. *Different doesn't mean better…* She chanted the same mantra that had gotten her through every meeting with her family members for the past few decades.

Athena's eyes immediately narrowed in on the debris in Delta's hair. Her eyes darted about, most likely finding other bits and bobs tangled there. Thankfully, she kept her mouth shut and simply bustled about the kitchen, making her own cup of chamomile tea with a sprinkle of lavender. No wonder Athena was always so relaxed; sleep and sleepy tea.

Anyone who could sleep like that didn't let the world's worry bother them a bit, Delta decided. Even after learning about the deals being struck between demons and witches, despite her ire, Athena would categorize the information and then file it away under a mental lock. She was good at that; they both were, or they never would have survived their mother's parenting. The difference was that Athena filed things away to forget and Delta filed them away to remember.

A bundle of raw energy burst through the kitchen door followed by a gasp. Julian stopped just inside the kitchen, rubbing sleep as well as what Delta suspected to be tears from his reddened eyes.

"Malth, I thought you left me." The child hiccupped with a sniff before wiping his nose on the back of his hand.

Gross.

Athena tried to discreetly pass a tissue to the boy, who used it to wipe his eyes.

"I told you I'll tell you when I leave. I wouldn't lie to you." Malth spoke the words carefully to the child. "I did pinky promise you this." He didn't berate the boy for his fears or his tears, simply reassured him that all was as it should be.

"I-I know," the boy stammered.

Delta waited for his "but." Clearly, he'd been let down by people in his life, and she suspected the child's mother was at the top of his list.

"I know." Malth whispered the words back in understanding. It was as if the two could communicate without words, and perhaps they were. Perhaps some of their shared experiences allowed them to do so.

"I bet Malth is hungry." Julian made this announcement quietly to the room, as his own stomach let out a rumble.

It took Delta a long moment to puzzle out what Julian was saying. Then it hit her: the child wasn't going to ask for something for himself. He'd learned along the way that the world didn't work that way for him. A protective instinct flared within her chest and momentarily she understood Athena's desire to mother Julian.

"Pizza," Delta blurted out. Kids loved pizza. Well, and so did she, truth be told. He deserved a treat, and not just scraping a few pizza rolls out of the bottom of the freezer. Besides, Athena had probably microwaved them, not even knowing that baking them was clearly superior.

"Malth, do you like pizza?" the boy asked as he held his own stomach, before adding hopefully, "I like pizza."

"I love pizza." Malth's reply was gruff, but perhaps he feared coddling the child would bring fresh tears. "What's your favorite topping? I like everything, especially pepperoni and sausage," he prompted.

"Me too! I like pepperoni, but I pick the other stuff off."

Ah-ha! Malthazar knew his shit, and he knew how to talk to the little man. He'd spent time around the youths he rescued, and that time have given him insight Delta doubted she would ever have.

He also shook his head slightly no when Delta would have given him some of the cola that surprisingly Athena had added to the order for herself. Maybe the boy couldn't handle his caffeine, like Delta. She offered him some of her iced hibiscus tea, at which he subtly wrinkled his nose and offered a polite no thank you. Mentally, Delta frantically poured over the drink options in the house, before Malth suggested water, which the boy happily drank two glasses of. Water… Who would have thought?

Pepperoni and some everything pizza on the sofa during a movie night. A movie that Delta had never seen, but Athena had flipped through the children's choices until a slightly positive reaction from Julian told them they had a winner.

Despite not speaking up for his own needs or wants, the boy was a chatter box and chatted through the first movie, devouring an entire pizza while he did it. Then he chatted through the second movie while he lay his head on Athena's lap. She ran her fingers through his hair, seemingly mesmerized by the boy. Occasionally, he would pop up to offer an excited opinion about the on-screen action that Delta wasn't following. Malth had eaten two pizzas himself. Thankfully, Delta had ordered extras knowing they would eat it all that night or the next day. To her dismay, Malth didn't stick around for the second movie and made some excuse about scouting the yard and street.

"Julian," he commandeered the boy's attention for a moment. "I'll be back," he promised, before sliding his knit cap down low on his head and shrugging into his jacket.

Would it be too obvious if she went outside under the pretense of picking special leaves under the moonlight? Not even a full moon, but who would know? *Ugh*, pretty much anyone in the house would see through the act, except maybe Julian, and he was pretty astute so she might not even fool him. Now it was her turn to keep glancing toward the door, but Malth never reappeared.

Despite having slept nearly a full day, Julian began to yawn and pull at his eyes before the middle of the third movie.

CHAPTER SIX

Obtaining a hand of God to burn might sound impossible, but in reality, a spellcaster looking to summon rain can easily find a fern.

*D*elta managed to crawl out of bed after another restless night. She'd given up poking Athena in the ribs to move her over and continued scooting to the edge of the bed all night long until her sister was nearly on top of her. At one point, she'd gotten up and moved over to the other side of the bed, the side Athena swore was "her side," but still sleep didn't come easily. Darkness still filled the house as she crept into the kitchen with her robe pulled tightly around her body.

With quiet, careful movements, she filled her kettle with water and began putting together a tea mixture that might get her through the day or at least the morning. Maybe if the goddess smiled down at her, she might get a nap before the forty-eight-hour deadline required they begin tracking Ibis. Delta hadn't checked the time when she'd given up on sleep, trying to creep out without waking her sister. It was still dark out, but that could mean it was 5:00 a.m. or 7:00.

Would Julian sleep in or would he be up early? Did kids his age take naps? Yesterday had been an entire night's sleep and six days worth of naps rolled into one. Maybe today, he would be up more, and if he was up, it stood to reason his temporary guardian would be up as well.

Light on his feet, Malth slid stealthily into the kitchen. If she hadn't been looking toward the door, she wouldn't have known he came in. How late did he come in after making his rounds? Delta wondered. She hadn't heard him come in last night or this morning, but perhaps he'd planned it that way.

Side-eyeing him, Delta tried to take all of him in without being too obvious. All things considered, he looked like he was well rested. Wordlessly pulling out another mug, she fixed a cup of tea for the man, similar to yesterday's. After adding two cubes of sugar, he'd drunk the entire mixture, so she could assume it was at least satisfactory. This time, she added the sugar before passing the mug to him. She could feel her eyes growing wide when she realized she'd given him the Dungeon Daddy mug and hoped he didn't read too much into her fixing his tea in it. Damn Eva, and her book boyfriend mugs.

Nodding his thanks, Malth took up a sentry position at the back door. He leaned against the wall, staring into the yard as he sipped his tea, not seeming to notice the words scrawled across the mug. Delta tried to determine if she should remain standing, sit down, or start cooking something. Well, put something in the microwave or toaster. Damnation, except for last night's pizza, she hadn't eaten all day and had forgotten to place some sort of grocery order. What did people even eat for breakfast? How had making a decision like that suddenly become so awkward? Staring at the man's broad back, she realized that in the barely two days he'd been there, everything about her felt out of sorts. More so than usual anyway, she admitted to herself.

Taking another sip of his tea, he stared out the doorway before doing a double take, leaning closer to the window as if the few inches might bring some clarity to what he was seeing. "Why is there a hellhound in your back yard?" Lowering the mug to his side, his previously relaxed shoulders straightened and he covered the doorway with his body, as if he could physically stop the perceived threat.

"Oh, that little devil is back, is he?" Delta thought something was seriously wrong by the way he'd shot off the words. "It's Eva's Big Boy or Baby Boy, depending on the mood. Surely, you've heard about him? The pup that was with her when she was taken? They've sort of bounded or something during captivity, and he likes to come by the house."

In fact, she'd been spending more money on treats for the beast and the neighbor's dog Apollo than she had on her own groceries. It was imperative to keep them on hand and ready to feed them, as her sister had learned. Who knew when they might come begging for treats, and the doorway needed to be open for them. The hound clearly could get around the door as well as take a few treats, but apparently, he liked being hand fed the goodies after being welcomed into the home.

"*That's* the pup she held in her arms when we found her?" Incredulous, Malth stared out the window, eyes flicking back and forth, following something Delta knew she wouldn't be able to see.

"Don't lock the dog door during the day. He likes to come in and out, and he really likes it if Apollo can as well." Delta paused in her clean-up of the tea. "Wait, you can see him?" Although Big Boy let himself be known, often with a muzzle butt to her hand, the treats moving around, or simply by bringing his buddy, Apollo by, she'd never actually laid eyes on the creature.

Malth gave her a sardonic look with a half turned up lip before turning his gaze once more out the window. "Yes."

"Like sees like," Delta muttered softly to herself. How could she forget that bit of info?

Without looking back at her, Malth offered softly, "Mostly, but if you wanted, I could allow you to see. You need to have your third eye opened."

Delta bristled at his response. Her third eye? Surely, he jested. She was the most open-minded witch she knew. She burned white sage, practiced yoga, and even meditated when she could.

But maybe he meant something different than the metaphysical world of the witches? She chastised herself for falling into the trap of thinking only like a witch when the entire world was out there.

She walked to the window with her tea to watch out the window, knowing that for the past weeks she'd wished she could see the beast. It was one thing to read about them and hear others' accounts, but to actually see him. Incredible!

The neighbor's dog Apollo had joined the hellhound for a play date. The Great Pyrenees mix bounded around the yard, twisting and turning while playing with the unseen hound. It would be pretty amazing to see the demon pup. As far as Delta knew, she would be the only witch in existence to actually lay eyes on it, and it would definitely make it easier to hand the hound his treats. Generally, she tossed them in the air in the direction she thought he might be while he scrambled and thumped against the linoleum, trying get it before it hit the floor. On occasion she held it out, but she could be holding it into thin air while the pup smirked at her from several feet away.

"Make up your mind, here they come." Malth pivoted away from the dog door that took up the entire half of the door while pulling Delta along with him to safety before the flap whipped open. Thank the goddess; she'd been bowled over by the beast more times than she could count.

"Definitely," Delta decided as Apollo slid to a stop

and the braided rag rug inside the door seemed to magically slide halfway across the kitchen. "Wait, is this a deal?" She hated her suspicious mind for asking the insulting question, but years of experience had taught her that being tricked into a bad deal was pretty much the worse thing she could do.

Malth grimaced but shook his head. "I don't do deals. Consider it a freebie or payment for the last few nights." Placing his tea-free thumb and forefinger across her forehead, he whispered, "*Daemones videre et ultra.*"

See the demons and beyond, Delta mentally translated as she gazed into his eyes. The snap of energy pulsed through her head, as his fingers settled the magic into place. The warmth spread quickly from the top of her body and downward as his silver magic settled over her. *Silver.* Delta sighed. Not black magic but beautiful, shimmering tendrils of silver magic emanated from him.

For a moment, her breath hitched in her lungs as she stared into his brown eyes, tiny flames flickering high before settling back down, and it took all of her strength to not pull him closer and lose herself in those eyes. Were his curls as soft as they looked? What about his horns? Were they rough and rigid or smooth? Her body tingled, beginning in her forehead and moving down her chest and through her arms. Apparently, his magic wasn't done with her yet. Delta gasped, catching her breath as she wondered whether that was the magic working or simply a byproduct of standing too close to him.

This was the closest they'd been since he'd arrived, except when she sat too close to him on the sofa that first night and he'd shifted uncomfortably away. She wasn't going to count that bit of awkwardness. Malth seemed to instinctively avoid touch. Sure, the first night she'd slid a plate of sandwiches toward him, along with the soup that he'd reached across the table for. This morning, she'd handed him tea and he'd managed to take it without as much as a brush of his fingers. He seemed to shy away from even the boy he traveled with, seemingly fine with Athena taking over the bulk of his care.

"Now look," he whispered, the scent of cinnamon and cloves wafting from him.

A slight tremble moved through her, as her mind clicked the image of him and the sweet smell together. Delta knew she would never be able to drink what she would now think of as Malthazar's tea, without connecting it to him and this moment.

Turning her head, she skeptically scanned the kitchen, only half believing she would lay eyes on an infamous beast of hell.

"Holy Mary, Mother of…" Delta gasped and shot backward, twisting as she fell. She would have face planted into the door, but Malthazar caught her. "Goddess," she whispered, not sure if she was referring to the dog or Malth's arms around her.

For a moment, the world stood still. Sure, yes, the dogs were still bounding around the kitchen, bouncing precariously close to the two of them, although Malth held them in place. Apollo even let out short yips, telling the world his friend had come to visit or perhaps reminding her that it was treat time. All Delta found she could focus on was Malth's face and arms around her, and the feeling of wet warmth as her tea dribbled down between them.

"It's okay," he said calmly, as if his entire world wasn't imploding. "I suppose this was the little pup I saw Eva with the day we rescued her. I didn't realize it had bonded." More than likely, Malth mistook her speechlessness for fear, and Delta wasn't about to admit that it was him who took her breath away. Instead of admitting such a thing, she reluctantly turned to focus on the creature currently eyeing her expectantly.

What sat before Delta was certainly no pup, and if she'd known how large he was, she might have left the house the first time he and Apollo begged for treats. Apollo sat sweetly, tongue lulling out, waiting eagerly for what he'd come to expect. But what sat next him absolutely dwarfed the full-grown dog. Fur as black as night covered him from head to toe, not a hint of color marring his fur. Weeks ago—or had it been months now?—when Eva spoke of the beast, she'd called him a fuzzy little thing. Apparently, the puppy fuzz no longer covered his body; instead, the wiry fur of what might be considered an adult hellhound sat before her with his tongue lolling out as well. His pink-and-gray tongue was the only color on his body, unless you counted his red eyes that seemed to dance with flames. The fur around his neck was thicker, almost like a lion's mane, and it framed his face as he turned his head back and forth, looking at her expectantly. And the size! How was Apollo even playing with this monstrosity without being hurt? Baby Boy or Big Boy was at least three times the other large dog's size. Delta didn't want to think about what allowed the hound's teeth to shine so white and bright. If Apollo's head reached mid-hip when he sat before her, this *pup's* head was above her waist.

Impatiently, the hellhound tip-tapped his front paws, waiting for the expected treat before letting off a light woof, which Apollo mimicked while prancing briefly in a circle. He spoke? Not only could she see him, but she could hear him as well. Her lack of whatever had literally kept the pup silent and unseen.

"I've only been giving him two treats at a time," Delta whispered in awe and a bit of fear, reaching for the treat bag without taking her eyes off the pair.

"Just keep doing that," Malth warned. "Otherwise, he might get spoiled, and he seems perfectly content with the setup."

Yeah, if the perfect setup meant an open dog door and hand fed treats, then he was content.

Apollo nearly choked on his first treat, he swallowed it so quickly, and the second took at least three bites before he swallowed deeply. Big Boy took his treats carefully, and dare she say daintily, into his mouth before lying down near a wall. Spitting one out, he held the other between his front paws and began to slowly chew the first while he returned her look, as if he understood her trepidation and was trying to show how careful and gentle he could be. Time had clearly taught him to lie away from the middle of the room; she'd tripped over him several times, not realizing how large he was. If she had, Delta would have definitely given him a wider berth.

"Don't treat him any different," Malth ordered in a low, husky voice that gave her a light layer of goose bumps down the back of her neck. "He understands the order of things here, and you don't want a spoiled hellhound on your hands."

Without realizing it, Delta had pulled herself closer to the half-demon behind her. She *knew* it was the same hellhound she'd been chastising for weeks about tearing up her hawthorn and burdock before she had a chance to harvest them. Hell, once she'd threatened to withhold treats if he didn't quit climbing the elderberry tree. Crap, she'd accidentally whacked him with a broom when Apollo wasn't around because she had no clue he was visiting.

"Have you ever seen a spoiled hellhound?" Delta questioned what havoc a spoiled one might bring, when this one seemed to spill chaos all around the place.

"No." Malth's low laugh rumbled through his chest, leaving her with a warm feeling as it caressed her back. "But I can imagine. To be honest, I've never seen a domesticated one either. He's much larger than when I saw him last," he admitted, eyeing the creature appreciatively. "I think Eva poured more than a bit of her succubus energy into him and caused this… growth spurt?"

Malth sounded as if he were talking himself through whatever it was he found strange about the hound. Surely, he didn't expect a response from a witch who had never laid eyes on any hellhound, regardless of age or size. If Malth said he was unusual, then Delta would have to take his word for it. It made sense, though. As Eva had evolved, she not only took energy from life, but she could also gift it. As a half-human-succubus hybrid, she instinctively controlled life forces without awareness, but with practice she could control it at will.

Mind blowing! Delta had no idea the *little* guy was quite so massive, while he also tried to take up as little space as possible. After eating his treats, as well as licking up all the crumbs, the pup lay near the wall, watching her intently, as if he knew things had irrevocably changed between the two of them. For several minutes, they watched each other, determining how to handle the change. Ears perked, he stared at her with dark eyes that flashed red at her as if waiting for her to scream. Or was he trying to communicate? Delta didn't dare ask the inane question aloud, but at this point anything seemed possible. The hound broke the stare-off first, looking away from her with another tilt of his head as his pointed ears rotated, searching for a sound that she wasn't hearing. Lifting a lip to expose an incredibly bright white canine, he sat up even taller, if that were possible, while looking past her toward the closed kitchen door, waiting.

Delta shifted uneasily, aware that the warm giant behind her hadn't immediately moved away, even as she leaned deeper into him. The heat of his body enveloped her, and she gulped with the realization that the demon in front of her might not be as dangerous as the one she was leaning into. She felt herself flush with the knowledge that the danger didn't immediately come from the stories whispered under a full moon about demons and their evil progeny. This primitive danger came from her. Her own wants and desires.

The kitchen door swung open as Athena herded Julian into the room, breaking the spell Malth's body had placed upon Delta. Julian rubbed sleep from his eyes, but most likely his stomach had won out over sleeping longer. Between irregular sleep and even more irregular meals, he had absolutely zero schedule they could rely on. Malth smoothy slid a proprietary distance away from Delta, so quickly she thought she might have imagined that she'd just been leaning against him.

The instant Julian laid eyes on Big Boy, his entire face lit up, sleepiness no longer an issue. Delta prepared to assure him that the scary-looking hellhound wouldn't harm him, but apparently, he hadn't gotten the memo about the beasts that the rest of humanity had.

"Puppy!" he shrieked, his voice going to a higher

octave then Athena's, if that were possible. He leaped across the floor, all traces of sleep gone as he fell to his knees, sliding the last few inches straight into the hellhound. Burying his face against the rough fur, he let out a giggle as it tickled his nose. "Good doggy," he said, his voice muffled by the fur but his loving tone difficult to hide.

Surprisingly, the dog handled the new visitor quite well, bopping the boy in the cheek with his nose and following up with a quick flip of its tongue.

Delta looked at her sister in astonishment. Despite not being able to see the hellhound, her face displayed panic at the boy's exuberance. Unless Malth had done the same trick on him that he had on Delta, the boy was definitely a demon, despite appearing totally human. Seeing him with the demon hound cemented it firmly into place.

Like sees like.

"Did you get me a puppy, Malth?" the boy asked, finally tearing his eyes away from the beast to look at the man.

Malth glowered at the question. "No, boy. This one belongs to the house or the house belongs to him," he admitted with a glance at Delta. "There is a good chance that the house is feeding him magic as well, since Eva did."

So, the pup was basically an enormous, unpredictable beast on magical steroids. Lovely.

Apollo had enough of being ignored and shuffled over, bopping Athena's hand as if he could trick her into another treat or two. Without looking, Athena patted the large, *normal* dog's head while watching the spot in midair that Julian snuggled against. Decision made, snapping back into older sister mode, she ordered Julian to wash his hands so he could eat. Ignoring things even when they smacked you right in the face was the family's way.

After complaining that Delta's non-existent bread was moldy, Athena found two boxes of frozen waffles in the porch freezer that Delta had forgotten about. Apparently, even Eva resorted to frozen food at times. Athena considered asking if they were still good after their months in the freezer, but after looking at the two males' hungry faces, she decided it didn't matter if they were a hint freezer burned. Enough syrup could hide a plethora of problematic tastes.

While her sister bustled around popping frozen waffle after frozen waffle into the toaster, where she most likely mentally cursed her about the lack of food choices, Delta racked her brain for more food ideas.

Digging deep into the freezer under the refrigerator, she emerged triumphantly with a package of bacon. Julian squealed with happiness and even Malth looked interested in the package. Ugh. Recalling how much the half-demons had eaten yesterday and the day before, she realized this might be an appetizer. Digging deeper in the porch freezer, she found the other package and waved both in hand. After filling the sink with hot water, she dipped a finger in, swirling it around as she muttered an incantation to heat the water more and thaw the bacon quicker. Damnation, they needed to get a grocery order delivery. Last night's pizza delivery had been satisfying, but even Delta knew that kids needed better food than she was currently offering. The other part of her reminded herself that in a few hours, the food inside the house would no longer be her problem.

In no time at all, the four of them were sitting around the small table now covered with crispy bacon, and waffles.

Both males ate like they hadn't eaten the night before, and Delta felt guilty that she hadn't offered enough subsistence to the two of them. Clearly, they'd been fleeing for a long time before they stopped and had been thankful for what they'd been offered. Delta could feel the weight of her mother's disapproval at her offerings. Shaking off the feeling, she reminded herself, as her online therapist had suggested, that she wasn't her mother. She wasn't her mother. *She wasn't her mother.*

Julian let out a long burp after he stuck the last bit of bacon in his mouth, drawing a look from Malth. "Excuse me," the boy said happily, as if the look hadn't chastised him in the least. Nothing about the brooding man seemed to give the boy even an ounce of fear.

Apollo and Big Boy had taken up spots under and near the table. Delta pretended not to see it as Malthazar broke off and discreetly passed small pieces of bacon to the eager dogs.

Not spoil them indeed... Delta bowed her head to hide her smile each time she saw the exchange.

"I think you should leave Julian here with me, while you two go off on whatever mission you've been assigned." Athena pushed the words out quickly and without any inflection of tone or volume, clearly expecting them to immediately disagree. Raising her chin, she stared at them as if daring them to argue with her.

Delta's eyes flew from her sister to the brooding man. This wasn't what she'd expected to hear this morning, and why, oh why, was her sister telling him what to do? Did she have no respect for anyone? Of course not, she was the Maiden. The Maiden didn't make requests; she ordered.

Malth sighed, but before he could affirm or deny her request, Athena pushed onward, ticking off her reasoning. "Whatever magic drew you two here knows this is a safe place. The house is hidden from the world if it wants to be. No amount of magic can see into it. It sounds like you guys are in a hurry to start this mission, or you should be." The last words sounded suspiciously like an accusation.

Those words nearly drove Delta to interrupt. Athena had no idea at all about the missions she'd been on, and it sounded like she was claiming that Delta didn't take her job seriously enough. The job she knew nothing about. Sure, Delta enjoyed her down time, but work was work. It wasn't like they were sitting around waiting. Their orders had been clear:

they needed to wait to start, almost as if someone knew Malth needed to eat, sleep, and recuperate before they began tracking.

"I can arrange a food order. We don't even have to leave the house, the yard," she amended, before adding in a firm but shaky voice, "I'll keep him safe   or die trying." Athena's words were shaky and lacked the usual high-pitched nasal quality, but Delta could hear the truth in them. As if she expected Delta's skepticism, she added shortly, "Of course, I can order food. I've seen it done enough."

Goddess, her sister was…. infuriating? A leech? For someone who claimed she didn't want to be useless, she sure embraced being, well… helpless.

Eyes darting back to Malth, both witches held their breath, awaiting his answer. Julian, blissfully unaware, wrestled on Big Boy's back while the hound patiently nudged him back and forth, occasionally opening his jaw dramatically wide to gently mouth on and lick the boy's arm.

Sighing, Malth slowly shook his head. "I thank you." Holding up a hand to quiet the protest escaping Athena, he added, "Aye, I thank you, and I agree. I've been listening all morning and it's been quiet. I think I'm to leave him here. The hound remains close by and will guard him. It's in his blood. Maybe the house even called him here for the job. Hell knows, stranger things have occurred."

Athena's relieved smile broke across her face, but Malth held up a hand as he continued. "For now. For now, he stays," he repeated, "then we'll see what the magic holds."

"Awesome!" Julian screeched; apparently, he'd been listening, "It'll be like I have my own dog. Did you hear that, boy?"

Both dogs' tails pounded in excited agreement against the linoleum.

"Where will he go?" Athena whispered as the boy galloped with the two dogs into the living room. It had been the silent question the last few days, and she'd finally asked it. The sisters hadn't even dared to ask each other what might come of the sweet child, and Delta found herself thankful that Athena voiced the worry.

"I don't know yet," Malth admitted. He sat, quietly examining the two women before drawing a conclusion. "There are a few hidden settlements that take halflings like him. I take them where my magic tells me. It tells me where they would fit in, how much demon versus magical lineage they have, if any. Right now, he is to stay here with the beast and you, of course. After that, we'll need to see where he fits."

For a moment, it crossed Delta's mind that Malthazar hadn't offered to allow Athena to see Big Boy, despite being left with the boy as well as the hellhound. Her guilt smashed down the sense that he'd shared something special with her. What was wrong with her? They were preparing to go on a mission and this boy's life was in danger. Her sister, who never seemed to think of anyone outside of herself, was offering to help, and all she could think was she was glad the sexy man wasn't touching her.

Delta had no intention of sharing with Athena that she could now see the hellhound. Warmth spread through her. She had something her sister didn't. Something more, something secret, and for right now, it was her own.

"I'll clean up in here," Athena offered, clearly happy with this arrangement. "You two can plan whatever it is you need to plan for these missions. Delta, I blessed a mojo bag and your go bag or whatever you call it. I also cleansed the bag after your last… mission." Hesitating, she looked at her younger sister before adding, "Something tells me it's important to wear, and you will know when to open it. If you would put it on before the day ends, I would… like that?" Normally confident, Athena seemed to falter as she made the offer.

Delta's mind went blank. Athena had made a mojo bag for her mission bag? Athena had recognized the bug out bag for what it was, not any old piece of luggage, as well as the fact that she'd taken it to California with her. Apparently, she knew that Delta's trip to California had been more than silly escapades, but nonetheless, she'd played along. "Thanks?"

"No worries." Athena brushed off the words, but her strained smile relaxed as Delta accepted the offer.

As Athena bustled around, happily cleaning up the after-breakfast mess, Delta briefly considered taking a picture to send off to Mother Hecate to show her that her precious Maiden was, in fact, perfectly capable of everyday tasks. Just as quickly, she dismissed the idea. No reason to break the unstable tranquility of the moment.

CHAPTER SEVEN

Goat's foot added to a spell should be warning enough of its danger, but morning glories might not scare the user enough to recognize the dangers of its hallucinogenic effects.

Shoving his hands into the pockets of his comfortable jeans, Malth followed the boy to check on whatever he might be up to. Neither woman seemed to know much about children, and they most likely didn't understand that a quiet child, especially a quiet half-demon child, would be up to no good. The older one would learn that soon enough, and hopefully the house didn't suffer too badly while she learned the lessons.

Thankfully, Julian wasn't up to any trouble. He'd found a ball and was rolling it back and forth across the floor to each of the dogs, who in turn would nose it back toward him. After a moment, Julian looked up at Malth with eyes that seemed too large and too knowing for one so young.

"Malth, my head hurts." Julian whispered the words, breaking Malth's hardened heart a bit. For

Julian to trust Malth enough to admit pain and weakness meant the boy was growing comfortable and attached. He hadn't led a life where a scraped knee might lead to a Band-Aid and a kiss. No, Julian most likely would have earned a sharp word or a cuff on the head for such carelessness. Still, the child yearned for comfort and care; he hadn't yet given up on the world.

"Here?" Malth pointed to his forehead. Perhaps the child needed more sleep.

Shaking his head, Julian pointed to the top and sides of his head. "Here."

Sighing, Malth settled down onto the sofa, gesturing for the boy to come closer. "Lay your head here, boy," he ordered, the blunt tone not seeming to bother Julian.

Springing up from the ground as only the young could, Julian complied quickly. He listened well. *That might keep him alive in the years to come, no matter where he ends up*, Malth thought guiltily. No, best to remain positive; he would end up in a safe place. Once the boy settled down with his head on Malth's lap, Malth began massaging the problem spot. "Your horns are coming in." He could feel the tiny nubs under the boy's shorn hair, although they were too small to see yet.

"Horns, like yours?" he asked, sighing as Malth massaged away the ache he knew the boy had.

"Aye, horns like mine, or close enough." Horns could grow up and over like his, or out and alongside his head. Horns meant he couldn't go to one of the three regular communities that Malth usually took the foundlings to. Depending on how closely the demon genetics came though, it meant that a deeper hiding spot was needed. Some halflings ended up looking entirely human and despite their larger than normal size, they could fit in. Others who had horns, or a strange skin tint, or even webbed appendages went deeper into hiding for their safety and the safety of those they lived with. A tail could go either way, depending on how large it might grow. The boys were integrated into society as much as possible. For some, their world became very small, but that was better than the alternative. Death was better than the alternative.

Julian hadn't spoken much about his mother. It was more than likely the witch had held him at arm's length, knowing her time with him was limited, caring only as much as the contract required. This was yet another *mother* who wouldn't gain the power her selfish contract offered; in fact, she would never create another contract again. Few of the boys asked after their mothers, so at least he didn't have to lie to them. Simply letting them know they would never see her again sufficed to comfort them.

The sisters had wandered in, most likely after another moment of quiet arguing, to hear the end of the exchange. Delta wrinkled her forehead in concern while offering, "I could brew some yerba bruja for the aching?"

She seemed eager to help, but Julian shook his head a bit, mumbling softly, "Feels good," as Malth continued to massage the area where the horns were pushing through.

"He'll be fine, for now. If it doesn't let up, we can consider it in a bit." Massaging usually helped the aching, and the boy had relaxed enough that it seemed unnecessary to have him drink a bitter concoction that might or might not help with the pain.

"It's commonly used to help erectile dysfunction as well, but it really works well for headaches." Delta half shouted the words and then slapped a hand over her mouth, looking like she hadn't meant to share this bit of knowledge.

"Aye." Malth honestly wasn't sure how to respond to that. "I'm fine as well. I don't have a problem with that, but I thank you for your… offer."

Athena shook her head at her sister, obviously as confused as he was at her shouting out the fact. She didn't even pretend to lower her voice when she hurled an accusation at her sister. "I'm starting to think you don't get as much D as you claim to."

What an odd pair of women. Possibly even more confusing than most, which said a lot, since Malth disposed of witches who sold their offspring for power. Of course, he would be the first to admit that his knowledge of women might be limited as well as skewed.

Thankfully, the off-the-rails conversation was interrupted by a sharp knock on the door, startling the group to temporary silence.

Malth shifted to stand up but hesitated, not

wanting to wake the now sleeping boy. It had been a long, hard few days. His magic hadn't flared, so nothing at the door was a danger, but he didn't like to be surprised.

Athena beat Delta to the door. Apparently, this time they'd heard the knock and they rushed to answer it, pushing each other as if a prize lay on the other side of the door.

"Delta?" a low male voice questioned the woman, who thankfully didn't respond right away. If she switched back to that nasal tone, it might wake the boy. But whoever it was surely expected Delta to answer. The thought had a low rumble building in the back of his throat, as if he could scare the male away. Turning his head, he sought to see the man without rising from the sofa. The speaker stood far enough back from the door so as not to appear to be a threat, but also putting him out eyesight.

"Right here." Delta wiggled past her sister. "Right now isn't a good time for a visit, Jackson."

Apparently, they knew each other, and even Apollo popped up from his spot on the floor to wander to the door, tail wagging for a greeting. The hellhound opened his eyes from his spot on the floor but didn't bother lifting his head from his paws. Was this Jackson a regular visitor Delta had? Malth didn't want to consider what the fire that flashed through his chest at the thought meant. Mentally, he berated the hound for not forcing the man off the property and away from Delta.

"Apollo? You over again? Your mom and dad are going to think you're leaving them."

Despite craning his neck, Malth couldn't catch a glimpse of the mysterious Jackson, who seemed to be making himself right at home as he apparently bent down to pet the treacherous dog. The hellhound made a snorting sound, as if he could read Malth's mind before closing his eyes again.

"He comes and goes." Delta rushed the words out. "I told them I don't care how often he visits. No one knows how he's getting in and out, but he's no bother," she lied. The hellhound somehow picked his friend up and dropped him off after visiting. But of course, no one would believe that.

Malth could finally see the man who stood up after greeting the dog. He focused on the women in front of him, not seeming to realize that Malth and the boy sat inside. Jackson's inviting smile and relaxed stance looked so different from his own, and for some inexplicable reason Malth hated him a tiny bit. There were too many things at stake; Delta needed to send this man on his way.

Athena was still strangely quiet, and she sent a sharp elbow into Delta's side.

"Oh yeah, Jackson, my sister Athena. She'll be staying here... awhile. Athena, this is Eva's friend Jackson. He stops by to fix things or whatever, but nothing's broken today." Delta spit out the words of introduction, thankfully trying to get the man on his way.

Even from the sofa, Malth could see the confused look on Jackson's face. Had he rendered the older sister mute? Hopefully. *Not very observant*, Malth judged. This Jackson still hadn't noticed him sitting on the sofa. Glowering, he considered what an enemy bent on harm might do to one so unobservant.

"Nice to meet you, Athena." Looking between the two with a tilt of his head, apparently trying to differentiate between the women, he ventured, "Twins?"

Athena giggled a little, startling Malth. Perhaps there was more to this stranger than he'd first thought.

"Nope," Delta gritted out, sounding a little stressed, in Malth's opinion. "Just regular run of the mill sisters. Regular old sisters."

"Eva called and asked if I could get the winterization done, and wanted me to double check the outside spicket. I figured I would take care of it today." Jackson brushed his hands on the sides of his pants before crossing them across his chest. His eyes flitted around the room, but still he didn't mention seeing anyone else.

"Did she?" Today's visit obviously wasn't what Delta wanted. "Of course, if Eva said so, then it must need looked at." Clearly reluctant, she stepped aside to allow him entry.

Malth was glad he'd pulled his knit hat on this morning by instinct. Despite the others knowing his horns existed, it was automatic for him to hide them. His first thought was that Jackson hadn't noticed him, but just because he hadn't acknowledged him didn't mean he hadn't seen him. Malth suspected this Jackson knew and saw more than he let on. His relaxed smile was just more practiced.

His suspicion was confirmed when Jackson stepped farther inside, then, without missing a beat, greeted him in feigned surprise.

"Hey, man, didn't see you there. I'm Jackson." He offered a hand before slowly withdrawing it. "Oh, I see you've got your hands full there with the little fellow."

For a long second, Malthazar gazed at the intruder, studying him to determine what the man's angle might be. "Good to meet you, Jackson," he responded dryly, attempting to cut off any further chatting, knowing it was fifty/fifty if the man would insist upon knowing his name. This congenial act seemed to inspire openness in return, but Malth hadn't trained in the pits of hell to give up any information freely.

Unbothered, Jackson nodded in agreement with Malth's lackluster welcome. "I'll take a look at the faucet, get the winterizing done, and get out of your way." Without waiting for agreement and ignoring the less than warm welcome, he strolled toward the kitchen with the confidence of a man familiar with the house. The two women watched him go, while Malth watched them. He reluctantly admitted to himself, that some woman might find the tall man handsome enough.

The unconcerned hellhound opened his eyes, this

time raising his head to follow the man passing through the room. Even if the house let him in, the beast's reaction to the man cemented that he was no threat to its inhabitants.

"Have you slept with him?" Athena had finally found her voice and she used it to lowly hiss the question at Delta.

Malth suddenly found himself very interested in the answer as he shifted his legs against the weight of the still sleeping boy.

"What? Hells bells, Athena. No, I haven't slept with him." Delta's shock was too authentic to be a lie. "Goddess, what a question. I cannot deal with you today. He didn't even know who I was for sure. He thought you were me? Remember, that was a whole thirty seconds ago. Like I would sleep with someone who couldn't tell me from you."

"Just checking." Athena pursed her lips together, as if she were the offended party.

Interesting.

"I'll admit he does fill out a pair of jeans pretty well. And that hair…" Delta's words had Malth ready to go toss the man from the property. Athena's huff of indignation reflected Malth's thoughts perfectly.

"The boy is in your charge." Malthazar found his voice, preparing to tone down the tense situation between the two sisters, as well as cut off Delta from complimenting the interloping even more. Apparently, there was a history here that he didn't want to be privy to. "Delta and I will leave in twenty minutes."

Despite Athena's grating voice and bossy attitude, she did seem to care deeply for the boy despite having just met him. This place was as secure as any safe house and perhaps even as well hidden as the communities that took in the fledglings.

Malth stood in front of the small two-seater car an extra hour after he'd stated they were to leave. Delta called it a smart car and declared it would safely take them anywhere they needed to go. Even if Malth managed to fold himself into small enough pieces to get into the seat, he was doubtful it would hold his weight.

Delta had spent twenty minutes poking around in her bag, adding a few items before taking a few out, testing its weight before placing the bits and bobbles back into the bag. She'd certainly repacked it at least twice, wedging items together to make them fit before tossing a toothbrush into the top of the bag. After that ordeal was finished, she headed out to the back yard, removing her shoes before stepping barefoot onto the grass, seeming not to notice the late fall temperatures. Raising her hands to the sky, she muttered incantations that Malth could barely hear and couldn't understand at all.

After standing in this position for an impossibly long time, she slowly lowered herself until she lay prone on the ground, her lightweight clothes no help against the morning's frost that hadn't quite melted away. Just when he was ready to sharply order her to the car, she pulled an ugly-looking root out of her sleeve and set it to burning.

Sighing, Malth stopped himself from interrupting the ritual. Despite his eagerness to leave, he wasn't about to misstep in spell casting. The root burned and smoked up the yard while Delta watched it intently, going as far as to raise her head to see the smoke trail away across the property.

Jackson didn't seem to notice anything odd about the woman's actions. After sorting through a few of the tools on the back porch, he tinkered with the outdoor faucet access on the back porch while a well-rested Julian chattered his ear off. Neither seemed bothered by the unusual behavior, and Malth began to suspect this Jackson fellow had some ties to the paranormal world as well.

"Do you have any better options?" Delta was getting cross and clearly impatient to get started, seeming to forget she was the reason for the delays in the first place.

Admittedly, Malth didn't have any better options and was looking around the driveway and front yard, hoping the shrubbery might give him some answers. The ride-share that had dropped them off a few nights ago might have worked again if he had any inkling at all of where they were going. He also suspected a ride-share couldn't take them as far as they might need to go. Then he spotted it. A savior.

He gestured toward the older Suburban parked

under the awning on the side of the house, farther down, well past the end of the driveway. "That."

Immediately striding toward it, Malth determined that any ride was better than the little tin can she was insisting would work. The death trap wouldn't even hold his gear bag, let alone both of them. Without looking back, he took long, even steps toward the vehicle and slowly walked around it to examine its road worthiness. New tires, and the passenger side door looked to have been replaced as well as both rear and front bumper. Despite being an older model, it had clearly been well maintained.

"Oh." Delta bumped into his back when he stopped abruptly. "Oliver did fix this up pretty well. He claims it runs better than new."

Knowing Oliver, this old beast probably had been made bullet proof and a new engine dropped in it. Even Delta would have to admit that having a mini tank like this was a much better option than her tiny car. He silently waited for her to agree without him having to insult her car even more.

While the two stood silently trying to out wait the other, Jackson walked around the side of the house. "Oh hey, you guys wanting to take the old beast?" Digging in his pocket without missing a beat, he pulled out his set of keys. "Here, take my keys. Leave them in the bowl by the door when you're done."

Malthazar didn't know what Eva had told her friend, but he seemed fairly accepting of new people squatting at her home, as well as using her things without question. Grunting, he accepted the keys, while Delta sighed and loudly exclaimed, "Thanks, Jackson."

"Oh yeah, no problem." Nothing seemed to phase Jackson. The thought irritated Malth more than it should have. Despite being ignored and cut off by Malth, he continued talking as if they were both civilized.

"Your son is cute. He wants to help me fix the faucet and replace the spigot. After I grab some parts, I'm gonna put him to work, if that's okay with you. We've got a few things that still need winterized around the place, and the furnace filter needs changed."

Malth nodded, but for whatever reason, Delta spoke up. "Not his son," she sing-songed. "We're just babysitting. Well, now Athena is. But Jackson, it's very important that Julian stay here at the house. Don't let him talk you into running any errands with you. He's a handful, that one, and, well, he's a runner as well. We can't have him getting away from you."

It was much nicer than what Malth had been about to say about keeping the boy inside. Jackson seemed to take the words seriously despite not being threatened with impending death and dismemberment, as he nodded in agreement. "Absolutely. I'll bring back something to eat while I'm out as well. Your sister said there was an accident or something with the fridge? Do you want me to look at it too?"

Delta crinkled up her nose and forehead before

informing the man with a badly placed lie, "Oh no, nothing to worry about there. My sister isn't used to the fridge and she left the door open all night. All night and day. So, everything went bad."

For whatever reason, she was disparaging her sister instead of just saying no. Malth wanted to get out of there, before she let the man know they were off across the country to track down a magic user down and put them down. Words seemed to explode from her mouth without any thought, and Malth preferred his business be kept a bit quieter. Why give out information at all? Especially when there were so many variables. Despite her smart mouth, Delta had the survival instincts of a bug and Athena even less. However, only one of the two gave him the urge to wrap his arms around her and shield her from whatever might come.

Chapter Eight

A quest to find the seed of Horus would simply lead you to the not so elusive horehound plant, which then might sooth your sore throat and cough.

Delta took long, deep breaths in through her nose and out through her mouth. Watching the large, silent man out of the corner of her eyes, she tried to decide the best way to determine what the plan was—outside of getting in the vehicle and driving aimlessly. Annoyance and impatience rolled off him and even with her slight view, she could see his jaw clenching and relaxing as he fought the urge to say something to her.

Tossing her hair back over her shoulder, she lowered her chin and forced herself to keep her eyes forward. *What does he have to be annoyed about?*

Malthazar had made the proclamation that they would leave within the hour without consulting her, his supposed partner. Apparently, she had no voice in the matter. Taking an hour was a crunch when she was trying to track magic from nothing.

Athena's mojo bag had been paced on the top of her magic bag, tied tightly with a leather strap, and Delta could see strands of her sister's purple magic threaded through the bag. She'd placed a powerful blessing on it, and Delta had to trust that she would know when to open it as Athena had promised. She dropped it around her neck and it settled into place next to her hag stone.

You couldn't rush the goddess; these things took time. They had limited knowledge on the magical being who still went by the name Ibis and claimed to be Ravyn's sister, or at least what remained of her magic. Delta had tasted the magic Ibis had left behind. It wasn't quite like anything Delta had seen or felt before. Its heavy stain saturated the compound where Ravyn had been held captive, giving Delta free rein to study the demon magic before it dissipated. Ibis had powered up any magical creature retained by the now-trapped wendigo, willingly or unwillingly. Finally, this previously unknown magic was recognizable and once that happened, Ibis could also be tracked. Delta's weakness after the event hadn't allowed her the strength to study it deeply, but it had been enough.

But Malth hadn't asked about that. He'd simply taken the keys, stomped around to the driver's side of the old Suburban, and heading southwest. He'd tossed a bag that Delta couldn't remember him having last night into the back seat. She'd sat her own beat-up leather duffel bag primly on her lap, not really caring that he insisted on driving but more perturbed that he hadn't even asked her.

Malth drove casually with one hand, while the other was propped up by his elbow on the window ledge. He had the heat turned up on high, blowing the dry air right into their faces. After a few minutes of the heat drying out her eyeballs, with a huff, she turned her side of the vents off. He didn't seem to notice or care. He acted as though it were late afternoon and they were pulling out; it was still before noon and well before the forty-eight-hour mark her mother had requested. Or had that been a requirement? A smidge of guilt that was as quickly squashed. When a mission was assigned, the assignees got to manage it how they saw fit. Even if it were Malth calling the shots, Delta wouldn't miss a chance at thwarting any of her mother's instructions.

Not enjoying the silence settling over the vehicle, Delta flipped the radio on to an upbeat tempo, which Malthazar immediately flipped off. Turning the full force of her annoyance toward him, she eyed him with eyebrows raised—which he ignored.

"Excuse me?" She drawled the words out, hating being ignored. After suffering a lifetime of it at the hands of her mother, she refused to allow others to act like she didn't exist. "Where are we going? And what's with the radio? Shotgun gets to pick the tunes, it's an unwritten rule. Hell, it might even be a written one." Being sexy as sin didn't give someone the right to be an asshole.

Pursing his lips together, Malth gripped the steering wheel tight enough to turn his knuckles white. He didn't take his eyes off the road. "I told you, you didn't need to come along. You don't look like you're carrying a single weapon, so I'm not sure what that has to do with the radio or tunes."

How did he know things like not giving a child soda, and what a pinky promise was, but not know what "shotgun" was? The pause was so long that Delta began to think he wasn't going to answer her other questions, and she began preparing a scathing speech in her head. Instead of opening her mouth, however, she flipped her phone over in her hand, hoping to distract herself and her ire with some mindless scrolling. *Shit.* Despite being on a charger all night, the phone was dead, refusing to power on or even hint at any life left in it. Tossing it to the floor, she stared out the window, determined not to recite the list of grievances forming in her head.

"I need the silence for tracking. The silence is what will tell me where to go."

"Oh." Delta considered his explanation for a moment. "I'm guessing the silence hasn't told you jack shazam yet?"

This finally made him take his eyes briefly off the road, glancing at her as if he hadn't realized she knew it was bullshitting. "No," he admitted. "I figured this way was as good as any to start. Ravyn is still in Missouri with Sebastian. It's doubtful that Ibis has given up and might be headed toward her."

It was all over the news that the actress was taking a sabbatical. The news had been intentionally released, knowing that Ibis still considered Ravyn her best chance to regain her immortality. This time, instead of the vampire hiding out from a stalker, she was relaxing with Bash's family in their wolf-shifter compound, waiting to draw her prey closer to her and her entourage.

"Yes, but I think going straight to Ravyn is out of the question. Currently without a few witches under her, Ibis is powerless, but she's not stupid. She needs to get herself another coven of sorts before she attacks anyone."

"Sadly, we don't know where she could do such a thing. We do know with certainty that she'll eventually make her way to Ravyn."

"Right, all powered up on the juice of a bunch of black magic witches," Delta argued back. "Getting to her now, while she's weaker, is the best idea."

Gripping the steering wheel with both hands now, Malthazar bit off, "I. Know. That. But until we have a clue on where she is, we need to head in the direction she's going."

Delta examined her fingernails, picking out a small piece of what appeared to be rosemary from under one nail. "Well, partner…" She bit out the "partner" with more sarcasm than necessary, but something needed said. "What if I told you that we're heading in the wrong direction, and that I know where she is? The general area," Delta quickly amended, looking up from her examination to see him shoot her a glare. Finally.

"Then I would say, what the hell?" Malth finally looked at her, settling the full fury of his gaze on her. "But also, doubtful. You seemed a bit intent on packing and doing your witchy mojo in the back yard. Even I know winter is the wrong time to plant seeds or whatever you were doing."

"Eris…" Delta felt the curse fall from her lips at his lack of… anything at all. *This?* This was who she was expected to work with? How was it she knew so much about him, but despite her working for Oliver for over a decade, he didn't even appear to know anything about her. In the next breath, she considered the problems with cursing using the name of the goddess of discord and chaos. By doing so, she might be calling more problems down on them. A quick mental apology, along with a promise to do better, hopefully appeased the goddess. How was it just a few hours earlier, she'd wanted to wrap her legs around Malth and now she wanted to punch him in his cocky face? Although even his annoyed eyes had her wanting to lose herself in them.

Too soon, he turned his attention and those eyes back to the road in front of them.

Delta took a few deep breaths in and out before she spoke, this time attempting to censure her temper as well as her words. Despite being a redhead, there was no reason to perpetuate the redhead stereotypes. "It was important I pack for every possibility on this mission. Some of us need more than the clothes on their back." Mother Goddess Tiamat, she hadn't packed any clothes! So focused on packing lodestones, herbs, and magic supplies, she'd completely forgotten a change of clothes.

That was a problem for later. First things first: getting this bull-headed man to drive in the right direction.

"I wasn't tossing seeds into the air for planting. You saw I was burning a root," she grumbled. "I was tracking which direction the magic lay. Instead of southwest, we can head northwest and cut her off before she gathers an army. I'm estimating northern Iowa or Minnesota. Most likely Minnesota," she amended after consideration. The land up there was mostly unruled and if they were careful enough, an entire coven of witches, rogues, and beasts could hide out for centuries without being noticed. These would be precisely the witches who would be attracted to the power Ibis offered and vice versa.

"You never thought to tell me this earlier?" Malth bit the words off sharply, pretending he weren't the one driving off half-cocked and failing to communicate.

"Well, I figured as partners, we would talk and make some sort of plan. Sharing of ideas and whatnot."

"Why Minnesota?"

If he was going to be perpetually angry, this was going to be a long mission. Hopefully not too long, though, because she'd forgotten a change of underwear too. "I track magic. I wasn't just rolling around in the back yard burning dead leaves, you know. They were giving me directions. Plus, a lot of freelance witches like to settle in Minnesota. They don't want to be a part of a coven or if they do, it's a "take care of yourself first" type of coven, and they're sort of easy pickings for someone like Ibis." "Freelance" might be a generous term for the witches they would find, but Delta suspected Malth had met up with even worse during his missions.

This kept him quiet for several long minutes, as he swung the Suburban around in the median with a sequel of tires.

They rode in silence for a while, only the thumping of the tires turning along the road marring the quiet.

"How does your…" Delta began to speak at the same time Malthazar snapped a few words.

"Could have mentioned it an hour…" Both stuttered off, waiting for the other to continue.

"Go ahead," Delta offered magnanimously with a wave of her hand. "You were saying?"

Malth's jaw tensed and relaxed before he continued. "You could have mentioned an hour ago we were headed in the wrong direction."

Glancing at her phone, Delta pertly corrected him, not bothering to hide her smile, "Actually, it's been two hours. Yes, I could have, but you kept insisting on silence. But in my defense, my GPS is telling me if we take the next exit and follow the next highway, it will catch us up pretty quickly."

Malth glanced at her with a hint of smile of his own before admitting, "I have a few things I could work on. I'll do better."

Not "try." He said he would "do better." Delta nodded in agreement and found herself prepared to offer to do the same.

"Shit," Malth muttered as he hit his hand on the dashboard. Glancing over his shoulder to check the traffic, he added, "We need to pull over for a minute. Says it's overheating."

He eased off onto the shoulder of the road as a hint of steam rolled out from under the hood. They stopped a few hundred yards from a service station. "Oliver gave this thing an entire makeover," he muttered as he shut off the Suburban. Picking up his phone from the console, he punched an angry finger at its screen before letting out an annoyed grunt and setting the phone down.

"Maybe it's out of water," Delta asked weakly, having no idea if any place in the vehicle even took water. Glancing at his phone, she realized it wasn't lit up despite his attempts. Had his phone died too? Digging around in her bag, she scowled when her search didn't result in a phone charger. She swore she'd packed it, but maybe not. After all, she'd neglected extra clothes. One problem at a time, and the phones being charged couldn't happen until the Suburban was running again. It might be worth walking down to the gas station to pick one up, if they were going to be stuck here a while.

Malth side-eyed her before responding dryly, "Yeah, maybe… Just stay in here. I'm gonna pop the hood and check it out."

Only a few minutes later, he was back in the driver's seat. "We've gotta wait for it to cool down, but we can pull up to that station. Little low on oil, and the radiator let out a little water. So much for his team giving it a once over," Malth grumbled as he cranked the key in the ignition and slowly rolled down the shoulder to ease into the station.

The two sat in silence, this time not even the noise of the engine to break it up.

"What did you want to know about my magic?" Malth finally offered up to an astonished Delta.

He was offering information?

Turning sideways in her seat, she tried to hide the eagerness she felt. Her experience with demon magic was limited. She knew Ravyn had something, and Ibis had something, and clearly Malth had something, but it wasn't as easily defined to her as the magic she'd been surrounded with since birth. The tomes she'd read through barely mentioned it, and if she hadn't searched through the libraries, she would have never known it existed.

"How does your magic work? You said you need silence to track? I mean, I suppose you track. Oliver called you the best tracker he knew. Which is saying a lot because, well, he knows me. But I can only track magic and it sounds like you track much more than that. Like, can you track anything and everything? Only things touched by magic or other things? Do you have to focus just your mind or open your third eye?"

Malthazar's mouth opened and closed silently as he turned an incredulous look at her, again gripping the steering wheel tightly in both hands. Dammit. She knew she could be a bit much. Delta clamped her lips closed to refrain from pouring out an apology, an explanation, or anything else that popped into her head. He would answer what he wanted, if he wanted.

"My mother was a witch, much like Julian's, but also not. Perhaps even more powerful, but my memories are short. As with others who are… bred… this way, I have a unique combination of demon and witch magic. None are the same. The pairings are always different, even if the demon and witch strike a repeat bargain."

Delta's stomach twisted at his words. He meant that boys like Julian and him were like livestock, bred between the species to see what they could create. Clearly, there was value in that to both the demons and the witches, but even she knew to not voice that thought aloud.

"My magic allows me to search for a track from whatever I focus on. Years ago, I was gifted a pendant that amplifies and focuses my magic. On my own I'm good, but with the amplifier, nothing can hide from me." He grumbled the afterthought, "That is, if the magic decides to do its job. Then an instinct takes over and I simply follow it. That, as well as chance and fate, lead me. For example, if there is a crossroad ahead, one might be blocked by an accident or a broken-down car, but the other way clear. I follow the clear route."

The last few days, he'd rubbed the pendant hanging around his neck, almost as a habit or security blanket. It had been easy enough to assume it was important, but Delta hadn't been rude enough to ask straight up about the stone hidden under his shirt.

"That happens at every intersection or every road exit?"

"No," he said, shaking his head. "If there is nothing, I continue straight on. Sometimes I do end up take a meandering route to get to where I need to go, even if there was a straight route. I assume that fate is watching my back and that if I'd chosen a different way, things would have gone differently."

"Your magic keeps you hidden from the possibilities as well," Delta mused, nodding as she considered. "That could be why the car overheated or why we went so long in the wrong direction." Perhaps it wasn't her being bull-headed, and her obstinance was actually fate saving them from some sort of catastrophic event. Magical fate was an idea she could get behind.

Malth considered the events thoughtfully before nodding slowly. "It could be. Or it could be just some shitty attitudes." His grin told her he wasn't claiming she was the only one with an attitude. "Obviously, it's not a perfect situation, but also I have no inkling of what's coincidence or what might have been."

"Right, the magic may have you fight low-level problems, which seems not so great, but if you'd taken a different route, you would have had to fight a boss demon, which would be much worse. Sort of the burnt toast theory, but magical. Being delayed or redirected to a different path for protection. The outcome being you get where you need to be." The pause sat in the air between them as Delta beamed at Malth, happy to have learned something new about magic. No matter what she learned, there was always more.

Malth finally nodded, hesitantly agreeing after some thought. "Yes, maybe something like that. Although always the best outcome is to avoid any demon or hell-bound creature altogether. Oliver and I tried a few studies to see the outcome of things if different decisions are made. He would take the path the magic set forth and I would try the other route. Just on simple things, things that didn't matter. But maybe a child was crossing a road, and that slowed me down, or there was a camera on one route and not the other. Mostly, though, we couldn't tell. The consensus was to trust the magic, and that's what I've done and always do."

Malth opened the door, leaving it open to the cool air as he popped the hood, hiding him from view, as Delta considered his talents. Her stomach growled a reminder that it had been a few hours since she'd eaten, and with so little food in the house, she'd felt bad taking any of the remnants for snacks. Hopefully, Athena would manage to feed the boy while she cared for him. A hungry child might be more destructive than an annoyed hellhound.

The well-stocked station had a few options, and it took Delta several minutes to peruse the aisles and decide on what might best satiate her driver's hunger. If Malthazar could pump the gas, she could try to keep him fed. He hadn't complained, but if she was hungry, he must be famished. Her arms were laden down with bags of goodies when she returned to the Suburban. Malth must have seen her coming, because he hopped back out to open her door and offered to take some of the bags. Waving him off, she settled back into her seat, offering him a couple of cheeseburgers she'd picked up from under a warmer. After he inhaled the burgers, she slid one of the extra chicken sandwiches toward him, perfectly content to eat one and then nosh on the snacks she'd purchased. Pulling carefully onto the road, Malth glanced over at her when she propped her now bare feet up on the dashboard. It had felt good to stretch at the station and walk around a bit, but lingering too long wasted time. Digging through her white plastic bag, Delta found the colorful bag of Skittles and the travel-size bottles of vodka. Thankfully Indiana allowed the sale of the tiny alcohol bottles. If they had reached Illinois, she would have missed out on making this little treat without a liquor store stop. Ripping open the bag with her teeth, she carefully added several of the colored candies to the bottles before shaking them vigorously. Smiling as the colors began swirling throughout the liquor, Delta set them aside and pulled out another tiny bottle of rum. Opening the cap, she slugged down the bottle in three gulps, savoring the coconut flavor as it warmed her thoroughly. She could feel Malth's eyes on her, and she shook one of the vodka infusions vigorously, before opening the bottle and enjoying a tart sip of the liquid.

"Are you allowed to drink that?" Malth asked sharply as he glanced from the road to her and back again several times.

"What are you talking about? I'm of age," Delta informed him as she drew another sip, before screwing the cap back on. Those flavors needed to mellow together a bit more. Dropping them back into her plastic bag, she pulled out a bag of gummy worms. *Oh, those would have been good in the bottle as well.* Maybe next time. She ripped open the bag and alternated bites of the gummy worms with the remaining sour candies. "Anyhow, it's caffeine you're thinking of, and who told you that?" she asked suspiciously.

"No one." The words came out so quickly that she knew he lied. "Isn't it illegal to drink and drive?"

Delta snorted, any of them really followed the laws of humans when they didn't want to. "Who told you?"

"Your sister," he reluctantly admitted. "When you were switching out some herbs, she whispered it to me." Delta waited while he continued, "Oliver may have mentioned something about it in the mission instructions. But still, I don't know that drinking alcohol is—"

Delta waved off whatever he was going to say. "I barely had any. I made that up for later. Besides, plant-based alcohol opens up my third eye, so I can grasp things within the fifth dimension better. It's a witch thing you wouldn't understand."

Malth roared with laughter that startled Delta enough that she pulled her feet down from the dashboard. "You're a terrible liar," he finally gasped out, before laughter overcame him again.

"I am not," Delta lied, before erupting in giggles herself. She *was* a terrible liar; it was amazing that her mother and sister didn't see through the lies when she told them outrageous stories. The more outrageous and poorly told the more they believed, and sometimes she forgot that others weren't so gullible.

"Should I be referring to you by your title?" Malth didn't take his eyes off the road when he asked the question once his laughter subsided. He seemed so earnest after his infectious laughter.

If Delta had thought his smile marvelous, his laughter warmed her better than the alcohol did. "Title?" She was puzzled. Did he mean like the title of Witch or Oliver's Witch? She'd been referred to by both, but personally she preferred her name. Truth be told, mostly she accepted her name. No one seemed open to the idea of allowing her to pick a new one for herself.

Malth deadpanned, "Princess. Seems like I heard a lot of titles rolling around back at Eva's house. Wasn't sure if I should be referring to you as royalty."

Delta snorted, then choked in surprise, gasping to catch her breath as she fought to cough and breathe at the same time.

Malth's eyes, wide with concern, shot over toward her, not sure if he should pull over or pound her on the back.

"No," she gasped, choking on the saliva in her mouth. "Absolutely not."

"Sounds like your family is some sort of witch or magical royalty."

Delta shook her head. She lay back against the seat, closing her eyes. "No, *I'm* absolutely not royalty. My mother and my sister are," she corrected, "but I'm not."

"I don't think it works that way," Malth questioned her statement hesitantly. "Does it?"

"In my family, it absolutely does," Delta replied firmly without opening her eyes or raising her head from the seat. Hopefully, her tone conveyed to him that this line of discussion was over. "I'm the witch who isn't supposed to be."

Ding, ding, ding.

The alarm interrupted whatever either of them might have said next. Malthazar looked at the dashboard in dismay. What issues could the vehicle be having now? The red light next to the gas gauge flashed the low gas warning, letting them know they were in danger of being stranded.

"What the hell?" Malth muttered, as he gestured toward it. "I just filled it." He smacked the dashboard a few times with the flat of his hand. "It's got to be malfunctioning."

Delta nodded in agreement, not sure what might be malfunctioning. Either they had gas or they didn't. Right? "We passed another station a little bit back, and I'm not sure how far ahead we might be looking for one," she admitted, worried that she might have to walk miles if the car stalled.

"We'll turn around," Malth decided immediately, turning wide and throwing up dust and gravel as he used the shoulder of the road to make the turn. "It should have a few dozen miles left in it, but I agree. Don't want to take the chance."

They arrived at the gas station, and Delta had the door open before Malth had even shut the truck off. "I'll grab another drink. Want anything?"

"No. Well, a couple water bottles," he amended.

"Really." Delta shrugged. Who didn't have a list of road trip snacks they immediately went for? He had declined her offer to share her snacks, and she thought maybe he had a preference. "Suit yourself." Gathering up her trash to deposit on her way inside, she hurried so their stop wouldn't have to be quite as long as the previous one.

By the time she returned, he had it filled up, ready to go. Arms full of drinks, she managed to pull the door open with a few fingers, catching it with her hip before it slammed shut. "They had Icees!"

Malth looked at her a bit put off, so she apologized quickly as she hopped in sideways. "Sorry, the line was long for the Icee. Then my credit card wouldn't work so they called authorization. But I got your water." Delta offered him one of the cold ones, before dropping the others to the floor of the SUV, "If you really want an Icee, you can have mine." She generously offered; while internally hoping he would refuse it. Silently Malth took the water from her. Cracking it open, he lifted it to his mouth and drank deeply, nearly finishing the bottle in one go. Maybe she should have offered to get him a drink at the previous stop? Clearly, neither of them was cut out for this partnering up stuff.

CHAPTER NINE

Ivy or a cat's foot might be used in a love spell or a banishment spell, depending on the mood of the caster.

"No, but thank you," he finally said. Maybe he'd considered her offer. "I'm glad you found something to your liking." The shift in his tone drove the dark mood in the car to a somewhat more manageable acceptance of their situation. It was an old car and sometimes things went wrong with old cars, but it was still moving them forward.

Did Malth not get much in the way of adult interactions? His words often seemed rehearsed or delayed, perhaps he wasn't sure what the correct response might be. Was he overthinking every word that left his mouth? When he didn't hesitate, didn't consider every word, he was nearly fun. Did he ever hang out with people? Despite Oliver and him claiming a friendship, they didn't seem to see each other that often. Goddess knew Oliver rarely let his guard down to relax, talk, or have fun, although that had changed since Eva had come into his life. Still,

Malth didn't seem to have anyone he could just "be" with, and it didn't seem to come natural for him. Children barely out of the toddler years couldn't offer too much in the way of stimulating conversation, although Delta had to admit, Julian was pretty entertaining for a kid.

"What is that?" Sniffing the air, Malth asked the question after less than thirty minutes of silence.

Maybe things have already improved, Delta thought hopefully.

Hesitantly, maybe unused to requesting information from someone, he clarified, "That smell, it's familiar, but off."

Scrunching her face in confusion, she didn't stop what she was doing but did sniff the air. "What is what?" Goddess, did she stink?

"That stuff you keep rubbing on yourself? Some sort of pheromone?"

Bewildered, she paused rubbing the lotion on her arms, not looking at him so he wouldn't see the pleased expression she was sure filled her face. Projecting, much? Sniffing at her arm, she didn't notice anything strange about it. Just the typical coconut sort of chemical smell one might expect.

"As if," she snorted with a half-smile. "If you're feeling something, that's all you. This is my sunscreen." Tilting the package toward him, she showed him the SPF 65 that she'd been applying regularly every hour. The old vehicle's windows let in every bit of the late fall sunlight, and she refused to let it burn her sensitive skin. "I'm a redhead," she explained, "fair-skinned, and I burn easily. Just because it's getting dark earlier doesn't mean the sunlight can't damage me."

"Isn't there a spell or potion for that sort of thing?"

"I mean, zinc oxide is sort of a potion. But no, I tried to make my own potion." Wrinkling her nose in disgust at the memory, she added, "In short, it was a disaster. It smelled like cat piss and pond scum. So, I stick with my SPF 65 and remain burn-free. I just have to apply it often."

"Why did it smell like cat piss and pond scum?" Malth was suddenly full of questions.

Delta found it amusing that sunscreen could be such a deep topic to discuss. But it beat him wrinkling his nose at her eating habits.

"Most likely because that's what I used in the potion." Delta laughed at Malth's incredulous expression. "Sue me, I wasn't trying to get FDA approval to sell the stuff, I just wanted sun protection. But goddess, I stank!"

They laughed, and Delta reveled more in the ease in which the half-demon relaxed as the laughter flowed through him. He leaned against the window with one hand propping his head up and the other casually on the steering wheel, still softly chortling.

Delta felt a sense of pride at getting him to relax. If she found him handsome when he tried to ignore her, his smile nearly had her climbing over the armrest that separated them.

As she was considering flipping the armrest up and scooting into the middle seat, a *thunk* outside of the vehicle interrupted her ideas. The SUV rattled as the *thunk, thunk, thunk* continued beating against the side of the vehicle just behind her.

"Damnation," Malth cursed, his smile immediately lost. He glanced in his mirror as he sat up straight and began carefully slowing down again. "Seriously? Can't we even go a hundred miles…"

"What is it now?" Suddenly her heart pounded in her chest as the clambering on the vehicle remained steady beside them. Were they under an attack?

"A flat." Malth grumbled, "a flat tire, but we need to take care of it before we drive any farther." He eased the thumping SUV off to the side of the flat road, giving passing vehicles plenty of room to move around them. "Seems like maybe we would have been better off taking your tin can. But it shouldn't be a problem to change it out. Just takes a bit of time."

Delta found her heart settling down. She'd thought… No, it didn't matter what she'd thought. It was simply a flat tire. She'd had one of those once, and a quick call to AAA had her back on the road within an hour. Clearly not an ideal delay, but much better than the alternative. Thumping her head with the palm of her hand, she let out another soft expletive. Two stops at service stations, and two times she'd forgotten to purchase a phone charger. There was no calling someone for roadside help. Had being around Malth made her adle-brained? It wasn't like she hadn't been around good-looking—make that great-looking—men before. Why couldn't she remember the simplest tasks?

Sitting for a moment, Delta wondered awkwardly if she should get out and offer some sort of assistance. Admittedly, she had no idea how to change a tire, but manners dictated that she should offer to hold a flashlight or something. People held flashlights for people working on cars, right? The sun had dipped lower in the sky, a flashlight might be needed. *Did Malth have a flashlight?*

Mind made up, she slid out of the SUV and gasped when she saw the shredded back tire. It looked like an animal had ripped its claws through the rubber, fighting to escape it. The passenger side door regaled her with a loud screech as she pushed it closed. Oliver might want to recheck the mechanics work on the old vehicle. Wrapping her arms around herself, she attempted to look like she might have an idea or suggestion on what to do.

Thankfully, Malth didn't seem to expect her opinion on the tire. With a grunt, he lowered himself to the ground, sliding under the truck at the back. Delta stepped back and tilted her head before seeing that a tire was attached underneath. She hadn't known it was under there, but she decided not to share her lack of knowledge with Malthazar as he manhandled the tire with expert ease from under the car. Opening the back hatch, he lifted the underside of the trunk, revealing a plethora of tools. Did her car have all that stuff in the trunk? Clearly not all of it, but even the smart car maybe had at least a small jack. Could she have changed her own tire before? Malthazar didn't seem fazed by the task, acting like it were an everyday thing, like brushing one's teeth.

Laying out the tools, he closed the truck before examining the shredded tire. "Bit of bad luck," he mused.

"Seems like if we didn't have that, we would have no luck at all," Delta quipped. As soon as the words left her mouth, realization hit her like a brick. "Damnation," she repeated his earlier curse.

A quick glance from Malth had her explaining. "All of this isn't coincidence. Ibis has herself a catalyst. I'm willing to bet money on it. Of course, the way things are going, she would probably make me somehow lose that bet. Heading in the wrong direction, the petty arguments, no gas, phones going dead, my credit card, bit of tempers, overheating, and now this." Delta ticked off the list, wondering if anything else had slowed them down without them realizing it. Guilt flashed through her when she considered how long she'd lingered over her magic bag, unnecessarily checking and rechecking while she delayed their departure.

Perhaps it was a low-level one, and she was simply boosting their power to deter anyone from trying to find her. Perhaps that was the reason her mother's people had lost her trail. Nothing blatant, nothing quite dangerous, yet minor annoyances designed to slow them down, to deter them from the trail. Delta couldn't be sure if it was aimed directly at them or anyone who was looking for Ibis. Considering the possibility of her knowing who exactly would be sent after her, it was a generic blanket effect—one that perhaps now they recognized it would be shaken off.

"Fuck!" Malth ran a hand across his face as he tried to open the back passenger door. And then her door. Peering into the SUV, he asked her sharply, "Did you lock the doors?"

"No, I just got out. I don't think I can even lock the doors from this side. It's old."

"Well, I think your catalyst locked all the doors on us."

"You have the keys with you, right? So, no problem. Get the tire changed and then we unlock it." Fine, so recognizing it didn't shake off the magic. But they would get things under control and be back on the right shortly.

Tight-lipped, Malth shook his head. "Idiot," he mumbled to himself.

Delta peered through the window. There the keys sat on the middle of the seat, almost tauntingly. Were they really mocking them through the dusty windows? No, not possible.

Sighing, Malth continued, "No, apparently, I didn't bring the keys with me. And the doors are locked. Any chance you can magic open a door?"

Gravel crunched as a car pulled in behind them. Delta found herself shielding her eyes from the sun, as she tried to determine who had pulled in behind them. Friend or foe? Either was possible and at this point, she would be happy to see an enemy if it would take Malth's irritation off her. Her answer came soon enough when the red and blue lights began flashing from the unmarked car.

Dusting his hands off on his pants, Malth casually stepped in front of her, shielding her from dust and the view of the trooper inside the police car. If everything wasn't going so damn wrong, Delta might have found herself considering his protective action a bit more. Instead, she filed it away for later, focusing on the issues at hand.

Damnation. Just what they needed, the law checking on what they were doing. The dust had settled down before the state trooper set a single foot outside the car.

"Afternoon," he offered up, friendly enough despite the hand resting on his sidearm.

"'Officer," Malth offered up in a matching tone that Delta found a hint unbelievable. He'd settled into a casual stance that led Delta to believe he was prepared to spring into action as needed.

"Bit of car trouble?"

"Yup, blew a tire and getting it changed," Malth offered up, shifting the tire iron in his grip.

Nodding in commiseration, the trooper glanced behind him at the traffic. "I'll hang out here with my lights. That tends to make even the idiots move over."

Malth nodded, and Delta prayed to the goddess he

would simply change the tire and not challenge the officer. Apparently, Malth decided that was the best course as well.

Grunting, he began pumping the jack to raise the SUV off the ground. Despite how quickly he made it happen, the trooper didn't seem inclined to simply wait in his car.

"Either of you Miss Nance?" The officer appeared to be making casual conversation while Malthazar made even quicker work of the lug nuts. "Says this here vehicle is registered to Eva Nance out of Ohio."

"She's my sister," Malth answered with a quick glance up from the tire, but he didn't offer any additional information. Delta stood quietly watching the exchange, wondering if she was supposed to be quiet. Crap, what if this officer asked to see some identification? Did Malth even have an ID or, shit, a driver's license? Panic ensued, as Delta considered the possibilities. If she could get to her bag... Belladonna, perhaps, but just as quickly she discarded the extreme idea. The officer wasn't a lover looking to forget them. What were the chances she'd packed some dried morning glories or forget-me-nots? Slim to none, for sure. Mental note, grind up some of the memory herb for the future.

"Sister?" The man questioned it like it wasn't possible for Malthazar to have a sister, and Delta opened her mouth to confirm the relationship.

Malth casually beat her to it. "Sister-in-law. Married to my brother. Half-brother, different fathers.

141

She loaned us her truck." Looking up from the tire, he nodded toward Delta. "She drives a little bitty smart car, she calls it. I couldn't spend an hour riding shotgun in that thing."

The officer snorted before nodding in agreement. "Damn right. Whoever decided to call those little things smart sure seemed dumb. And ma'am, you are…?"

Delta wasn't fooled by his good ole boy act. "I'm Delta. Delta Blair." She matched the last name of her current license. Her mother would kill her if she gave out the family name.

Nodding slowly, the trooper looked around as another car slowed down, giving them a wide berth. "Another sister? His sister?"

"Oh no, Eva is also my sister... in... law. But us..." She pointed between herself and Malth. "We're not related at all." She trailed off, stopping herself from slapping a hand over her mouth. Goddess, he'd better not ask her to explain relationships any better. Why didn't she just agree to be Eva's friend? That wasn't a lie. What if he asked questions about Eva? Without her phone, she didn't even have their numbers to call to confirm the vehicle loan. "We also locked ourselves out of the car."

Delta's eyes grew wide as she overshared. She didn't have to glance down at Malthazar to know he'd gone stiff at her declaration. But hell, it was going to be obvious in a few minutes when Malth lowered the car and they couldn't get back in it. Sure, maybe she could magic open the lock, but what if the officer waited around? Were they going to hang out on the highway, waving at the officer until he drove away?

"Damn if your family reunions don't get crazy." Adjusting his hat, the trooper sighed. He watched a semi pass them, blowing more dust in the air. "It's an old car; let me get my thing."

Malth and Delta were silent as the trooper walked back to his car and pulled out a wedge and rod. "Don't get a chance to do this much anymore with all the smart cars and apps. Hopefully, I'm not too out of practice."

Wiggling the wedge into the car door, the trooper began working the thin rod into the gap, as Malth lowered the jack and then released it.

"I got off ten minutes ago, and my wife's got a hot dish calling my name. Y'all ever had a hot dish back in Ohio?"

"No sir, I don't believe so, but I'm from Illinois," Delta admitted, not really knowing what he was talking about.

Malth grunted, which the man must have taken as a negative.

"I know a couple of good cooks in Illinois who could make a mean hot dish. Nothing better than a meat and potato casserole after a long day." The man kept his focus on the Suburban, wiggling the rod into place as he talked to the two of them without seeming to wait for an answer. "You folks heading to Minnesota?"

They didn't bother denying it. The direction they were heading meant they were either stopping right before they got to the state or heading there.

"Suppose you've never gotten to try a Juicy Lucy either."

Were they still talking about food?

"You folks should try it while you're there. Got to have someone who cooks it up right for you, so it's not raw in the middle."

Yup, they must be still talking about food, but what was it? Raw?

In less than two minutes, the familiar click of the lock had the trooper grinning happily. "Haven't lost my touch." He wiped his hands on his pants before he folded the rod up slowly, clearly not in any hurry yet either, despite his talk of wanting to get home to his wife and his dinner.

Still, Delta found herself clapping her hands together as her new hero pulled open the door, proving that wiggling his strange wire around had worked. Even Malth's dour glance couldn't stop her excitement. "That's amazing! Thank you." Bouncing on her toes, she turned to shoot a happy smile at Malth. The stranger had unlocked the door without magic and she didn't have to admit that she might not be able to do so even with magic. Their run of bad luck had to be turning around; as soon as she could, she would sort out this catalyst magic and take it apart. Nothing could stop them.

Then he surprised her. Malth smiled. Smiled *at*

her. The sides of his mouth turned upward, white teeth peeked out, crinkles filled around his lit-up eyes, and he focused its full glory straight at her.

Without another single thought, Delta stepped forward and kissed him.

If she'd thought his smile glorious and his laughter intoxicating, his kiss took her straight to heaven. Of course, at first, he stood frozen as she wrapped her arms around him, pulled him to her, and planted her lips straight on to his. Eyes closed, for a split second, Delta considered that she'd made a huge mistake. Getting caught up in the moment, then jumping in without restraint usually took some effort, but this moment felt right.

It only took a second for his lips to relax and match hers. Another second, and his arms tightened around, her lifting her a bit off the ground.

Did her toes curl? *Do* toes curl? Suddenly, the romance books that Eva enjoyed reading made sense to Delta. Delta thought she'd even kicked her foot back a hint as she mashed her lips deeper against Malth. Suddenly, it wasn't a kiss in celebration of the door being unlocked. It was... something else. Something shifted. The overjoyed eagerness that began the kiss developed into something else as Malth kissed her with more urgency. Just as her hands itched to move up his body, reality settled in.

"Eh, hmmm..." The forgotten trooper cleared his throat. "Good thing you're not sisters. Am I right?"

Delta broke away from the kiss, although Malth

didn't release her from his arms. He relaxed his grip enough that her feet were once again firmly planted on the ground. A quick glance at the trooper showed him standing there, awkwardly holding his tool, waiting to get past them back to the safety of his own car.

"Thank you." She tapped her forehead against Malth's chest and knew her voice was muffled.

A grunt of surprise escaped her when Malth picked her up and pivoted her with ease out of the state trooper's way. Poor man, he wanted to get home to his wife's hot dish. *Wait, was that some sort of euphemism?* No. No, it wasn't. It was dinner, that's all.

Even Malth should be impressed with the ease with which the man had unlocked the door. However, he immediately entered the driver's side of the Suburban and slammed the door, leaving her feeling a sort of cold abandonment outside in the cool evening air. Delta stood by the passenger door, waving cheerfully at the trooper as he quickly eased into traffic, eager to finish his work day. Hmmm, maybe the trooper would have shoved off if he hadn't known their predicament, but now they had the car unlocked and hadn't needed to resort to breaking windows.

Grinning, she ignored the fact that Malth hadn't unlocked the door yet. A smile plastered to her face, she watched the trooper's car disappear in the distance, attempting to hide the fact that she was worried he would pull away and leave her standing alongside the highway.

Click.

Relief rushed through her; thankfully, no awkward attempt to get home needed to be made. Sliding into the well-worn leather seat, Delta relaxed, knowing that they were at least one step closer to their destination.

That kiss. What had she been thinking throwing herself at him like that? Although he'd seemed to reciprocate, perhaps she had all of her wires crossed and magic signals scrambled. Goddess, he probably felt like she'd attacked him, and he couldn't push her off in front of the human law enforcement. Maybe she should say something? Maybe apologize?

"That's no low-level catalyst," Malth rumbled, as he turned his signal on before carefully re-entering the highway. "Thought we were gonna get hauled off."

Okay, apparently this was how it was going to play out. The kiss hadn't happened. Or maybe Malth had thought it was part of their cover and he went along with it? Goddess, all the options were horrifying.

So, yes, pretending it didn't happen was the correct way to go.

Consummate professional that she was, Delta went back into tracker mode. If he wasn't going to examine her actions, then she would happily go with the flow. "Ibis is definitely boosting." Now that she recognized what was happening, she could examine the magic. The catalyst magic stream was faint and completely saturated with Ibis's strange dark magic.

"Already she's drawing others to her," Malth grunted out in agreement.

Still a bit light-headed from the kiss, Delta

graciously declined to tell him, "I told you so."

If this was Malth's experience with witches, no wonder he was clearly disgruntled at having her around. Between making deals and creating half-demon babies bound for hell, and then witches making more deals with Ibis to expand their own magic and power, of course he thought they were evil, power-hungry beings.

Then she'd *forced* him to kiss her. Damnation, she might be as bad as those he hunted.

CHAPTER TEN

*Juniper, when combined with thyme, can be used to
promote physic visions.*

The redheaded ball of energy trapped beside him in the
SUV bewitched him. It took everything Malth had not
to look at her constantly. All day long, he'd tried to
ignore her. That didn't work. He'd engaged with her,
hoping that the constant stream of chatter would shut
off his brain until she became background noise. That
didn't work. He'd belittled her food choices. That
didn't work, and she even got him food. That made
him feel even worse.

That kiss. Had she done it to appear more human,
more natural to the trooper? The local law had seemed
to accept them for what they appeared to be. Then
why? She was that happy that the door was unlocked?
It felt like more than that, though; something
spontaneous that she'd done on a whim.

If the trooper hadn't been there, hadn't reminded
them he was there, Malth was about five seconds away
from having Delta against the side of the SUV. He

hadn't wanted to hitch her up until her legs wrapped around his waist. He wanted to fist those wild curls and lose himself in her sparkling green eyes. Malth wanted… he wanted to devour her and lose himself in her at the same time. Clearly, he couldn't easily handle spontaneity, if his first reaction was to lose himself in her. Mission? What mission? Doing that got you or someone else dead.

Damnation, she asked a lot of questions. He couldn't get an answer out before she peppered him with five more. But he was beginning to understand the part in Oliver's orders that firmly instructed him not to allow or give Delta any caffeine.

The order also informed Malth that he was to trust her tracking and give her the lead as needed on this case. Malth had grumbled a bit when he read this. Oliver knew Malth worked alone, and to give a witch the lead on a case was double the trouble for him. But if Oliver trusted her, then Malth trusted her. Malth knew that he and Delta were the two people Oliver's own personal alarms went to. They alone had the codes to deactivate the wards. Despite the fact that they never seemed to cross each other's paths, both of them were clearly important to the vampire.

It wasn't like Malthazar had gone out of his way to avoid the witch, but he did avoid most witches as a rule, so he hadn't gone out of his way to meet her either. Oliver knew it would be trying on Malth to work with a witch, but after meeting Delta, it wasn't for the usual reasons.

Simply said, she was stunning. The vibrant reds and golds of her hair reminded him of the warm fires on the demon plane. Despite the other memories of the place, the fires always brought comfort to him. Her curls begged him to twist his hands up in them, pulling her closer to look into her green eyes. Most of the drive, he'd kept his hands firmly attached to the steering wheel to keep from reaching over and touching her to reassure himself she was real.

While Julian seemed attached to her whiny sister, Malthazar had absolutely no interest in that witch. Out of habit, he rubbed the pendant that hung around his neck. Sighing mentally, he cursed the magic within him that was staying strangely quiet. The magic that most likely had come from his own witch mother, aka the reason he avoided most witches. Compartmentalizing witches kept him from delving into the sacrifice his mother had made and the flashes of memories that caused his heart to tighten even if he couldn't quite remember the loss. He hunted witches or he worked with them. Still, Malth avoided spending any real time with them or the boys he saved. He had a job to do, amends to make; that was all. Nothing more, nothing less, until he died.

His reasons for avoiding the boys after dropping them off didn't take a therapist to unravel. Relationships were a weakness that could be exploited. To care about someone meant you could lose them, and it was easier to continue with a hardened heart than to let any of them in. He'd done enough by saving them from a fate worse than death; he sure as hell wasn't going to sit around with them, braiding each other's hair and singing "Kumbaya."

Since laying eyes on Delta, he couldn't quite remember why he had the rules he had. What good did they serve? Oliver trusted him with the witch, trusted him to work with a partner to destroy the threat to those he cared about. He owed Oliver that and more.

That kiss.

Now. The voice inside his head ordered, followed by a punch to the gut.

Taking a hard right, he left the middle line with the screeching of tires to make the on ramp. "A heads-up would be nice," he grumbled, keeping the old vehicle steady as it hit the ramp.

"Well, I told you two miles back I wanted to stop, but you didn't answer me, and then you snap when I repeat myself," Delta informed him, as if he didn't know he'd gotten snappy with her. "Make up your mind. Acknowledge me if I speak to you, then I don't have to repeat myself or assume you've heard me when you haven't." Propping a foot up on the seat, she leaned on her knee while she looked out the window.

Malth paused, uncertain if it would be more offensive if he told her he hadn't heard her but was tracking. He glanced out the corner of his eye, trying to gauge her anger level. Tense shoulders pulled back even as she tried to relax by looking out the window, but the posture really told him Delta was putting her back to him.

Staying silent about it all seemed like the best idea; something told him that she disliked being unheard.

Clearly, she knew he'd been caught up in his own daydreams and hadn't heard her, but he'd been rude since the moment they met.

Clearing his throat, Malth offered, "I'm sorry. I've been out of sorts with this whole thing, and I've been taking it out on you. Not your fault I don't like having a partner." He wasn't ready to admit that he was flying blind, with silent magic and an uneasy dependence on a somewhat flighty witch.

"Accepted," Delta chirped, turning her head toward him and smiling. "But I have to admit, my magic hasn't shown me where we are to stay the night. And we're still in Iowa? It doesn't seem to have a lot of hotels to offer. I thought for sure Minnesota should be coming up soon, but I've not seen any signs saying so."

They'd been on the road for about ten hours, if his guess was correct. He couldn't be sure; the old car didn't have a clock and their phones were dead. The sun had dipped low in the sky, which meant they needed to find a place to stop for the night soon.

"Can you wait a bit to stop or do you need to immediately?" *Dammit,* he would try to take into account others' feelings even if it killed him. Consider this lesson number one—or even number twenty. The strands of magic they were both latching onto seemed to be leading them on a very meandering route. No signs stated that they'd crossed the border yet, and his damn phone wouldn't turn on to check a map.

"I can wait a bit more."

"We'll stop at the next rest stop we see, and see if we can get a hit on our next move?" Malthazar offered up, before glancing over at Delta. "Sound like a plan?"

"Yup."

The late full sun went down quickly leaving it fully dark when they pulled into the rest area at the border of Iowa and Minnesota.

A rest area combination welcome center at the border had a mix of flashing lights and arrows pointing to various attractions the states offered. Delta twisted in her seat, trying to examine one flashing sign on the side of a red barn.

"Did that say casino?" she asked, astonished. Flipping her head back around before he could answer, she added, "I think it did. Why would a casino be in a barn? Is that a thing? I've never been through Iowa before. There are a lot of fields. Did you see how they have the gates that close off the interstate? I bet that's what they do when it closes because of the snow. They must get a lot of snow in Iowa. I mean, we get a lot in Illinois, but we don't have gates like that. And even though I was in Ohio, I've not been there in the winter, but I think they get a lot of snow there too."

Malth found himself breathing in and out for her. How could she not take a breath?

"Let's both focus for a moment and breathe. See what we can find or what finds us."

"Remember, I need to use the restroom. This took longer than I thought it would. Hold that thought, and I'll be back in a jiff."

She wasn't, in fact, back in a "jiff," but she was silent and ready to focus when she did return.

They sat in silence, him with his eyes closed and rubbing the pendant asking the magic, the universe, where their prey was hiding. Where should they go next? Nothing.

Sometimes his magic sat at the ready, forcing itself forward even when not called upon. Sometimes it made him sit and wait. Another lesson, surely? Patience. That was one lesson he'd learned repeatedly over his long years.

Opening one eye, he peered at Delta, who sat on the cold grass a few feet across from him and to the side. All day she'd been in a state of movement; even when still, a part of her moved. However, now she was completely still. Other than telling him the general direction that they were to head, Delta hadn't mentioned the tracking at all. He wondered if she'd simply deduced the direction, which his magic confirmed, or if it had been magical intuition? The catalyst magic could be leading them in circles, and they had to hope it wasn't tricking them both all the time.

Delta sat silently, a few herbs crushed in front of her. Despite the rest area being quiet this time of night,

155

that could change quickly, and unpacking a lot of witchy supplies on a cold night would certainly gain more attention than they wanted. How much had she trained herself to fight against her nature to move? How hard it must have been for an energetic child to sit still and just be. Mesmerized by her motionless form, Malth nearly forgot his own searching.

Guilt flooded him. Here she was, sitting and trying so hard to find out where they needed to head next, and he couldn't even focus on where they might stay the night. Oh, that was it. He'd been focused on the wrong things. Closing his eyes, he opened up his mind while focusing on their most immediate need. Where would they rest tonight?

Delta cleared her throat softly. "I think I know where we've gone wrong. We've been tracking Ibis, or trying to," she amended, a frustrated note entering her voice.

Malth let out a grunt of agreement. Of course they were, that's what they were supposed to be doing.

"But the catalyst magic is strictly sent out as a general avoidance for Ibis. We keep trying to work our way around that but also keep searching for her. The magic is making us disagreeable and probably lost, as well."

The impatient voice shouting in Malth's mind for Delta to get on with it meant that yes, the catalyst magic was still creating shit to keep them from Ibis. Knowing about it hadn't caused it to dissipate.

Between their magic and the lack of

communication between the two, their day had been spent driving too far or too long in the wrong direction. Course correcting and then having some sort of battle with whatever the catalyst witch was throwing at them. Delta had murmured at one point that she should sever the magic but just as quickly talked herself out of it. Doing so would definitely alert the user that they were being followed. At the time, Malth hadn't considered her deliberations, too busy focusing on where the hell Ibis could be.

They were searching for Ibis, but there was a good chance she was standing next to the catalyst witch. Malth had also pointed out that there was just as much chance she'd boosted a witch's spell and then left, so tracking that magic directly might take them completely in the wrong direction.

"I know earlier I thought it would be a mistake, but I think we need to stop focusing on Ibis completely, and track the magic trail this catalyst witch is putting out. I think even with Ibis's boost, this witch still isn't too powerful. Mostly what we've faced has been distraction and irritation, nothing to completely take us off the board. So, I'm doubtful this witch can cover her own tracks while covering Ibis's magical signature. We need to forget Ibis for a bit, and focus on the trail right in front of us. At this point, we have nothing to lose, we've been at it all day." Even without the distractions and irritation being thrown their way, the day had lasted too long. They should have stopped hours ago to reconsider their strategy as well as rest for the night.

It came to him almost instantly, when he shifted his mind. Of course, he was so frazzled he couldn't even think of the right things to look for. Once Delta laid it out, it seemed simple. *Magic*, he scoffed. Sometimes it was worse than an unruly child.

Clearing his throat quietly, he interrupted Delta. "I think I know our next move now." He nearly whispered the words. Yet another one of his secrets to lay bare.

"Awesome, because I wasn't seeing crap. And my bum is freaking freezing." Delta stood up, stretching, and Malth found his eyes focusing solidly on said bum. With a jolt, he stood as well, towering over her and suppressing the urge to wrap his arms around her to warm her up. He placated that part of himself by promising that shortly they would have a warm place to stay the night. The faster they began, the sooner it would happen.

"What I'm going to tell you is a secret. Like secret, secret. Oliver doesn't even know. Normally, I would never ever, under any circumstance, share this secret, but if the magic says so; well, who am I to argue?" Malth found himself rambling like Delta, and it crossed his mind that perhaps she did it when she didn't want to face something head on? Or perhaps it was her way of facing it head on.

Delta tilted her head, looking up at him, waiting with her arms wrapped around herself, the sweater barely holding off the cold of the night.

He paused to look down at her before drawing in a deep breath.

"Malth, I can keep secrets. I keep lots of secrets," she whispered with a promise, speaking of deep knowledge of hidden unknowns. "I assure you, whatever you tell me will be safe."

Nodding, he bit his upper lip before opening and closing his mouth.

Delta nodded too, before taking one of his hands in her tiny ones. "Go ahead," she encouraged him.

"There are ways of traveling that are faster than what we're doing. I only use it when I need to or when it's the only way to travel." Beginning the explanation made the rest of the words come easier. "I have a stone that is used for inter-dimensional travel, with limitations," he cautioned. "It allows me to not only travel from one place to another nearly instantly, but it also allows travel back and forth between the demon dimension and here. I'm telling you all this because I'm being led to believe it's time to use it. I'm not sure where it wants to take us; it's quiet on that point."

"Whoa, wow," Delta replied slowly, her eyes widening as she took in the possibility and the implications of traveling vast spaces in seconds. "That's a… that's huge."

Malth could see her mind working as she considered the possibilities of such a thing. Like anything, it could be used for good or evil, right or wrong.

Squeezing his hand with her smaller one, she

promised, "I won't tell secrets that aren't mine to tell. This is safe with me, especially if it's getting us somewhere warm with a bed."

A secret from the depths of hell. If he wasn't a wanted man already, the fact that he was sharing this information might put him squarely at the top of hell's Most Wanted list.

It was a huge trust. Delta didn't need to tell him that. Not much was known about travel between dimensions, especially earth side. Hell gates such as the one at Houska Castle were a one-way ticket to earth. No turning around halfway, either. There was a bore hole in Russia that offered travel both ways between dimensions, but it was hard to find and had been capped off for decades. It could be opened only by whomever was the most recent key holder on the demon plane who controlled the comings and goings. Only those traveling on sanctioned hell business were authorized to use it. The humans who were instrumental in clearing the path were mostly dead now, so few living knew its secrets.

Silently, Malth pulled out the stone hidden deep in a small compartment he'd added to the pockets of every pair of pants he owned. Rolling it around in his fingers, he felt the warmth of it and the familiarity from years of use. He barely remembered a time he hadn't carried the stone on his person. Holding it up between his forefinger and thumb for her to look at, he offered it to her for closer examination.

For a moment, the simple stone sat dark and

unassuming between his fingers, as Delta examined it without touching it. Tentatively, she reached out to touch the offering when the magic reacted, pulsating rapidly in his hand, reaching out for his magic, attempting to drag it to the surface. The gasp that escaped her caused him to jump slightly as well.

"Did you see something?" Curious. The magical pulse, while easily felt, wasn't something that he could see, and he didn't think others could either. The boys he'd stolen away to safety using the stone had never even noticed its existence.

Her nose scrunched as her eyes darted around the stone, seeing something he couldn't. Nodding slowly, she blinked rapidly, refocusing her gaze on the item.

Gesturing with his hand, Malth offered it again for her to examine. He had no one to talk to about this thing, this magic he possessed, and he was curious as to her reactions. Delta seemed knowledgeable about many types of magic and their uses; he wouldn't turn down any insights.

"This is it? This is how you slip through dimensions? It flashed colors when you held it, but now it's quiet." Delta eyed the small black stone skeptically as she rolled it around in her hand. He knew it was difficult to believe that such a small thing could hold that much power, that much potential. But she'd seemed affected when it pulsated, so maybe she saw more than he thought.

"It's not just a stone. It's the stone from a fire demon's shit. A very rare, valuable stone." Malth explained the stone's origins. "To retrieve the stone means walking thousands of leagues across the Desert of Endless Flames before you can even possibly find one of the nearly extinct fire demons. Following it, hidden for days, until it, well, you know… and then digging through its shit before it hardens like lava. Very dangerous because you can't wait too long, but if you move in too quickly, the fire demon will kill you."

"What!" She tossed it up, prepared to let the supposedly precious stone fall straight to the ground as his words measured in her mind.

With a deep laugh he rarely felt, Malth caught the stone as it defied gravity and flew back toward the palm of his hand. The connection between them was strong and had only grown stronger as the years passed. "Just kidding, sort of. It's actually formed in its gullet, not its bowels. Thank the gods."

That was it; he'd done it. The redhead was rendered speechless—at least temporarily. Of course it wouldn't last, but he liked the shocked look on her face.

"Big bad hunter has jokes." She paused before adding, "You have a nice laugh. You should do it more often." Then she smiled, a smile to rival the setting sun, just before the darkness enveloped the world.

After she said the words, he swallowed the smile on his face. looking down at the stone in his hands so he wouldn't have to meet her eyes. An unfamiliar feeling settled in his stomach. Not an uncomfortable one, but interesting, like he wanted to make her smile like that again.

"Its magic has bonded to you. Does it always return to you?"

She'd noticed the way the stone had defied gravity when she dropped it. Not much slipped past her even when she didn't seem to being paying attention.

"It always has," Malth admitted. "I couldn't lose it even if I tried. Our magic bonded together, not one or the other, but both, equally." It was difficult to explain and harder even to understand, but his magic reached out to the stone. Even the few seconds it was out of his hand had his magic reaching out, aching to have it back on him as well.

"It *is* very rare and hard to find; and it *is* created from a fire demon. Sort of like the dragons you tell stories about. Fire demons themselves are rare and deadly. Legends say it takes a thousand years for the stone to form before they spit it up and hide it away. It's dangerous to retrieve and even rarer than the fire demons themselves. Currently only three are known to exist." Malth attempted to get an entire explanation out before she began peppering him with the inevitable questions. "They're such loners, they only reproduce asexually."

"Parthenogenesis," Delta murmured, before clearing her throat. "Self-reproduction. It gives a dying species a chance to survive. Mother Nature outdoes herself."

Malth snorted. "Mother Nature has nothing to do with these bastards. They would just as soon eat their young as raise them. A young fire demon's best hope is that a clutch is laid and then forgotten. The books say it takes a thousand years to hatch, to give them such a chance. The first one that hatches has the best chance. It gobbles down its nest mates as they exit their shells."

CHAPTER ELEVEN

The thin leaves of the knotweed resemble a sparrow's tongue and are thankfully more obtainable than catching a bird for one's tinctures.

"**W**ill I see the portal open?" Delta wasn't sure if it was nervous or excited energy coursing through her. She hoarded knowledge like a dragon might hoard its treasure, but this wasn't knowledge from a book or theory or conjectures. This was stepping out of the library and directly into the real thing, the role-playing games she played with friends had come to life. Magic was a fact, but folding through space? Mind blowing, and she'd agreed not to tell anyone. But knowing about it was enough to give her shivers, and she was getting ready to step through a portal.

A portal!?

"No, nothing so fancy that you can see. If you blink, you'll miss it." Malth considered it for a moment, before adding, "Actually, when it happens, you'll feel liked you blinked in slow motion." He rolled the iridescent black stone vigorously between his palms, both warming and energizing it.

"Does it lose power?" Delta couldn't help the questions. Even as a child, her questions had been limitless, driving those around her mad—especially, she learned, when they were unable to answer them.

"It's limited to a jump every several days if the distance is long. Shorter distances a bit more often, and if I were to only move a few feet, I could do that less than a dozen times in a row. I don't know if it charges between jumps or if that's all it's given." Then, perhaps anticipating her next question, he continued rubbing the stone between his palms. "I prefer to do this to keep it calibrated to me. Its magic connects to mine, but the contact energizes the stone as well. After all these years, it's probably not necessary. I don't want to take any chances, so I do it regularly anyway."

Delta watched as Malth shared energy with the demon artifact. How she would like to get her hands on it, to study it. When he'd tossed it to her earlier, she hadn't realized the importance of the small item. Now she regretted returning it so quickly, although she could admit Malth had been pretty funny. Demon crap? Goddess, even dried, she didn't want to handle that. A stone formed in its gullet was infinitely better. Maybe she could change a few things and work it into the next adventure game.

Guiltily, she thought of her gamer friends, the human friends she'd left without a word months ago when she fled to Ohio for solitude. These weren't online gamers who expected people to hop on and off at random. No, these friends had a weekly set time to play table-top, role-playing games. Like clockwork, she'd attended every meet, even going as far as to occasionally sign up for a weekend of non-stop adventure. She'd left them without so much as a goodbye.

She sucked as a friend. She knew that, but she also knew her role-playing group would be jealous if they knew she was off having a real-life magical adventure. None of them knew she was a witch, and she fought to keep from arguing when other players spouted "facts" concerning the paranormal or magical world. One of the reasons she liked the dragon fantasy world better when gaming was how no one was forcing incorrect details on her. None of them knew she was smack in the middle of the supernatural world or that the world, in fact, existed. To them, she was quirky Delta, who brought the best snacks to the group meet-ups and made every decision within the game as if it were life or death. Sadly, at the same time, Delta realized that humans expected people to come and go, and they would shrug and occasionally mention old friends when reminiscing. Perhaps they'd already replaced her in their game.

They'd already found a secluded spot in the lot where they could leave the old Suburban. Malth's phone was as dead as hers, so he wasn't even able to notify anyone where the vehicle was. He'd tossed his phone under the driver's seat like it was a brick to be discarded, but perhaps if it started working again, someone could track the vehicle if needed. Damnation, she'd forgotten to pick up a charger at the gas station. Still, she stuck her phone in her pocket, in case they landed somewhere with a charger.

Delta sprinkled a layer of salt over the Suburban's hood before deciding to add a sprinkle of the dust surrounding the lot. Then she carefully traced a witches' knot into the dust of both. The magic flared briefly as it took root, hiding the truck from anyone who might venture into the secluded spot. She added a blessing to keep the vehicle safe, in case that sort of thing was needed. Sometimes it paid to add some extras to the magic. Satisfied that even if it rained, the charm would hold for the seventy-two hours they needed, she dusted the salt remnants onto her thighs before facing Malth for the next part of their journey. Even if she didn't drive it much, Eva loved the old vehicle and its connection to her grandmother, and Delta didn't want it neglected under her watch.

Holding the handles of her go bag in both hands, she waited for Malth to take the next step. She hoped they wouldn't have to walk far. Even standing there with it in hand made her shoulders ache. It had been packed for usefulness, not lightness.

In comparison, Malthazar had a large backpack on his back that she suspected weighed much more than her bag and her combined. While hers carried potions, herbs, talismans, and other small magical items, his more than likely carried weaponry. It was a stark reminder that this mission was a dangerous one, not simply a jaunt around the countryside.

Hmmm, perhaps it was time to ask Oliver for another raise, although he'd been paying her rather generous salary the entire time she was on her sabbatical. That realization was followed by a flash of discomfort, but immediately that feeling was squashed. She was still at his beck and call as needed. She'd just returned from going to the west coast for him, she reminded herself. Helping Ravyn and trapping a wendigo was an adventure she couldn't replicate in a board game.

Realizing she had an opportunity to leave the city had her running out the door with a few changes of clothes. She couldn't stay near the city as it closed in around her, tighter and tighter each day. Everywhere in and around Chicago reminded her that her mother didn't know what to do with her, so basically, she did nothing with her. Delta was beginning to suspect the position she held at Oliver's was as much for her mother's benefit as her own. The job kept her busy and out of sight of, well, everyone. Delta was bone weary of being her mother's guilty little secret, as if it were Delta's fault alone that her mother's actions had put the future leadership of the coven and the entire northern region in such a precarious situation. Delta hadn't chosen to be born the second child in a line of witches who only gave birth once.

Her mother, Hecate, had nothing to fear. Not from Delta. She didn't want to rule or be in charge. That was Athena's destiny, and Delta's birth didn't change that no matter how much it worried the coven. Only one daughter would inherit the title, the magic, and all the shit that went with it. No, thank you!

Delta focused on Malth, following his every move as he finished rolling the unassuming stone around to his satisfaction. However, this time when he held it up in the dark shadows, she could see it ripple as its magic coursed through it, preparing to be used.

"Grab a hold…" He didn't even get the instructions out before she slid her hands through the handles of her bag so that they rested on her forearms. Grabbing his forearm with both hands, she opened her eyes wide to prevent any blinking and possibly missing what was to come.

It did no good to fight it. As Malth had explained, in a blink things shifted sideways. As soon as the feeling came, they landed elsewhere and her legs gave out on her, crumbling almost to the ground before Malth caught her. That didn't stop her bag from falling from her arms to the ground.

"Easy there," he murmured. This time, sadly, she didn't get a chance to enjoy being in his arms.

"Oh my…" Delta managed to eke out before turning and vomiting the contents of her stomach, regretting her choice of road trip snacks. Goddess, who would have thought the blue slushy would still be sitting in her stomach along with the plethora of junk food she'd greedily devoured along the way? Oddly, the swirling colors reminded her that she'd forgotten her concoction of Skittles and vodka underneath the passenger seat of the Suburban. When her stomach rolled at the thought, she quickly amended that perhaps that was for the best.

Malth didn't appear fazed by her reaction. Perhaps he'd expected it but had chosen not to warn her. He carefully pulled her hair back over her shoulders and rubbed her upper back with one hand while the other moved her bag an arm's length away.

His careful ministrations embarrassed her even more than her vomiting. Could she die already?

"Sorry," he murmured. "I'd forgotten what it's like for those who are unused to such travels." To his credit, he did sound sorry, and that made Delta feel a smidge better. He hadn't done this intentionally to her.

Closing her eyes as she hunched over, Delta managed to ask, "Did you travel with Julian this way? How did a child handle this?"

A low chuckle left him. "Much better than this, actually. Portal travel doesn't seem to bother young demons at all. Better equilibrium, perhaps? Thankfully, I rarely have to see these effects on those I move from place to place." He seemed without judgment, though, as he pressed a half-filled water bottle into her hands.

Delta wished the ground would swallow her up. Of course, a child could handle this better than her. "Goddess," she muttered, "wherever we're staying the night had better not be far; I don't think I have it in me now. And a shower or bath. A bed, a shower, and close by. That's not asking too much, is it?" Taking a deep gulp of the lukewarm water, she swished it around in her mouth before spitting it onto the ground. Repeating the procedure twice more seemed to settle her stomach as well as clear the taste of regurgitated cheese puffs from her mouth.

Malth stayed quiet, apparently not sure how to answer this question. Delta continued steadying herself, not wanting to start the vomiting all over again now that her stomach had settled a bit. Who should she thank that this day was nearly over?

"It doesn't appear we're walking far at all. This cabin is meant to be where we stay," Malth announced happily enough that Delta brought her eyes up off the ground to see their accommodations. "I've been here before. It's an excellent safe house, everything you could hope for."

Enough said. Delta looked in the direction he'd gestured with his head and nearly fell over in relief. The heavy moon in the cool night sky lit up the area like a streetlight. If it had been cloudy, she never would have seen the cottage right in front of them. The pastoral, graying split-wood cabin looked like it might be off the pages of an outdoor magazine. One that said, "Take your shoes off and enjoy your tea on this quaint little porch." The land around the cabin had been cleared of trees, removing any shadows that otherwise would have hidden it from view.

If Delta hadn't known better, she would have thought the grounds around it had been recently landscaped. The meadow grass seemed content to grow around calf-high, with an inviting dirt pathway where scattered leaves led them toward the door. The moonlight couldn't hide the bushy lovage planted along the base of the porch. The underlying scent of sage suggested that some had been planted out of sight, but still just as prolific. Re-energized, Delta had barely taken two steps toward the cabin when the dark branch on the ground in front of her raised its head and hissed at the two of them. Screaming, she hurled herself backward into Malth. Sweet Isis... Had Ibis sent a viper after them now? They weren't focusing on finding her, she promised the universe, as she scrambled behind Malthazar.

"R-rattlesnake," she stuttered out, having recognized the six-foot-long, splotchy brown reptile curving its thick body into an S shape. Any minute now, they would hear the unmistakable sound of a death rattle before it struck.

Malth wrapped a protective arm around Delta, pulling her fluidly behind him as he pivoted toward the danger. It struck Delta that he might be protecting the snake from her screams as surely as he was protecting her. The way the day was going, it could easily be either one. His arm relaxed a bit as he shook his head. "No, it's not. Rattlesnakes aren't local to this area."

"Tell that to the rattlesnake," Delta interrupted, her voice rising in panic. He was protecting the snake. "Ibis could—"

"It really isn't. It's a bull snake, although usually by this time of year they're underground with a colony, staying warm. It's rare they're out at night or this time of year, but I'm going to guess he got confused."

A colony? There were more of them! Even the bright moonlight wouldn't be able to expose them if any were hidden in the grass. Delta shifted uneasily at the thought, but Malth didn't seem to show the same concern she had.

"I'll move him over to the tree line, and then lead the way to the house," Malth assured her, even as she grabbed the back of his shirt to hold him in place.

"Wait, don't they bite?"

"They can, but he won't. Even if he did, which he won't, he's not venomous, just cold and confused."

Still, Delta scanned the ground continually around Malth as he edged over to the snake, cooing to it like it was a child. Handling it with care while Delta watched wide-eyed, he moved it closer to the tree line as promised, releasing it with a few words too quiet for Delta to make out.

CHAPTER TWELVE

Lovage planted around your home wards off unwanted visitors, but also men might bathe in it to attract women.

He'd barely gotten two of the lamps lit in the small cabin, casting a dim light across the room, before Delta's entire mood changed. Again. Unfortunately, it was for the worse.

"Oh no, no, no…" Delta's mood switched sharply despite her not having made her way around the room yet. The glow of the lanterns lit up most of the neat area, allowing Malth to quickly scan to see if there were any more snakes or mice that perhaps had riled her up. Heavy footsteps led her around the room, as she glared, flipping her hair over her shoulder.

Malth watched in confusion at her obviously angry inspection. A bed and a shower. Lighting another two of the lamps filled the small, cozy cabin with soft but bright light. They even had the possibility of a warm dinner. His stomach churned with the thought that after she'd thrown up everything in her belly, she would be fairly hungry.

It had everything she'd asked for; the magic had seen to that. The bed was even larger than some places he'd been led to. Pushed against the wall, it unassumingly had two pillows and a large quilt covering it that hung to the floor. Across the room, a small kitchenette sat waiting and surely had a few canned goods they could make use of.

Delta pushed the two doors open, violently slamming them against walls. Malth caught a glimpse behind one abused door, revealing a small, if not useful, standing shower and toilet. Another proved that the house provided a fairly stocked pantry, of at least jarred goods. It was obviously not a luxurious accommodation, but the fireplace would keep them warm through the night and, thankfully, this was appearing to be a fully stocked hideaway. A night's worth of dry wood sat next to the brick fireplace, alongside bits and pieces of dried kindling in a small basket. Was it too simple for her? Obviously, she came from royalty of sorts, but did she look down on this place?

Settling her angry eyes on him, Delta finally explained. "Absolutely not. I've read this book and attended college in the nineties. It's so not happening."

This explanation made as much sense as her anger over being led to exactly the type of place she'd wanted. A bed and a shower.

Pointing an accusing finger at him, she continued, "You're telling me your magic led you here. Here to a cabin in the middle of the woods with a single bed. One pillow and one blanket and a door to a bathroom that won't close completely. Your magic is a horny little bitch."

"There are two pillows." Malth only understood maybe half of her angry words. "A book?" he finally stuttered out. She was angry about a book. He hadn't even seen any books in the practical cabin.

"Oh yeah, you know: a book. The one-bed trope," she continued with a hint of disgust in her voice. "Two attractive people, some sexual tension, and bam!" Clapping her hands together loudly, she announced, "It's all bumping uglies and wet spots."

"You—you find me attractive?" was all he could stutter out after her tirade.

A blush rose that nearly matched her hair, before she waved her hands toward him up and down. "Of course, you're all… this… Who wouldn't? But this is such nineties frat boy crap." Dropping her voice, she continued, "Oh, you've had too much to drink to go all the way back to your dorm. Stay here and sleep in my bed, and I'll take the short, uncomfortable couch."

No couch sat in the tiny cottage. Aside from the bed, the only bits of furniture were a wobbly-looking table between two equally unsteady chairs—chairs that Malth had already determined he couldn't and wouldn't sit in.

"Are you asking if I want to have sex with you?" Malth asked cautiously, knowing he was missing something, but also, dare he say, hopeful?

"NO!" she shrieked. "I think you're trying to have it with me." Shaking a finger at him, she continued, "No beasts with two backs, no hide the snake. Nothing. Nada."

Her face turned even pinker as she continued her tirade.

"I apologize if I've done anything to make you uncomfortable," he began, feeling a hint of guilt at the way he hadn't been able to stop thinking about her the entire endless day. And damnation, that meant the kiss had purely been for the benefit of the lawman. But it wasn't like she'd allowed herself to be forgotten. During the long drive, she'd huffed and puffed when she shifted position. The redhead had giggled while scrolling through her phone—until it died, of course. That moment had been marked with aggravated sighs while violently hitting the phone several times against the arm rest. When she wasn't peppering him direct questions that she rarely waited for him to answer, she was talking to herself in whispers, tilting her head like she could hear a response outside of the vehicle.

He'd been aware of everything she'd done, including the moment she'd slowly twisted her hair into a bun on top of her head. Mesmerized; it was all he could do to just watch her out the side of his eye as she twisted the long, unruly strands up off the curve of her pale neck where the shoulder of her thin tee slid down. Surely, she hadn't noticed his glances?

Understanding hit him slowly as she stood before him, hands on her hips, one foot tapping frantically as she stared him down. Feeling he personally had led her to this moment, forgetting that he'd offered for her to stay behind. Nearly insisted, but here she was.

Three long strides had him next to the bed. Brushing past her without looking, he could still smell the mixture of earth and herbs that he would forever associate with her. His knees snapped slightly as he squatted and flipped the over-sized quilt up onto the bed. Damn, the years were slowly catching up with him. Grabbing the metal frame under the bed, he jerked firmly before recognizing the release mechanism still needed pushed in. Standing up, Malth pulled the smaller trundle bed out from under the larger bed in the same movement. A small blanket covered it. Grabbing one of the pillows off the top of the bed, he tossed it down.

"There" he grunted, "problem solved. Maybe next time, you can wait a breath before you overreact." As soon as the words left his mouth, he regretted them. He turned to take them back already and saw Delta's shoulders slump. Who was she to be hurt by his comments? She was the one accusing him of orchestrating whatever it was she thought he'd orchestrated.

A mumble escaped from her direction and Malth's eyes shot back over to her. "Pardon?"

"I'm sorry." This time, the mumbled words were a hint clearer, at least clear enough to understand. Clearing her throat, Delta repeated a bit louder, "I'm sorry. That was terribly rude of me. And… you've done nothing, nothing at all for me to accuse to you of."

This conversation had run its course, and she made his head spin. For a moment there, it sounded like, well, he should forget what it sounded like. When this was done, there would be loads of fighting and sex, he silently promised his libido.

Delta might be able to survive on snack food, but the gas station burgers he'd scarfed down hours ago were long gone, leaving only a dull, aching pit in his stomach. Yes, better to focus on hunger rather than whatever had just occurred.

Clearing his throat, Malth made himself busy opening the kitchen cabinets. He'd been guilty of more than a few elicit thoughts, but he would never cross any lines. "No worries," he found himself mumbling with his back to her, intently looking at cooking pots for a meal he hadn't even decided upon yet. "You went to school in the nineties?"

Every time she spewed out a mash of information, he learned something new about her, especially when she was wrongly accusing him of things. Yeah, there was only one bed in view, but calm down for a second. How was that the first thing she noticed? Malth immediately squashed that thought. Thoughts like that caused… situations.

"Yeah… yes. I wanted to have some independence after decades of living under Mother Hecate's thumb. Funny enough, my roommate situation in college was probably even worse than this one."

Malth tossed a look over his shoulder before moving on to the pantry, behind one of the doors Delta had opened and slammed in a rage moments before. "How so?" Exploring the contents, he found they had enough good canned options that he might be able to piece together a quick, decent meal. Decent. Hell, he wanted to make something that caused the witch's eyes to light up in delight and made her exclaim how good it was. Practical was one thing, but he wanted her to eat her fill of a feast.

"I really, really wanted to live on campus and have the entire college experience. But we had to fill out this huge questionnaire about our likes and dislikes, what type of person we were. Trying to match us up with similar people to not cause too many clashes. When it asked if I was spiritual, I put yes. I mean, of course I am, to a degree all witches are guided by the goddess. Of course, I like nature la-dee-da sort of things." Delta paused, seeming hesitant to continue.

Malth turned around, placing some canned goods on the counter. "That seems fairly honest and consistent with what I know about you," he offered.

"Right." Delta laughed, relaxing a bit. "Except, I was matched with a Mormon girl from Utah. Needless to say, her idea of spiritual didn't match up with my idea of spiritual. And her idea of communing in nature was riding her horse, not dancing naked under the midsummer moon."

Malth stiffened. Suddenly, all he could think about was Delta naked, with moonlight dancing on her skin.

Slowly blinking, he attempted to clear his mind of such things. No good could come of thinking like that. He cleared his throat, as if cobwebs from lack of speaking so much needed cleared out as well.

"Did one of you move during the first semester?" He'd never attended college, didn't need to in his line of work, but some of the boys he'd rescued had. They'd spoken about semesters of college work whenever life brought him into the communities they lived in. Eagerly, in fact, like he needed to know that they'd done something after he'd uprooted their lives, proving that he'd made the right choice in saving them from the pits of hell. But they didn't need to prove anything, certainly not to him, of all people. No child deserved that fate. He nodded, never asking for details, but still they reported if he came across them. He would listen quietly, filing away the information and then insist they had nothing to prove.

"No, surprisingly not," Delta admitted with a laugh, slowly returning to her normal confident self as he asked her questions. "We roomed together for four entire years—two off campus, even. She still sends me Christmas cards with a family picture and some years a little newsletter. She's married with half a dozen kids and a grandchild or two."

"Is she curious about you? Or why you don't age like she does?"

"Not really. After graduation, she spent a few years teaching back in Utah. Then she fulfilled her marriage obligation and starting popping out kids. She was too busy to really keep serious tabs with an odd ball roommate from college who stank up her room with herbs. I don't do social media and a few years ago, I sent a picture of Mother Hecate and claimed it was of me. That should pacify her for decades. She'll probably never leave her side of the country again, so it's really an ideal amount of knowledge."

Malth popped the seal of the jars with his thumbs after sorting and verifying what he wanted to use. "What did you major in?" Although he'd started the line of questioning to cover the awkwardness of her apology, he found himself interested in what she'd experienced. Interested in a way the boys' discussions of college and university life couldn't draw him in.

"Ironically, I took a bunch of classes on religious studies and botany. I suppose I could have called it a weird double major, but in the end I didn't actually graduate. I think the university would have happily kept taking my money even if I never intended to graduate. I already knew a lot about plants, but I enjoyed the classes, the discussions, and the experiments. Grafting plants opened up a whole new world."

Smelling the jar of pressure-cooked meat, he considered what it might be. Venison? Not that it mattered to him, but should he give Delta a heads-up? After viewing her eating habits, he suspected game meat might be out of her comfort zone.

Delta surprised him by asking her own question. "How old are you anyway?"

Malth considered his answer; in truth, he wasn't sure. Those early years had run endlessly together. "Old enough to have seen the rise and fall of countries and even a civilization or two."

Delta hmphed. "That's not exactly an answer, more of a non-answer."

"That's the best I can do. You're not exactly a spring chick yourself. College in the nineties? You're looking pretty youthful to be, what, in your fifties?" Malth examined the old, simple two-burner stove. After adjusting a few knobs and sniffing the air, he carefully lit the pilot light of one burner with wooden matches kept beside the stove.

"I'll have you know I'm quite young for a witch. I went out on my own years before my peers did. Some might even call me a prodigy." Delta raised her nose in a vain attempt to look haughty before a giggle broke out. Despite her words and her nonchalance, she wrung her hands together before wiping them discreetly on her shirt. Was she still feeling bad about her outburst? Probably, but as he'd quickly learned, she would push through.

Malth let out a deep laugh that even surprised him. "I'll bet they do." Moving on to the oven, he examined it before determining the battery spark ignition would ignite the propane to heat the oven.

"During your oh-so-long life span, did you ever go to college?" Delta asked the question hesitantly, perhaps knowing the answer already but not wanting to assume.

"As if," he mumbled, but not as hurt by the question as he once would have been. "My formative years were spent in hell. They aren't really concerned with that sort of higher education there."

Looking up, he saw Delta open and close her mouth like a fish as she struggled to formulate a response. He hadn't wanted to make her uncomfortable, but it was what it was. "Yes, literal hell. And no, it's fine you asked. Unlike Julian, there was no one there to rescue me." He turned away, focusing on the bounty before him even as wished he could take back the words. Take back the truth. Delta didn't need to know the ugliness in his world.

"Why don't you check the pantry for some grain or even better, flour, and we can make some biscuits to go with this stew?" Maybe Delta had the right idea. When things got uncomfortable or awkward, just push through.

CHAPTER THIRTEEN

*Hecate's torches or mullein was a gift from the gods to
literally light the way when coated with beeswax, and
can be used in numerous spells and rituals.*

Delta knew her mouth constantly got her in trouble.
She had no filter and typically, people didn't know
how to respond to her. She could blame her mother.
Hecate had at best ignored her and at worse given her
attention when she said outlandish things.
Disappointment, but never correction. A therapist
would have a field day with her, but being self-aware
meant she knew what she was doing yet chose not to
correct or change her actions. Besides, she'd unloaded
enough in therapy over the years; a girl has to hold a
few things close to her chest.

With Malth, however, she found herself wanting to
bite her snappish tongue. When she found herself
prattling on and on, she mentally begged the goddess
to put a muzzle on her. The more time she spent with
him, the more she found she didn't mind the silence
that often settled over them, especially now that the

catalyst wasn't tormenting their every move. Also, when he spoke in that quiet, gentle voice, she found it easy to stop talking and listen to him. Malth didn't fill the quiet with chatter, and when she spoke, Delta could see him analyze and consider her words as he *heard* them.

Malth had created a hearty stew out of seemingly nothing. At the same time, he'd quietly given her instructions on making a small batch of simple biscuits. His first seemingly innocent direction of getting out the flour evolved into scooping a few cups into a bowl. Thank goodness, she hadn't needed to mill the grain. But scooping into a bowl was within her lacking range of culinary talents. Malth followed up with requesting she held out her hand before he poured salt into her palm and instructed her to sprinkle it over the flour. Handing her a spoon, he asked her casually to add a spoonful of baking powder to the mix. Powdered milked whisked with bottled water poured over the top.

Before she knew it, she was sliding a sheet of biscuits into an old hot oven without even realizing the task she was on. Smiling proudly to herself, Delta crossed her fingers that they tasted as good as they smelled. She didn't cook; she mixed things together, but actually cooking? Nope. Malth had tricked her into cooking without her even realizing it. Or maybe she hadn't cooked, maybe she'd still just mixed some stuff together?

Delta leaned back onto the small counter area,

crowding Malth, who stood at the stove carefully sorting the spices the cabin had provided for them. "Hold on," she instructed, feeling unusually useful in the kitchen. "What flavors are you looking for? I have some freshly dried herbs that might work." Pushing herself away from the cabinet, she struggled with her bag to the table. After the long day and night, it seemed even heavier than usual. Lifting it with both hands, she strained to bring it to table height before releasing it with a thump that shook the rickety furniture.

"Um, basil, rosemary, oregano, sage, thyme, bay, or even marjoram?" Malth considered the options before he clarified, "It doesn't need all of those, but we can use anything like that you have."

Despite her usual blase attitude about life, Delta's bag was organized to the point that she could pull out the items she needed without even looking inside. Almost as if her life depended on it, and sometimes it did. When Malth nodded approvingly as she handed him an array of fresh and dried herbs, Delta found herself smiling in pleasure at being able to help with a simple task. *Basil for protection, clarity, and courage. Thyme for openness and receptivity. Bay for intuition, luck, and victory. Rosemary for wisdom and awareness.* From habit, Delta whispered their uses almost as an incantation or prayer.

"Casting a spell on us?"

"At this point, I figure anything might help us out," Delta admitted. The way the day had gone, it seemed downright lazy not to combine the cooking with a request for help.

Malth looked pleased by her words and nodded in agreement as he generously added herbs to the pot, stirring each in completely before adding the next.

"There's some canned butter in the pantry, and some honey, I think. If you mix that with your rosemary, we can use it with your biscuits."

"Canned butter?" Delta couldn't help the skepticism that filled her voice. "Are you teasing me?"

This time, it was Malth who grinned, followed by a deep rumble from his chest that sounded suspiciously like laughter. "It's not common, I'll admit, but it's a real thing. Someone told me once you could can anything, and honestly, I've yet to find something that can't be canned. Most of the safe houses I visit are stocked with the basics, but refrigerated items might not be used up if no one comes through for a while. So, it's canned goods and dry goods alone, along with a few spells to keep pests out. We lucked out with not just vegetables, but canned venison as well."

That explained the savory stew beginning to bubble away with potatoes as well as a previously unidentified meat bobbing up and down. Thank the goddess it wasn't snake. Delta feared that since Malth had begun mixing things together but had been afraid to ask. Despite being loaded with vegetables, Delta's stomach growled as the savory scent wafted through the small kitchen area. Maybe cooked vegetables wouldn't be so bad.

"Venison? Like Bambi?"

Malthazar scrunched his face as he considered Delta's question, probably concerned that the answer would turn her off dinner. Finding herself smiling at his hesitation, she refrained from reminding him that she ate cheese puffs; deer meat certainly wasn't going to bother her.

"Um, more like his father? Probably the old guy died of natural causes anyway." Malth lied to her with a straight face that caused her to laugh until her side ached. The look of relief on his face nearly caused her to start laughing again, but at the same time, he was so concerned about her eating that she didn't want to continue his misery.

"Um, honestly I'm glad it's not snake," she admitted as Malth laughed harder.

"Who cans and stocks the safe houses? Seems like it might be a big job." Delta wasn't certain how much Malth could or would share about his project, but he'd mentioned it and she wasn't specifically asking how many houses or where they were located.

"I've always assumed it was witches who support the work I do." He hesitated, pondering; he hadn't really considered who kept the food in place. "There are many moving parts for the missions I'm on, and it's safest for all if we don't know who else is involved. Even if it's their job to can food or stock some of the safe houses, it's not safe for me to know who they are any more than it's safe for them to know who I am. We each do our part and know that the others are doing theirs to keep things running smoothly."

"This mission is to rescue boys? Boys like Julian?" Delta wasn't sure if she should ask, but he'd found himself using her home—oops, Eva's home—as a safe house, albeit a temporary one.

Malth nodded, his curls bobbing around the tiny horns protruding from the top of his head, while continuing to stir the bubbling stew. "Yes, we rescue boys like Julian. Boys like me. We have other missions we're called to as needed, and the safe house serves several missions outside of those. But the only one I know for sure is mine." Before Delta could formulate a response, another question, anything at all, Malth continued, "Might want to pull out those biscuits now before they burn."

She might as well tear off the Band-Aid and admit the next problem, especially now that things were going relatively well and they were getting along since shaking off the witch's deterrent to seeking out Ibis.

"I forgot to pack a few things," Delta admitted uncomfortably as she rinsed off the dishes in cold water, after Malth had gone to turn on the gas to the small water heater that would heat a few gallons of water for a quick shower. No need to waste it on dishes.

Malth moved to grab a towel and dry the meager

dishes. Slowly, he responded, "I wouldn't have thought you would forget anything."

Delta wondered how he kept from saying the first things that popped into his head. Malth seemed to always pause before he responded, considering every outcome his words could have. "Yeah, well, I'm going to blame the catalyst, but I don't have a change of clothes, and I really need to wash these tonight." She gestured with a soapy hand to her clothes, which had streaks of cheese dust, pizza grease, and other unrecognizable food items—or worse—down the front. "I mean, I can wash them tonight and dry them all for tomorrow in front of the fireplace, but I could use something to wear overnight, if you've got it and don't mind."

Malth grunted in a way that Delta felt was affirmative. He'd turned off a few of the unnecessary lights, but now the dimmer lighting hid his expression when he looked down. If he really didn't want to share, surely, he would have said no.

The tee-shirt smelled like him: a combination of earth, wood, and fire. No sulfur, despite his warning when he tossed it to her. Surely, he joked about the sulfur. Nothing about him smelled like brimstone or what she might imagine hell smelled like. The gray shirt hung halfway down her thighs and the shoulders draped down low on her shoulders. Once Delta left the privacy of the bathroom, she refrained from burying her face in the tee to revel in his scent.

Instead, she casually detangled her hair with her

fingers, rubbing in clove and rosemary oil to tame the worst of it. Frowning, she considered putting her hair up, but in the end decided to leave it free for the night to dry. Tomorrow it could be twisted into submission of sorts.

Crawling into the small bed hardly off the floor, she pulled the covers up to her neck. Having no idea how much time had passed, Delta suspected they had only a few hours until sunrise. Tired to her bones, she felt herself sink into the comfortable bed. Hearing the shower begin, she closed her eyes and allowed herself to imagine Malthazar in the shower. The same shower she'd just been naked in, washing himself.

With a smile on her face, she fell asleep before the shower water even shut off.

CHAPTER FOURTEEN

The neem tree or bead tree can bear fruit used in making prayer beads for a number of cultures.

Malth shot awake, startled from his deep dream, the echo of his heart pounding through his head. For a moment, he didn't know where he was. He thought he was back in hell, facing a punishment that few came back from. The inky, dark dream sat heavily on his chest, and his breathing slowed as he reminded himself he was safe. He could touch the quilt, warm and heavy on his legs. He could hear the silence; there were no screams, no whips hissing through the air right before they snapped on flesh. He could smell the remains of the stew from dinner, the wood burning in the fireplace.

Whatever had jolted him awake, saving him from the emptiness, the hopelessness of his dream, sat silently now. Not a sound came from the small trundle bed next to him where Delta slept. She was already asleep when he'd come out of his quick shower, and he hadn't known whether he was disappointed with that or something else. Knowing she'd been lying in a bed wrapped in his tee-shirt had made him feel things, things he reminded himself once again that he shouldn't be thinking or feeling. Delta deserved softness and all the good the world could offer, none of which he could give her.

Malth reached out with his senses straining to hear, to see, to feel anything out of the ordinary hiding in the darkness. He refrained from looking directly toward the fireplace as his eyes adjusted to the darkness. A thin gleam of perspiration slid across his skin, despite the coolness of the room. The fire he'd banked earlier smoldered now, just a few embers against the darkness of the wall. Not much time could have passed; the windows were still dark but clearly struggling to hold out the cold.

Quietness settled over him as he listened to the nearly indiscernible breathing of the woman lying low to the floor to the right of him. Whatever had roused him from his nightmare hadn't woken her. Listening to her soft intake of breath followed by an equally soft exhale soothed him. With careful movements, he rolled over to peer down on her, hanging off the bed so he could make out her features even in the dark. Her curls were just as wild and willful as they were when she was awake. She looked like an angel with her pale face buried sideways in her pillow. *If angels sleep with their mouths half open...* He snickered to himself, unable to move his eyes away from the still figure.

Despite being awoken by the ever-recurring

nightmare, he was thankful that he finally had a chance to examine her features after spending all day with her. Quick glances hadn't given him his fill of her. He was entranced by the scatter of light freckles that dotted her nose and cheekbones. He found himself wanting to trace them like the stars in the sky. Damn, he never got tired of the stars. Seeing the constellations after decades spent in hell still brought him comfort. Seeing them drawn across her face brought forth feelings he wasn't even sure how to name.

Watching her was dangerous. Still, he couldn't bring himself to roll over and go back to sleep. If he had, he would have missed the shiver that trembled through her, the way her hands clutched at the blanket. A disgruntled sound escaped her as she attempted to wrap the blanket closer around herself. Guilt started him; his plush quilt was larger and thicker than the blanket she'd wrapped herself in. He hadn't even noticed. The fire couldn't wait until the morning sun made its way into the sky.

The bed squeaked slightly as he eased himself down to the end. Pausing, he waited to see if it woke her. Silence, except for the occasional soft snap as the dying fire attempted to find fuel.

The creaking of the floor echoed through the room, not hiding his normally light tread. Using the fire poker, he pushed the coals around until the heat grew slightly. He added the smaller of the pieces of dried wood until the fire snapped and popped, gobbling up the offering. Banking it with larger pieces, he fed the fire until the heat next to it might be considered by most as unbearable. Not for him, though. The scorching heat comforted him as it burned at his skin.

Closing his eyes, he allowed it to wash over him. The dream that had awoken him contained the unrelenting brimstone fires that surrounded them in hell. For a moment, he found himself back in the dream as it snapped at his ankles, driving him forward, away into the deeper circles of hell where only pain and death awaited. Fire could be both a comfort and an enemy, a cleansing and a destroyer.

No matter how it destroyed, he still found himself drawn to it. Seeing the fires meant you were still alive, and not all were so lucky. Blinking, he forced the down the screams from his dreams. This fire was warmth. This fire wouldn't destroy.

Delta was still wrapped in the blanket. In fact, it looked like she'd pulled it tighter around herself in the minutes he'd spent staring at the growing flames. His blanket was warmer. Perhaps if he were careful, he could remove her thin blanket and trade it for his heavier one. Malthazar didn't enjoy being cold, but he could handle it much better than Delta. Had she ever been uncomfortable? He hoped not. Despite her brash outspokenness, he found himself hoping that she never had to feel the heat of a million suns or cold that could freeze your breath before it left your body as it burrowed deep into your bones. Cold so deep you wanted to sleep and never wake.

Malthazar regretted having to tug her blanket free. Even in sleep, her hands clutched at it.

Finally easing the thin blanket free, he tossed it on the bed before pulling the bulkier quilt off the end toward him. Once in hand, he hesitated deciding the best way to cover her. Tossing it over her would result in a rush of air that might wake her up. The warmer and safer option would be to move in closer and carefully cover her with the blanket before tucking it in around her.

Nodding, satisfied with his decision, he moved forward with his task. Covering her with the blanket happened with perfect ease, and he imagined her sinking deeper into the bed as the warmth of the quilt settled over her. Frowning, he saw that the blanket gaped around her side and a foot. If he were careful enough, he could tuck those spots in, giving her a true cocoon of warmth.

Leaning over her, failing to ignore the soft fragrance rosemary and clove wafting from her, he tucked the blanket around her shoulders. Delta had come out of the shower working her fingers through her hair, massaging in the oil, and the scent still clung to her. Using all of his strength, he'd rushed past her to enter the bathroom—a bathroom so filled with the scent of her, he rushed his own shower.

Sliding his feet alongside the bed, he attempted to work his way down. Disaster struck in the form of his feet getting tangled into what he belated realized was her witch's bag of goodies that she always seemed to keep within arm's reach. That knowledge didn't stop him from stumbling and falling straight toward the peacefully sleeping woman. All he could do was attempt to roll a bit and brace his arms around her, hoping to not knock the wind completely out of her. Instead of fully hitting her body, his arms and knees took the bulk of the weight and the small trundle bed smashed under his fall. His head knocked into her stomach, pushing a banshee-like wail from her.

"It's me, it's me!" Malth tried to get the words out before she could continue her screams. "I'm sorry. I…"

Looking up, Delta's wide eyes met his and she opened her mouth, either planning on screaming again or berating him. Her mouth closed before opening, gulping in more air. Malth struggled to upright himself on the tilted bed, but the fragile trundle bed wasn't finished. With a groan and a snap, it collapsed, tilting deeper on its side and forcing Malth's face back against Delta.

Delta struggled against his prone body, and he was sure that if he wasn't pinning her arms down, she would be hitting him.

"It's me," he repeated, this time sternly. "Just stop, I was trying to—"

"I know it's you. And I don't care what you were *trying* to do. Can you get off me now, so I can breathe?" Her voice, husky with sleep, rippled through him, causing a rush of blood to flow to *all* parts of his body. When his overactive imagination had envisioned being close to her, this scenario had definitely not been an option.

Malth rolled off her and onto the floor with little more grace than he had when falling upon her. Lying on his back, he looked up at the dark ceiling, wondering if his face glowed red in the dark. For a moment, there was silence and then her laughter broke through the night.

"Hecate, Athena, Freya, any goddess who's listening. Goddess, you scared the crap out of me."

"I was afraid you were cold," Malth offered weakly as she continued laughing.

"So, you decided that scaring me from a dead sleep would get my adrenalin flowing and warm me up?"

Her teasing tone had Malth closing his eyes at his own ineptness, but she still wasn't done. "Are those the moves you pull out for all the ladies? Do they actually work for you?"

Apparently, snark needed no rest. Malth felt a strangle bubble moving up through his chest. He tried biting back the laughter building up, he really did. But damnation, how had his attempt to cover the witch go so incredibly wrong? Barking out his own laughter caused Delta to laugh even harder.

"I'm going to assume that's a 'no.'" Delta tilted her head up over the side of the broken bed to glare at him. She eyed him suspiciously before pounding him in the head with her pillow, only causing him to laugh harder. "You scared decades off my life. How am I supposed to sleep like this now? Three of the legs are broken."

"Woman…" He pulled the pillow out of her hand, dragging her along with it so the top half of her body ended up on his chest. He could feel his heart rate quicken and hoped that if she felt the rapid beating, she would think it was from their misadventure. "Looks like we may have to share the bed after all."

"I don't know..." Delta pushed herself up from his chest as he held her in place, her legs still on the broken bed.

"I know I broke the bed, and I apologize. It truly wasn't my intent. You looked cold, and I tripped over your bag. I know a true gentleman would offer to sleep on the floor, but I don't have it in me." When the options were sleeping on the ground or sleeping on a bed, Malth would always choose the bed. "It's big enough."

Delta's face was close enough that Malth could read her every expression as she considered his options with a scrunched forehead. Suspicion and uncertainty first, followed by consideration, before finally a begrudging acceptance. Malth schooled his expression, acting like he didn't care about her answer, but a rush of excitement flowed through him when he knew her answer before she spoke the words.

"Surrrre," she drawled out casually, not knowing that her heart rate had nearly doubled as she considered, "but only because I'm cold and I'm not sleeping on the ground either."

With a grin, Malth heaved her upward, tossing her over the pieces of the trundle bed onto the real bed. "Looks like all your college fantasies are coming true."

CHAPTER FIFTEEN

Needing ladies' fingers for a spell to combat curses and the evil eye is, thankfully, as simple as cutting okra and involves much less maiming than one might think.

Delta woke up in a furnace, a furnace she was lying on top of, and one that was snoring softly, so deep was his sleep. For a moment, she allowed herself to bask in the comfort of the man half under her. Slowly raising her head, she gave in to the desire to examine the sleeping man as much as she wanted.

Pushing her wild hair away from her face, she peered down at him. He'd grown a light, golden stubble over the last few days. Perhaps he didn't pack a razor or maybe he hadn't planned to be gone this long. Clearly, Malth's typical mission of tracking and rescuing boys before dropping them off at a community to be raised only lasted a few days. Unplanned side quests of tracking down magical beings formed from hell's demon magic didn't fit into his normal plans. It was all Delta could do, though, to stop herself from rubbing a hand over the stubble. His tawny, sun-kissed skin spoke of a love for the sun, a sun she was beginning to suspect he'd been denied for years at some point of his life. But that was his story to tell, when and if he chose to.

His soft curls were beginning to wrap around the nubs of his horns even higher. Except for pulling on his cap, he didn't seem too concerned with hiding them. The bony protrusions begged her to test them, to run a quick finger down them to see if they were as warm as his body. Delta couldn't stop a hand from reaching up to run two fingers along the short horn closest to her, smoothing the curls down onto his head, so she could feel where the horn met his skull.

Sucking in her lip, she marveled at the small curve. Damnation, how were corns so sexy? Delta had thought falling asleep wrapped in the scent of his shirt had been glorious, but waking up enveloped in his arms could make a woman do bad, bad things.

Malth let out a low moan and shifted in his sleep, causing Delta to freeze her movement, horrified that he would wake up and find her curious hands on him. Still, she couldn't help but caress the smooth appendage before pulling her hand back. So smooth. Did the horns have feeling to them, and had it been a coincidence that he reacted to her touch?

A flash of wrapping her arms around his head to pull him closer to her using his horns flew through her head, and she startled at the vividness of the vision as well as the jolt of excitement that ran though her.

Guiding him to her mouth, and lower… Damnation, maybe she should have gotten laid in California instead of fabricating an interaction.

What kind of professional was she? First time she'd been given a partner and all she could think about was… *Fuck, stop thinking about it.* Her body seemed to have a mind of its own; she couldn't help herself from arching against him to get even closer. Heat flushed through her, leaving her aching to touch him again—and have him touch her.

Malth shifted in his sleep, an arm instinctively pulling her closer to his warmth even as he softly murmured something, so softly that Delta couldn't decipher what he meant. It didn't matter. She was a professional. Damnation, she ached, though. Still, she didn't fight against the pull, allowing her hand to lie on his chest. Should she move her leg? The one that had drawn over him in their sleep?

"Stop fidgeting," his low, sleepy voice demanded as his arm wrapped lower around her hips, pulling her leg and hip farther onto him so that the rest of her body lay parallel against him. The hardness against her leg told her she wasn't the only one affected by their closeness. Could he feel the heat from her as well, the dampness that he'd just drawn closer?

This time it was him who caressed the curls cascading from her head. "Are you real?" he whispered as he ran calloused fingers through her scalp, touching her forehead with his thumb. "Temptress…" His voice shifted from sleepiness to something lower, more primal. "The power you hold."

Delta couldn't stop the sigh that escaped her lips at the feel of his hand against even that small part of skin. Instinctively, she hiked her hips closer to him, rubbing the aching spot that begged for those same hands. The arm that had wrapped around her urged her closer, pulling her ass to him when she might have held back.

His hands locked her in place for a second against him. "Tell me you want me to stop." Malth moved the leg she'd wrapped herself around, brushing along the heat of her core, clear in what he was offering and just as clear they could stop.

"No," Delta whispered back, nearly screaming when the movement paused. "Don't stop." Who was this woman who begged? Who was this wanton woman who wanted to explore every part of him, while he eased the aching between her legs?

Still, the infuriating man hesitated. "Are you sure, Delta?"

"Never more sure of anything,"

That was all he needed to hear. Malth pulled Delta onto him so that she straddled him. She knew how she must look to him; the dark lust in his eyes told him. Straddling him, she couldn't stop from grinding against his rock hardness. They were separated by too much, too many clothes. Still, she could feel his cock twitch against her as she rolled her hips, begging for more of him.

"Patience, Princess, let's do this right." Malth sat

up on the bed, pulling her hips closer to him while his lips reached for hers. If the impromptu kiss along the side of the road had been fireworks, this kiss was nuclear. No longer tentative or exploring, Malth devoured her. Urging her closer as he took her mouth in his, he simultaneously pulled the gray tee-shirt over her, only releasing her lips long enough to pull the shirt over her head.

Then she broke apart.

CHAPTER SIXTEEN

Gathering graveyard dust might be as easy to find as patchouli, but results will vary if a spellcaster doesn't know one from the other.

The fire had died down, leaving the room heavy with the damp cold that seemed to settle in so quickly. The urge to build it up to keep his woman warm wouldn't allow him to linger in bed. It wouldn't do for her to be uncomfortable, even if it might drive her to remain in the heat of his arms. At some point during the early morning hours they'd finally slept, her wrapped around him while he tucked her head under his chin. Reluctantly, he began to extradite himself from her hold, determined to let her sleep as long as needed, but wanting to warm the room.

Even in her sleep, she was reaching out for him. A moan and a soft grunt of dissatisfaction left her before she tossed her leg back over him, rolling into him. A bare leg hiked up onto his waist, which he reluctantly eased off, tucking the blankets around her to hold in the remaining heat. Kissing her head, he whispered that he would be back.

"Bathroom," she muttered in the same husky, sleepy voice that had whispered filthy things to him. Tossing aside the blankets he'd tucked around her, she pulled on the tee-shirt that lay on the broken bed she'd started the night in.

With a half-smile, Malthazar watched as Delta stumbled out of the bed to the bathroom, her hair flaring in all directions, barely closing the door behind her. Wrapping his hands in her hair as she came on his cock had been better than he could have imagined. His redheaded princess was insatiable, exploring his body as eagerly as he'd explored hers.

It crossed his mind briefly as he pulled on his jeans that when he got the shirt back, he might never wash it. Long after she was gone, he would be able to breathe in her scent. She'd pulled closer to him in their sleep, reaching out, like breathing the same air and occupying the same space wasn't enough for her.

Attempting to banish these thought as he stoked the fire, Malth reminded himself that attachments were weakness. Attachments led to heartbreak and death. No, it was better for her if he kept a safe distance. Women like Delta were better than a one-night stand. She deserved more than that, more than he could give.

As she stumbled back from the bathroom with her red curls sticking out in every direction and a yawn filling her face, he broke all the promises he'd just made to himself and her. His tee was over-sized on her, reaching nearly to her knees, and shapeless over the slender figure he knew it hid. Still, he couldn't stop the tightening in his groin, and he found himself turning to stoke the fire in the fireplace to hide the evidence of his arousal.

"Damn, I slept so good last night," Delta admitted in a low voice as she made her way back to the bed.

Had she slept? There had been a bit more than that, but what did she remember?

Watching her out the corner of his eye, Malth continued poking at the fire, glad he'd brought more wood inside the night before. She rubbed the sleep from her eyes and pulled the quilt from the bed. Dragging it along the floor, she made her way to the hard, unforgiving floor in front of the fireplace. Malth captured a glimpse of her long, pale legs before she tucked them under the quilt and rolled it around her body.

Leaning toward the heat of the fire, Delta mused, "It didn't feel this cold last night."

Malth didn't know how to respond. He wanted to beg her to come back to the bed, and at the same time, he wanted to say something short and hurtful to drive her away. He couldn't bring himself to do that, couldn't bring himself to cause the hurt he knew would flash through her eyes.

As if Delta knew his dilemma, she soldiered on in Delta-like fashion, not once mentioning the hours they'd spent wrapped around each other's bodies. "I can't believe I forgot extra clothes. But I did bring eye of newt."

Was this how she wanted to play it? Or did she want him to reference it? Gods, Malth panicked momentarily. *Breathe,* he ordered himself. Maybe she regretted things said and done in the dark?

"Mustard seed. You brought mustard seed." With a strained smile, Malth said the only appropriate thing that came to mind as he poked at the fire. "You can buy it at any grocery shop."

"Yeah, but eye of newt sounds so much more dramatic," Delta pointed out as she wiggled across the floor, close enough to him to bump him with her shoulder.

Malth poked at the fire. "Next you'll be bringing out toe of frog and wool of bat," he said, referring to buttercup and holly leaves.

"Oh, someone knows a few witchy secrets." Delta's throaty laugh had Malth relaxing. Normal. Talking and joking was normal.

Breaking his riveting examination of the now roaring fire, he dared to look at the princess next to him. She'd wrapped herself from head to toe in the quilt and watched him with those intent, knowing green eyes, the flecks of gold flitting through them more vivid, if that were possible. He should look away. He should break whatever spell was being woven over them. But dammit, he didn't *want* to. What Malth wanted was to fall under her spell, to fall deeper and deeper into those eyes.

"I suppose." Delta broke the spell with her soft words. Clearing her throat, she began a bit louder. "I suppose I should go outside and see which way the magic might draw us. It's best with the rising sun. Not that I have such stipulations," she amended quickly, clearly not wanting to cast doubt on her abilities. "It's just clearest then."

The sun had risen hours ago and had already begun its trek across the sky, marking the beginning of early afternoon. There seemed to be no reason to point that out.

Reluctantly, she dislodged herself from the floor, rising awkwardly and trying to stay wrapped in the quilt, before she dropped it to the floor anyway. Standing up tall, she stretched, raising her arms high above her head, drawing Malth's tee up her thighs. Her legs. Her thighs. A sharp reminder for Malth to avert his gaze.

"I'm gonna pull on some clothes and head outside to see if I feel a pull strong enough. You coming?" she tossed over her shoulder as she gathered her clothes from the chair in front of the fireplace.

Malth wasn't sure if he wished them dry enough for her to wear, or damp enough that she needed to continue wearing his clothes.

Despite the cabin's security, he wasn't willing to jeopardize her safety by allowing her outside alone. He rose to his feet, his knees cracking from the effort.

"Suppose I should be on the lookout for snakes and things." Malth couldn't remove the dumb smile from his face, and already his body missed the feeling of her body against his.

Delta shivered visibly at the thought. "Definitely no more confused snakes."

Watching Delta flow through her movements, calling forth her own magic to search out other magic, mesmerized Malthazar. The same body that seemed in perpetual motion, unable to sit still, always moving, wiggling a finger, tapping a foot, sat completely still except for her slow, steady breathing in and out as she found her focus. Then her hands flew through movements so quickly that his eyes strained to keep up. Touching the ground, touching her thighs, touching her heart, her head, before reaching for the sky, fingers spelling out incantations he couldn't dare to imagine. Striking a match, she once again burned the strange-smelling root, frowning at it when it didn't appear to answer her questions.

This time, Malth stood close enough to hear the incantation she whispered.

May the bridges I burn
light the way.
May the footpath be shown
by the smoke of the fool.
Lead me, lead me,
don't let me stray.

Arms open wide, she searched and searched, before settling prostrate on the cold ground with her arms outstretched and her head raised to the sky.

She'd readily agreed to wearing his sweatshirt over her own still damp clothes. Hopefully, it made her a little more comfortable. The cold, heavy air felt like snow was coming, and Malth found himself examining the dark gray clouds in the distance. Delta had refused to spread the quilt on the ground, insisting she needed to be grounded and one with the earth. Besides, it was their one good blanket. Better a few minutes of discomfort than potentially a night of picking dead leaves and twigs from the quilt. Delta had to be freezing, but she didn't appear to even notice the cold.

Opening her mind and magic left her vulnerable. Every few minutes, Malth would reluctantly pull his eyes off her to scan the clearing and woods around them. He even searched the ground, in case another lost snake was drawn to her warmth. Opening his senses wide, he scanned as well as listened for any snap of sound, no matter how quiet, that might represent a threat to her. His own magic didn't appear to notice any portent of danger, but he refused to only count on one of his senses.

The sun was well into the sky before she rose from the ground, slowly shaking off the stiffness from the cold and the position. "She's still farther north of us. The catalyst magic is gone, faded away. But hers... I can feel her magic. It's black and sticky. Angry. Thick." Shaking her head, attempting to understand what she felt, she added, "Almost confused feeling, like it doesn't understand why it's being restrained. I'm starting to think it's her sheer determination to live that's holding her together. It's straining against her."

Rubbing her hands on her arms to return feeling, Delta continued, "Even if we don't find her, her time feels limited. I wonder if the twins somehow kept her together in captivity." She was referring to the twins who guarded the gateway from hell at Houska Castle. They'd kept Ibis under lock and key for decades after she was separated from the now human Anya. The dark magic that had made the vampire hadn't been able to return to hell and by reforming into the image of Ibis, it was able to create a different life form made purely of dark, evil magic.

"Could Anya be dying?" Malth offered softly. At ninety human years old, the former vampire turned human, now stricken with cancer, had limited days left on earth no matter the cause. The connection the two shared may not end at death; it may be drawing Ibis's life force to an end as well.

"That could very well be true," Delta admitted, "but without connecting with the twins, I don't know what they did and what tests they ran or what results there were. But we can't leave Ibis out here in the world. She's too unpredictable and too desperate to survive."

That couldn't be allowed to happen. Ibis had hurt too many people and destroyed too many lives. Not enough information was known to allow her to continue in the hope that her life force teetered out naturally. Things were happening too rapidly for anyone to attend to the twins, assuming they still lived at Houska Castle. They remained cut off from civilization, refusing to leave their guardian duty and only allowing a few to visit. One had to arrive and announce themselves before a determination was made. No one was sending a phone call or text to get approval beforehand. The twins remained truly cut off. The time to search them out had been days or weeks ago; now was too late.

Delta stumbled a bit as she attempted to walk off the numbness of her legs. Instantly, Malth caught her, holding her arm and refusing to let go as he led her into the house. Settling her back down on the bed, he immediately began heating water for the tea he knew would warm her up. The growling of his stomach reminded him that heating the remainder of their stew would be a necessity for her as well.

Sipping on the tea that surely wasn't as good as what she could make, Delta asked, "Are you feeling anything? Any of your tracker senses going off?"

Shaking his head while he rubbed the pendant around his neck, Malth confirmed, "Nothing, but I can't track the magic like you do. If you have a direction of up north, that's more than what I have.

"Eat," he urged her as he brought a spoonful of stew to her mouth. Surprisingly, she simply opened her mouth and accepted the offering. Seeing her savoring the flavor while she chewed and swallowed filled him with pride.

"What about your portal stone? Is it too soon to jump that direction?"

Despite the fact that he knew they would need another twenty-four hours to do a short jump, he pulled the demon stone from his pocket, rolling it between his palms, testing it. "It's too soon," he admitted. "Too vague, and too soon.

"I have a proposal," he added as he nudged Delta with his hip, urging her to give him some space on the bed as well.

"Good sir!" Delta feigned shock, putting a hand to her heart at his words. "Surely, it's too soon for a proposal!"

If he didn't stop smiling around her, the sides of his mouth might split open. Poking her in the side with a finger while she squirmed away, laughing, he rephrased, "I have a suggestion. I think since we're basically being told to wait, we could spend the day in bed, until a reason arises for us not to?" As soon as he said the words, his heart sputtered erratically in his chest. What if she said no? Since when did a mission get pushed aside for a day in bed? Ten minutes ago, he was sure she was ignoring what had occurred. Why was he such an idiot? What if…?

In the end, it didn't matter. Delta smiled in response before handing her warm drink to him and began removing his shirt once again. "I thought you'd never ask." The words were muffled as the shirt was pulled over her head, but the intent was clear.

CHAPTER SEVENTEEN

The burning root of the queen's delight plant may show you the way, but user beware: the sap will burn and blister.

Delta traced a complex series of lines across Malthazar's chest as he slowly drew a breath in before releasing it. Perhaps the witch was marking him as her own? Truth be told, she'd already cast a spell over him. The ingredients were her knowing smirks, wild hair, and flashing eyes.

He was bewitched, and he had no desire to break the enchantment. The day spent in bed might be the best day of his long life. They'd left it to break their fast. One bite of food wouldn't sustain her. Eating the cold leftovers of the stew and biscuits wasn't the best meal, but it filled their hunger without them leaving their bed for long.

"Are you be-spelling me?" Catching Delta's hand, he brought it to his lips for a quick kiss.

"It's protection," Delta whispered, sealing the unseen runes with a soft kiss. "It will help with the dreams."

Pulling his head up sharply, Malth looked down at her with a frown. "How did you…"

"You can talk about them if you want. I can actually listen. Sometimes the magic is in saying the things we don't want to say out loud. They lose their power then." Delta offered this as she continued tracing a line down and around his chest. At least she no longer caressed his horns; he hadn't realized how affected he would be with her running her hands through his hair and grasping his horns. Even the thought had him ready to climb on top of her again, but she needed to rest, as did he.

The boys. The boys he'd left behind and those he'd saved. It was always the boys. Malth found he did want to tell her. Tell her things he'd never whispered to others, the weight of which often crushed him, waking him and leaving him gasping for breath, besieged by guilt.

"They haunt me." Malth waited for her to ask who, but Delta continued her perusal of his body, running a single finger, sometimes two, around his shoulders, dancing across his biceps, brushing the edges of his ribs. There was no need for questions. He knew the past and knew what damage it had done to him. When she didn't ask but waited for him to find the words, he found he wanted to tell her even more.

"Unlike the boys I save and the ones still in hell, my mother loved me. Loved me deeply." A long, slow inhale, as Malth drifted for a moment toward that feeling that lay hidden within his soul. If he had a soul anyway. A little knot of hope, warmth, and softness that covered a face he could no longer remember. A smile that reached toward eyes whose colors blurred and remained hidden. A melodious tone that floated along in sunshine, tossing out words he could no longer decipher. A laughter of delight over the seemingly mundane things he'd done. Her delight in it all, as if she knew the time they had together was limited.

If he allowed the little knot to grow, it would fill the pit of his stomach. Once that hope, that love, reached his chest, he carefully molded it back down into the small hidden pit that held all the love he could remember from his mother. It was Malth's secret. He'd once been loved. And she'd fought to the death to keep him from his inevitable fate. Older now, he knew without a doubt that her fight had been futile, but still her love for him had been strong enough for her to fight until the light left her eyes.

"Run…" Her last whispered word had been seared into his brain, settling into his lasting memory, never to be forgotten. Her blank, colorless eyes that had just moments before been filled with light and laughter faded into nothingness. Damnation, why the hell couldn't he remember the color of her eyes? He hadn't run fast enough or far enough. His little legs didn't have it in them to escape the monster that chased him.

"Another boy down there must have known the same. Like knows like. He didn't pamper me; that would have been death. But he did better: he quietly instructed me on how to live, on how to survive." Malth remembered the taller, dark-haired youth. Thin from lack of nourishment, yet still Raz 'ga taught Malth how to fight for the few scraps of food they received. Showed him how to wipe away the blood and brimstone from that day's fight from the armor they cleaned. The best hidey holes as they were routed in and out of the battlegrounds that littered hell. The spots to look for that would camouflage their comings and goings. How to speak to the older boys, how to avoid the demons, and how to grovel, prostrate, and disappear if you were stupid enough to cross one's path. The older boy had shown him how to clean the wounds of the soldiers sent back each night, and how to clean the rags they reused day in and day out. Even after the older youths became soldiers, Raz 'ga still whispered instructions to Malth. What to prepare for, what to expect.

Until, of course, the day the young man didn't come back. They'd spent years together, working together, mostly silently cleaning weapons, spying, moving in and out of the lines. Promoted upward, taking on more responsibility, until the boy who had helped him became a man. One who was ready to lead a squad, even. One whose knowledge of love ensured that day after day, his squad would return. All of them. Until one day, they didn't.

Most of them did; make it back, that was. Tired, dirty, and blood-covered, the ragged squad hauled themselves back to the makeshift camp. Dragging feet, eyes downcast, every single survivor injured, two holding their own limbs separate from their body. Malth had eagerly awaited his friend. He'd always come back; the unit avoided his hopeful eyes.

"A part of that boy knew love and caring. So many of the youth had been deals made between witch and demon. Some by choice, some not. Few, if any, were loved by the creatures that birthed them. By the time they were five or six, their donors had collected their progeny and deposited them in hell to kill or be killed serving their masters."

No one would answer his unasked question, and it was days before the whispers reached him. His friend had been killed, ripped apart by a demi-gorgon, a wild demon that had never before been spotted in the region. Apparently, the team's success hadn't gone unnoticed, so dropping one unexpectedly into the maneuvers had upped the fun for their masters. It was Raz 'ga's sacrifice that had saved the few survivors, and for a few days, Malth had received a wider berth, an extra serving from a survivor, and eyes filled with pity and understanding.

This was why they didn't get close, another lesson hell deemed worthy of teaching.

Delta gasped lightly, and Malth lay his head down in his hands. "Don't pity me, I had more than most of them. At least for a bit, I knew… more."

"But why? Why would they do that?"

Malth barked off a snatch of laughter, biting his

hand to cut off the sound before raising his head to look back into the empty space ahead of them. "For fun, for entertainment. Half-demon spawn are pets, or less than pets. Humans wouldn't treat their pets like we were treated. These great demons on that plane have carved out bits of land, bits of areas of dirt to call their own. They collect children to raise them into soldiers. Pawns. To battle it out through childhood, serving where they can. Those who survive become grunt soldiers. The demons battle it out by day, sending in troops and soldiers to battle over the scraps of the shit hole each one had carved out as his own. Fighting, day after day, scrapping over a few feet of dirt or a rock."

Pausing, Malth brought his emotions into check; it did no good to try and understand the demons. "It's all a game to them, like we might play checkers or chess. When the game is over, the masters lay aside their weapons and plans, tally up that day's wins and losses until a winner might be declared. Then together, the demon masters celebrate with cups of grog, pretending that a few hours earlier they weren't sending boys and young men to their death against one another. Then they wake up and do it all the next day, and the day after that. Forever."

Malth needed Delta to understand. More deeply than he'd ever wanted something, he wanted this witch to understand. "To them, it was a *game*. A game to pass the time, only the pawns were real, living people. Moving pieces around, celebrating and parties to pat themselves on the backs for their strategies. We would fight for them, serve them, and thank them for the opportunity."

Malth felt a gentle hand settle on his forearm, tightening around his bicep, forcing him to look at her with just her presence.

"You did nothing wrong. You were a boy, a boy trying to survive. You did as any of them would have done."

She didn't know. After Raz 'ga's death, Malth's heart had hardened. He rose through the ranks at lightning speed. Prepared for whatever the players of that pointless war might throw at him. He didn't lose the part of him that silently modeled, if albeit exaggerated, how to survive to the newcomers. They either got the lesson or they didn't. But he stopped protecting the newcomers from the cuffs of the older youth. He didn't offer to show them the herbs that slowed bleeding or caused bruising to fade quicker. They needed those lessons as well. Not allowing them to receive them was a death sentence. The sooner they hardened, the longer they might live. He joined the ranks of manhood in hell. When Malth looked at the other soldiers' scarred and hardened faces, he saw his own countenance. To make it to manhood meant you could survive, and survive they did, no matter the cost or who was crushed under their rise.

"But you escaped; you're saving those boys now. They don't have to grow into soldiers."

Malth didn't deserve the admiration in her voice.

"Atonement," he admitted. "And a hell boy doesn't just escape. Even in death, if there is enough of you to resurrect, they will; over and over. Until the bits and pieces become too little and you're allowed to die. I was there for years, decades, I don't even know. I don't know what year I was born or how to tell the passing of time there. I rose through the ranks because I was good at what I did—killing others in the same situation that I was in."

"That was battle," Delta argued softly, "in a war not of your choosing. But still, you did what you did to survive. You didn't kill because you chose to; those deaths are on the demons."

She didn't understand. "I still made a choice—a choice to live and succeed." It hadn't gone unnoticed how good he was about sneaking in and out of places. His near sixth sense, probably from his mother's witch genetics, carried out battle plans and saw where troops might lie in wait. He could track a moth across the desert in the black of night. His existence and strengths were exactly why the demons made deals with witches. Between the two, they boasted an extended life and, in some situations, magical traits. That was the golden ticket the demons wanted for an edge in their game. His gut instinct was a strong magical precognition. It gave him an edge, and he'd honed it for his own survivor.

His skills hadn't gone unnoticed. Twice, Malth had been taken, prostrated before his demon lord, and questioned about his abilities. He'd answered carefully, well aware that one wrong step could lead to the demon deciding to behead him for disrespect or even from boredom. Then he could resurrect Malth and do it all over again.

Thankfully, that didn't occur. Obviously. The first time, he was gifted the stone he wore around his neck, the one that amplified and honed his untrained abilities.

The second time, the demon lord ordered him to stand, then examined him as one might judge livestock. Malth could still remember the demon's sigh of disgust as the creature wrinkled his snout at him, like he was the monster. After a long silence, his master grunted garbled orders: a mission deep into the bowels of the hell where they resided, past all that was known. He was ordered to track down a rare fire demon.

"The Desert of Endless Flames," Delta whispered to Malth, who looked at her in surprise. "I do listen, you know."

"Aye. I, along with three others, were sent out to search for the three remaining fire demons. Along with the hope that we could find the vomit they expelled from their gullet and that a thousand-year portal stone had formed."

"An impossible mission," Delta pointed out with a sad sigh, tears filling her empathetic eyes.

"Yes, but no," Malth admitted. "The demons knew it was time for one to form. Occasionally, every thousand years or so, they'd seen the mission a success. Of course, they had no idea which fire demon would form it. All the higher demons were forming teams to send out in search of it. Not only were we expected to battle the land and the fire demon, but also other teams, and then in the end each other. Only one of us was to return."

Malth let those words settle over the woman he'd spent the night and day with. He was no saint. By collecting the portal stone, he'd ensured that it bonded to him and was basically a job interview for the next position.

The stone allowed for nearly unlimited jumps between the dimensions when one jumped through hell. Jumping on earth had different rules. The stone needed time to recharge or whatever it did and only allowed a very small jump or maybe two within a twenty-four-hour period. The longer the distance traveled on earth, the longer it took for the stone to prepare for another.

Jumping back and forth between the hell dimension was pretty much unlimited or at the very least, Malth had never found an end to it. Maybe the stone re-powered when it returned home, maybe it built up or collected magic. These days, returning to hell wasn't in the cards for him. If he did that, all of hell would immediately know where he was. Even if he zipped right back out, they would be able to track him for days, hell, maybe years, based on that small imprint. He could never jump enough times or fast enough to stay ahead of the trackers in hell. Malth knew that better than anyone. He'd lived it.

His original job had ensured unlimited jumps. "Delta, I was a tracker for hell. My job became tracking down the babies that were on earth." He didn't want to say the words. He didn't want to watch the light die in her eyes either, as she realized he was a monster, but he forced himself to look. He deserved this, and she deserved to know what he really was—a monster shaped by the demon master he'd served.

Delta chose her words carefully. "You tracked down the children that the demons created, to bring them to hell to fight in their games."

"Yes." Shame filled Malth. Shame for all he'd done; he would never atone for those years.

"You escaped and instead of hiding away, you're trying to beat other trackers to these children and take them to safety?"

She didn't understand. It would take him another five hundred years to even match the number of children he'd stolen away to hell. He wasn't a hero. "Delta, I did this for centuries. I'll never make up for those I sentenced to lifetime after lifetime of pain."

"No, I suppose not." Delta blinked slowly at him, trying to expel the tears that welled up in her eyes. "But unlike others, you're trying. And maybe you can't make it up to all the ones before, but for Julian and the others you made a difference. A huge difference."

"It will never be enough."

"It never is," Delta offered gently. "All we can do

is try. Those you saved will remember you, and those you… did worse to… will understand your story. Your story is their story."

Malth felt her remove her hand from his arm, immediately missing the warmth and comfort it had brought. Despite her words, she'd pulled away from him.

Then Delta pulled his arm around her shoulders as she leaned into him. Frozen with surprise, Malth didn't immediately react as she wrapped both arms around his waist, giving him a firm squeeze. "All we can do is try to make our story better," she repeated as he slowly allowed his arm to relax and even pull her a hint closer, soaking up the contact and her forgiving words. Forgiveness he couldn't give himself.

The comfortable silence stretched between them, only the slow sounds of their breath breaking it, before Delta shared, "To quote the great doctor, 'We are all stories in the end.'"

"Who?"

"Exactly." Delta's voice was low, and if he hadn't been so close he wouldn't have heard her words. Words nonetheless that he didn't understand. Maybe she'd already fallen asleep?

"Your past doesn't have to define you. Yes, it made you who you are today. You're the one who wrestled control over the present and future. Don't let the past or others have undue, undeserved power over you, or you'll never really live."

Watching a spot above the bed, Malth considered

her words before slowly responding, "You're pretty smart." He needed to think more on what she was saying. Was redemption possible? If it were, then hope was as well.

"Like recognizes like, remember," Delta admitted softly.

CHAPTER EIGHTEEN

*Capturing fairies' horses is as simple as tracking
down ragweed.*

Delta lay on the bed with the quilt covering her from
the waist down, her soft, red curls framing her lightly
freckled face. They trailed down her pale shoulders
and brushed barely past her nipples, attempting to hide
them from his sight. By all the gods and demons, she
was beautiful. Never had he dreamed that such beauty
and goodness might be within his grasp. She seemed
to think there was hope for him, and if she thought
that, then perhaps there could be more. Things he'd
never thought possible could be possible. For him.
Maybe even with her.

A hint of a smile crossed her face as Malth
watched her. Pulling her forehead up in a questioning
look at his perusal, Delta continued her slight smile at
him as he stared at her. Malth couldn't stop himself
from returning her smile. Leaning forward, he braced
his forehead against hers before landing a light kiss on
her lips. Carefully, he ran his fingers down a curl

before lightly brushing over her nipple and following the line of her waist, settling his hand on her hip. Pulling her closer, he admitted, "You're beautiful." This was followed by another kiss to her lips. "Enchanting." Another soft kiss as she wiggled impossibly close to him.

Pulling his head back, he looked into her sparkling eyes, the eyes of a satisfied woman. "Are you a succubus? Tempting me over and over again? Was your father an incubus?"

Shaking her head, Delta let out a soft giggle. Biting her lip, she admitted with a bark of laughter, "As if my mother would lower herself to sleep with a demon."

The shift in the air was immediate. A bucket of ice water couldn't have been more efficient in killing the moment. Malth knew she instantly wanted to swallow the words back up. Both stopped, frozen by her words, and the building need between them fled quicker than it had begun. Malth moved first, withdrawing his hands as he felt his cheeks flush with shame as well as a hint of anger and embarrassment.

Rolling over away from her before she could see the hurt that surely filled his eyes, Malth let the reality of her words settle in. The words she'd spoken earlier were just that. Words. Hope was dashed. How had he thought this would be different? That he could be different or be seen differently?

Half-breed. Demon spawn. Witch's curse. Those words were the truth.

"Malth, no, that's not what I mean. You're different. You're you…"

Malth hated the way Delta's voice trailed off, her inability to explain that slumming it with a demon half-blood might somehow be fine. Pretty words could be spouted with ease, but the truth always came to light eventually.

Coldly, he spoke the first words that came to his mind. "What you're saying is that fucking me would infuriate your mother. Fucking a baseless demon is so degrading it's unimaginable except to revolt against your mother. I know exactly what you meant."

Malth rolled out of bed in one quick motion. Grabbing the tee-shirt that lay on the ground, he started to pull it over his head, when he realized it was the one saturated in her scent. Ripping the shirt away from himself, he balled it up and tossed it across the room. It wasn't anger that had him stepping into his jeans, but disappointment. In himself. In her. Tucking himself into his jeans, he didn't bother zipping them. He had to get out of here. He had to go... somewhere... somewhere that wasn't here.

"No, that's not…"

Still shirtless, Malth found himself by the door, holding his folded cap before she could finish that sentence. Pausing at the door and without looking back, he shot off, "You should probably go shower my filth off, you know, after rolling around in the gutter. We have a job to do, then you can run back to your precious mother and tell her what a naughty, fucked-up daughter you've been."

Ignoring the gasp of pain that came from the bed, he slammed the cabin door behind him. Feet barely registering the gravel and twigs as he stepped off the porch, his legs took him a dozen or so steps before the realization of what he'd said hit him.

The pain in his stomach bowled him over and for a moment, Malth wondered if he might throw up as Delta had after their portal travel. Half bent over with hands on his upper thighs, he scolded himself for his hasty, angry words. Worse, he could almost regret the hours of perfection he'd spent with Delta. A few poorly chosen words on both sides had reduced it to a tawdry event, like it wasn't worthy of being what it truly was. What was it, though? He could see, he could feel the possibilities. Being with Delta had felt more right than anything else he'd done in his damnable long life.

What had he done? What had *they* done? In the moment it had seemed perfect, but Delta wasn't wrong: a witch and a demon, even a half-demon like himself, wouldn't work.

They would never work. Demons and witches made deals. Good witches stayed far away from deals with demons. Despite knowing his mother had made no such deal, he couldn't help but wonder what trickery or force a demon had used upon her to ensure his conception. But knowing that didn't change who, or rather what, he was. No matter how good or how pure his mother had been, his sire was still a demon.

Nothing could change that.

Breathing deeply in and out, he closed his eyes against the barren ground outside the cabin. Mixing work and pleasure was a mistake. A mistake, no matter how perfect it felt, or how perfect she was.

"Well, helllloooo, handsome." A sultry voice interrupted his internal chastising, immediately sending him into an upright defensive pose, determined to find the source of the voice. "Youuuu are an unexpected bonus," she continued to purr, this time in his ear. Malthazar found he couldn't turn his body toward the voice, no matter how hard he strained. In fact, only his eyes could shift a bit back and forth.

Hell and damnation. He might have made a fatal error, wandered beyond the limited boundary of the cabin and lost himself in thought. Business and pleasure definitely shouldn't mix. Doing so caused distraction, and distraction could be the turning point between life and death. Ibis had distracted and separated them. They'd been so caught up in what they were doing, they hadn't even noticed she'd wiggled her way past the wards, catching them unaware, once again altering their emotions and leaving them vulnerable.

CHAPTER NINETEEN

Salt is the tried and true, perhaps one of the most important and simplest of items to include in a magical arsenal.

Delta wished it was possible to punch herself in the mouth or, better yet, swallow back the careless words. But neither was possible. Well, technically she could punch herself in the mouth, but it wouldn't take back the words spoken in a poorly worded jest.

Her words had been meant to show how unyielding her mother was, not as a jab at Malth. Unfortunately, the only thing it had proven was that she, as well as her mother, was a bigot and a classicist. She wanted to tell Malth immediately that she was an idiot, but her words did seem to say otherwise. There was no coming back on an insult like that. Malthazar had spent a lifetime proving he was better than his parentage, and she'd made a joke of it. An ill-framed joke had shown him that he wasn't, that he couldn't be the person he wanted to be.

He was better than that; Malth had more goodness

in him then she did. He had his freedom; he could turn his back on the entire mess and keep himself safe. Malth couldn't do that and didn't see that he wasn't simply making reparations. Everything he did was because he was a good person.

Eva's demon heritage had already shown Delta that there was more to demon kind than just hate and destruction. And Malth. Malth had stood right in front of her and told her his fears and experiences, and still she'd tossed the words out carelessly. Acting as if his existence was wrong or something to be disgusted by. What was wrong with her? Why did she blow up everything good in her life?

Stepping outside after spending too long in the shower was one of the hardest things Delta had ever done. It seemed like a good idea to let them both cool off and, at the same time, delay the words that she had to somehow string together. First an apology for her off-the-cuff, tasteless remarks, and then let him know that he meant something to her. Something that to a degree was undefinable and also beyond words. Malth was important to her, and when this was over, she didn't want to say goodbye. Didn't want to relegate the time spent with him as some titillating event to piss off her mother.

Several yards from the porch, Malth stood frozen in spot with his back to her. The weather was turning even cooler and here he stood barefoot, shirtless, with only his pants and cap to ward off the weather. He must hate facing her more then he hated the cold temperatures.

The thin sweater Delta had tossed on did little against the cold, and she rubbed her hands along her arms, knowing that going back inside to put on another layer would only delay the inevitable. If Malth could stand against the cool air after being raised amid fire and brimstone, so could she. Or at least she could until she could convince him of her regret and get him back inside the warmer cabin.

"Malth," Delta began, keeping her voice soft and apologetic as she called across the yard to him. He didn't move at the sound of her voice. Neither acknowledgment nor a hint of waving her off. "Malth?" She tried again, this time taking a few steps toward him. Of course it wouldn't be easy, but dammit, couldn't he at least look at her?

With a huff, she stomped closer to him, coming around his right side, ready to set a caring hand on his shoulder or give him a shake of frustration. Admittedly, Delta hadn't decided which before she realized that Malth didn't just appear frozen. He *was* frozen, staring straight ahead with wide, golden eyes that appeared to be stuck in a surprised state.

"Oh, fuuu…" Delta whispered, taking up a defensive pose as she whipped her head around the small clearing, looking for the threat that was written firmly across his face. A flurry of movement around her maneuvered Delta several feet away from Malth as she attempted to ascertain where or even what the damn threat was.

"How? Wards?" Delta sputtered out the random thoughts as her body and eyes whipped back and forth, following the blur. The cabin's wards weren't maintained, so keeping them small kept them efficient. Unfortunately, it also meant it was easy to step out of the safety of them.

Ibis stood in front of her, her face wavering and flickering about. At times she appeared to be the middle-aged Anya from the pictures Ravyn had shown her, and at others a crepe hag with sores and folds of skin hanging loosely from the bones of her face, as if they could barely cling to the woman. Wisps of fraying gray hair overtook the thick salt-and-pepper locks, if one looked hard enough. Her tall, proud shoulders hunched over if you could keep looking even longer.

Ibis had lied. She'd lied when she told Ravyn she was aging slowly. She wasn't aging slowly. She was deteriorating and rotting from the inside out. This body was but a façade, an attempt to hide the true reflection of the black magic that had made her. But alone, Ibis could only reshape her illusion for so long. Yes, she was magic and the magic was her, but it was dark, ugly, and rotting magic.

"Wards? What do you mean, wards? You were a beacon in this wilderness calling out to me. You wanted me here. Your magic invited me and thus, I am here." She opened hers arms as if her arrival was purely innocent and she wasn't holding the two of them in place.

Delta let her have her moment as she felt the

magic attempt to settle over her, whispering and crackling over her skin, but was unable to latch on. Let Ibis think that this magic bound her to her place. A simple flip of her wrist could have unraveled the flimsy thread of magic that tied them. It was insulting that the hag thought such a thing would hold her.

"I find you here with this creature. Your pet, I assume." Ibis jerked her hand, forcing Malth to his knees. "Good boy," she crooned. "Hell knows how to train them, I suppose."

Delta didn't need to move her eyes to know the fury that emanated from him. *Hold on*, she thought, hoping he understood they had the upper hand as long as Ibis underestimated their power. If Malth broke free, she would come at them with more.

Ibis tugged at Malth's cap, until it came free from his head. Tilting her head, she examined his horns with a cunning smile. Delta could see Malth strain against the magic; hopefully, it was a ruse and he wouldn't break free.

Delta nearly lost herself when Ibis began touching Malth, examining him with her hands. Running a hand possessively through Malth's hair, Ibis lingered her fingertips on his horns, surely knowing how the act would degrade him. "This one is much more appealing than some I've seen. I can see why you would sample him."

Narrowing her eyes on Delta as she ran an exploratory hand down his face and chest, she went on, "Yes, you've sampled him well, I see. You can keep him for now. I don't mind. We all have our little vices. I promise I can be so much more accepting than your mother."

Delta refused to be provoked and simply stared uncaring back into Ibis's eyes. Eyes she might pluck from the bitch's head when given the chance. She was throwing shit at the wall, seeing what might stick. Most witches had a problem with their mothers; nothing new there.

"I can see that you're interested in hearing what I have to offer, and that's understandable," Ibis continued, as if Delta had anything but an uninterested look on her face. "I want you. I want you to join me. I can almost taste your power in the air around you. It called to me. It wants what I can offer."

Batshit crazy, Delta thought. *This crazy bitch seriously only sees what she wants to.* Any second now, Ibis would be spilling her evil plan to her, not believing that anyone could turn down what she had to offer.

"A power without limits!" Ibis gleefully squealed.

Delta almost expected her to jump up and down while clapping her hands together, so wonderful this apparently was. "You have the power and with me, I can make it unlimited. Nothing would be beyond our reach. Together, we wouldn't need to surround ourselves with the unworthy waste of spaces that surround us."

Delta's eyes flickered to the two current "unworthy" acolytes flanking Ibis. They were so young, but somehow, Ibis had plucked them from whatever their circumstances were and promised them the world. Delta let her magic run over them, testing them and filing her findings away. Neither appeared to be the scryer who had assisted in freeing Ravyn from her bindings, and neither one the catalyst either. Either Ibis replaced followers often, or she already had a larger following than Delta had assumed.

The one binding them seemed a bit strained, but the other seemed untroubled by the dismissive attitude. Apparently, being called worthless was nothing new to them. Still, they allowed Ibis to channel through them and use their power simultaneously with hers.

Power corrupted. Delta couldn't imagine what unlimited power would do to a soul, especially such young souls. Even now, their magic was wound in the black, thick, inky magic that clearly belonged to Ibis. The strains of color in their magic should normally be hidden against the unnatural darkness, but still the colors fought in vain to break free.

"Child," Ibis murmured. "I see you. I see YOU. The second daughter in a line of single witches. Tossed aside, hidden from sight like YOU were the mistake. I wonder if your mother tried to rid herself of you while you were in her belly, knowing that she shouldn't have conceived you." Ibis seemed to consider the possibilities, tapping her finger against Malth's immobile head. "I'll bet she did. Easier to sweep away a mistake before others know of its existence. But you, my darling child," Ibis purred now, "you would have fought back. This magic of yours would have dissolved anything she sent toward you even when you were but a few cells in her belly."

Delta refused to speak to her, wouldn't give Ibis the satisfaction of responding to her tirade of half-truths. She attempted to keep her face bored and uninterested, hoping that Ibis wouldn't run out of steam in her monologue before moving them to her lair. Plus, it was damn cold outside.

"Your *mother*," Ibis spat out the word. "Your own mother couldn't see the possibilities you offered. But then I saw you. I watched as you took down the wendigo. Beautiful and strange. I didn't realize at first what I was seeing. It wasn't until later, after I'd fled. Yes, I admit I fled that foul creature's nest. When I had a moment to think, I realized you can see the magic." She made the announcement pausing like she expected applause, but Delta refused to even allow an eyebrow to twitch.

Damnation.

"You, child, cannot only see it but can manipulate the magic you see. You can use it against the user. You can unravel it, destroy it, but most of all, you can wield any magic you see. You go beyond unlimited—to complete and total power. I can boost and channel other magic users when permitted, but you… you have no limitations. What does that mean? What can we accomplish together? We could rule any dimension we choose. We could have demons bow before us. Men would fight to the death to be allowed to give us their blood.

"You can be so much more than you've ever been allowed to be," Ibis continued, acting like Delta were nodding along in agreement. "Woman or witch," she scoffed. "I've lived through enough times to know that it doesn't matter which you are, either is enough for people to hate you, to fear you. They'll burn you for either one, and it matters naught to them."

"In Salem, they didn't burn witches; they burned women." Delta found herself whispering the words, and Ibis didn't seem to have a problem hearing them.

"Exactly." Ibis beamed marking Delta as a star pupil. "Demon, vampire, witch. It doesn't matter to them. Being a woman is enough to warrant their ire." Caught up in her words, Ibis began speaking faster and faster. "You understand, don't you? You aren't feared for your power; you're feared and hated for being a woman. But together, we can be much more than that."

Actually, Delta wasn't following the woman's line of thought at all. That train had clearly derailed at the last station, and she was clinging to stereotypes and spouting off conspiracies faster than Delta could follow. Who was *they*? Man, or humankind? Was Ibis trying to convince her to join her based on magical power or on being women? The threads she was weaving together clearly didn't belong together. They were patched together worse than this deranged magical being's mind. Perhaps not as bat shit crazy as the wendigo, but the kind of crazy that made her more dangerous. Unpredictable with nothing to lose summed up Ibis. These were the rantings of a desperate creature.

Delta didn't even want to think of her as a woman, despite her clinging to the idea like a life raft. Ibis was discarded magic held together by hatred and stitched tighter with a desperation to survive in whatever state she could. Sure, if Ravyn could have made her a vampire again, Ibis would have taken that. But in her state of uncoiling, she was clinging to the hope that anything would save her. Ibis was unraveling, but would it take days or centuries for her end to come? That would leave the magic untethered and free, and from there, where would it go?

CHAPTER TWENTY

Capture a toad or gather toadflax to repel malevolent magic?

They'd unceremoniously been dumped in the back of a dark, windowless van. Balaclava-style face covers pulled backward covered their eyes but still allowed them to breath.

While the door to the van remained open, Delta could see the light flash around and the forms moving to make room for at least another person. Was that four people? Ibis. The two young witches. And one or two more. Who was the driver? There could be half a dozen. Delta wondered if they would add another layer to their heads to keep them disoriented, but after the door slid close and the darkness slid over her eyes, she realized that wasn't necessary. She couldn't see a thing and even if Malth could with his better eyesight, the windowless moving van wouldn't give much away.

They drove for what felt like hours, bumping along a winding road. Turns were made at breakneck speed, as if the driver didn't know that slowing down was a viable option. Perhaps they feared they were being followed? No spells had been laid to hide their progress. Even blindfolded, Delta would have felt the shimmer of such a thing.

After the first series of bumps, Delta thanked the goddess that she'd gone to the bathroom before she left the cottage, because apparently that wasn't something the witches were concerned about. Maybe if the magical paralysis had settled over her correctly, it wasn't something she would be concerned about either. Even without attempting to unravel the spell, her magic instinctively took over, removing it thread by thread until she was straining to lie completely inert, pretending it still controlled her. Without being able to see, she couldn't tell if anyone bothered watching her, so she didn't dare tense a muscle to stretch it out without them knowing the spell had failed.

Being carried out of the van was ridiculously humiliating, and Delta knew if she felt that way, Malth did as well. The witches who carried her grunted as they struggled to adjust their arms around her. This would be so much easier if they'd allowed her to walk. She wasn't that heavy. They dropped her feet with a resounding bang that jostled through her body, before they each grabbed her under an arm and hauled her up to lean on some sort of beam. Pulling her hands behind the beam, they zip tied her hands together, before adjusting her feet and tying them together. Thank goodness not directly to the pole, though. The covering was pulled roughly off her head, and she blinked as her eyes grew used to the dim lighting inside a well-maintained and thankfully clean barn. Damnation, that knit made a mess of her hair. She could feel the static electricity rippling through it, and she knew that between that and the fact that they'd put it on her wet hair she was a dang mess. A mass of curls fell in front of one eye, and she fought the urge to shoulder it off, instead maintaining the impression that the spell they placed on her held.

Delta felt magic float across her skin as the witch "removed" the spell that should have kept her frozen in space. Thank goodness. It was one thing to play dead while lying in a van, but it was really tough to simply not move a muscle while upright.

Forcing an angry scowl across her face, Delta hissed out of her throat, dry from the hours of not drinking, "My mother is going to kill you all."

She lied.

"Tell me something no one knows." Delta wished she could hold Malth's hand as she asked the question, but he was too far away. Ibis's minions had tied them to barn beams about eight feet apart as well as facing away from each other. Without talking, they'd maneuvered themselves to a seated position, unable to fully turn around to face each other. If Delta turned her head to her right as far as she could, she could see the length of his legs along the floor, but not much else of him. The barn floor was surprisingly clean and the barn itself empty of animals, although the faint smell suggested it may have housed horses not too long ago. A few animals would have been a comfort, but it also crossed Delta's mind that Ibis might not be above an animal sacrifice or two. Perhaps it was better that the creatures were long gone.

It was so quiet that for a while, Delta wasn't sure if Malth would answer her question. Despite him saying he understood and that he forgave the careless words, saying and doing were completely different animals. Delta twisted her head toward him till it ached, hoping she hadn't completely destroyed the tentative interest they had begun to explore together.

Finally, he spoke, his deep voice a whisper that carried across the dark cell easily. "You know more about me already than anyone alive."

Letting out a deep breath that she hadn't realized she was holding, she waited for him to continue.

"When I was a… soldier… one of the things I dreamed about was passion fruit. I swore if I ever got free, I'd eat my weight in them. How dumb is that? The entire world would be at my fingertips, and I all I could think about was the possibility of eating some fruit that I'd eaten occasionally as a child. I dreamed about it. When I cleaned blood from the weapons, I imagined cutting into the fruit and the juice running down my fingers. When I was shivering in the desert searching for the damn stone, I imagined how it might taste. How it might fill my belly."

"How was it?" Delta whispered, knowing that if that was what Malth had dreamed of, there was no way he hadn't eaten it at the first chance.

"Fucking delicious." He chuckled gravely after the admittance.

"I've never tried it. Passion fruit, that is," Delta admitted softly. "I guess sometimes when everything in the world is available to you, you tend to take it for granted."

This time, a full-fledged snort escaped him. "No, you just like your junk food, and if someone offered you fruit, you'd probably turn your nose up at it."

Delta let out her own out of place laugh that echoed off the walls. "I eat fruit, you know."

"I doubt very much you can consider those little gummy fruit snacks any sort of fruit at all, despite their name," Malth responded dryly, clearly referring to one of her gas station snack pick-ups.

Delta found herself smiling as she relaxed her head up against the cool beam. Despite the circumstances, she absolutely that knew they would be fine. Ibis didn't have the power she thought she had, and she knew absolutely nothing about Delta's magic despite how much she pretended to. This bitch was going to get what was coming to her. She would pay for torturing Ravyn and using Anya. She would pay for teaming up with a flesh-eating demon. And Ibis would live just long enough to deeply regret capturing Math and her.

"You still have your stone?"

"Oh yeah, they took it, but it's back already. They're just a bunch of kids, too scared to properly search, but too scared to refuse."

The pendant around his neck was gone, but they would get it back soon for him, Delta promised herself.

They hadn't even bothered searching Delta, and she felt a pang of annoyance. They'd left her sister's mojo bag around her neck as well as her hag stone. Maybe they were afraid to touch her? Of course, her weapons were her magic, but they could have at least assumed she might be armed. Hell, Malthazar was the weapon, and they still searched him, blind to the fact he was just as dangerous unarmed as he was armed.

Before she could ask her next question, Malth let her know, "It's too soon."

Despite the fact that he couldn't see her, Delta nodded her understanding. She wondered if they were being listened to and if, by chance, too much had been given away. Malth didn't seem to be worried about that, or Delta assumed as much, since she really couldn't see him.

"Want some light?" she offered. A small ball of light wouldn't take much energy or affect the battle that was coming. She wouldn't even need her hands free to conjure one up.

"I'm good," Malth stated. "I can see well enough." The strings of moonlight that trickled through the room mostly struck above their heads, with a few spots dancing on the walls.

Delta nodded again, not sure if "well enough" meant he could see her nod or not and just assumed he could. The darkness didn't bother her, and saving even that small bit of magic might make the difference later.

However, she was pretty cold and sort of wished they'd left the ski mask on her, but just turned it around so she could see out. A blanket had been tossed halfway on her, but being tied up hand and foot made it difficult to adjust it much.

Although with guilt, she quickly realized that they hadn't offered the same small gesture to the still shirtless Malthazar. Not even a hint of comfort had been offered to him.

"I'm sorry—" she began, before he let out a sigh, cutting her off.

"No, don't. It's not your fault they didn't give me a blanket, and I'm fine. I understand why you said what you said earlier. It's fine."

Disappointment stabbed Delta in the chest. Fine was what you were when you were far from fine. Even knowing they'd been manipulated into saying them didn't stop the hurt of the words. Had their other emotions been manipulated as well? Was what she felt even real?

"Thank you for never telling me to be quiet," Delta whispered across the darkness when the moonlight hid behind the cloud. What she felt for him was real. She was sure of it, because even now she was drawn to him.

"What? What does that mean?"

"I mean I know being stuck with me in a car for hours and hours, and then stuck in a cabin and now, held prisoner together. I know… I know I can be a bit much, but you haven't complained, not once, and I really appreciate that." If the moon came back right now, Delta would melt into the floor in an embarrassing pile of goo, but in the darkness, it seemed appropriate to admit her weakness.

Several long seconds passed, and Delta began to wish the melting bit wasn't a pipe dream. "Malth, forget it," she whispered, realizing that she needed to squash her thoughts and comments before they left her mouth.

"No, I was … considering." He didn't let too much time pass before he explained. "You're not too much. I like hearing you talk, and sometimes I even like it when you explode in excitement or anger or anything. You feel things deeply and to be honest, I'm a bit jealous and wish I could be as free as you. If anyone says you're too much or you should talk less, well, just punch them in the head."

Laughter shot out of Delta at the thought. "I think you're vastly overestimating how hard I can punch."

"Well, then, make it a figurative one with words that they're still trying to figure out years later."

"Malth"—she breathed out his name softly—"I'm truly sorry. Please let me say this. I blurt things out without thinking, but also, it's to push people away before, well, you know. I know something about being trapped by the circumstances of birth. I know what it means to be feared for my birthright."

"Delta…" Malthazar's voice carried a warning. "You don't have to explain anything. I forgave you the minute I walked out. I didn't even need to forgive you. You said nothing untrue."

"But I want you to know this. My family hoards magic, not unlike other witches, but we have our own way of doing things. Every generation is born powerful, but upon a parent's death, we inherit their power. No one lets a drop of magic go to waste. There is a fear of patricide, but in the end, it's more important to ensure a powerful line. For some families, loving children and loving families are important, but not mine. This ideal isn't common, and the legacy might be as bad as witches making deals with demons for power. But to ensure the line, there is only one birth per generation. Since the beginning of my line, I suppose that has been true, until me."

Catching her breath, Delta continued, "When Hecate is gone, the coven fears what would happen. Athena inherits it all? My magic demands it all? Or, heaven forbid, a dozen generations of magic splits between the two? The tradition is broken, and people fear the unknown. They fear me and what I might mean for the coven's future."

"Oh, Delta."

The pity in Malth's voice made her angry. "No, as you said, don't pity me. The coven never let me forget that if Mother Hecate hadn't been ignorant or willfully careless, then I wouldn't have existed. Now, in my developing brain, that meant if my existence was due to all that, then I must be too… I never embraced being ignorant, but I thrived on being willful. Maybe the goddess meant for this to happen. Maybe this is the generation where nature needed the power to split? How much can one witch wield or, more importantly, *should* they wield?"

Delta wished she had a drink of water. She swallowed hard, knowing she needed to get the words out before she lost her courage to bare her soul. "My mother seemed determined to prove to the coven that she wasn't unduly attached to me and that my magic benefited them. She had me trained as best anyone could, to dismantle and destroy magic. I guess she thought that would make me appear to be the best guard dog."

She let out a bitter sharp laugh. "Joke's on her. That made them fear me more. I mean, if I could do that to enemies, then I could unravel their magic just as easily." Shrugging although she knew he couldn't see her well, she went on, "They weren't wrong, but that's not what I wanted to do. Mother saw my magic as a weapon to dismantle and destroy. No one taught me it could be anything else. But who could have taught me? I'm not supposed to exist. I don't blame her. I did once, but not anymore. Oliver was the one who taught me there could be other uses for my magic. I could hone in and control magic, use it with cutting precision like a surgical scalpel. A healing spell—simple, nothing special—but I could take the most basic of spells that any witch could cast and use it like a scalpel. Cut away at the disease or burn away the poison, track down and heal an injury. Not boosting the spell, but controlling and using the magic with precision. No waste. My spells aren't special, but I can see the entire picture. I can search and find magic. Once it's familiar to me, I can trace and track it, I can unravel or break it, and I can strengthen it."

Delta paused, only hearing Malth's even breathing. *Say something now*, her mind screamed, but really, the next part was up to her. "I can unravel Ibis. I can *see* her. Her magic is already unraveling, but I can finish this. I'll need to wait for her to open herself to me, and I think that's what her plan is. And when she does, I'll have an opening. I need you to trust me and wait for my move."

CHAPTER TWENTY-ONE

Using unicorn's horn or devil's claw for medicinal purposes as well as traditional crafts goes back for generations.

Delta held her breath, waiting for Malth to respond. She'd given him no reason to trust her. She'd bared herself to him in all ways and she knew, absolutely knew, she hadn't been wrong in doing that.

"Malth, I—"

"Don't say it," his whispered, plaintive words begged her. "Not now, not here." Clearing his throat, he added, "Save it for after, at a beach somewhere, or under the sunshine. When you finish this up, then *we* can say it."

Despite their uncomfortable circumstances, Delta's face nearly cracked with her smile. They weren't done, and he trusted her to make the plan. Just as she would have spoken, the barn door let out a low moan as whatever barred it was slid out of place. Delta's head swiveled in the direction of the noise. Was it already time? She wiggled her fingers and hands in the restraints, attempting to regain the feeling in her numb extremities.

The large wooden door slowly creaked open a crack, but wide enough for someone to slip though. The light behind them disappeared quickly as the door whooshed closed. The figured leaned against the door, heaving deep, ragged breaths. Not Ibis, then. Someone else, someone very scared.

The girl—actually a small, underfed teenager—scurried across the floor, still managing to stir up dust in the mostly clean barn in her rush.

"I'm so sorry," she whispered, pulling a knife out as Delta flinched back. "No, I'm going to cut you free. I didn't know. She promised us things, but I didn't know."

Of course she didn't. They never did. The teenager looked fearfully over her shoulder toward Malth even as she drew toward Delta with shaky hands. Was she afraid of Malth? Or was it Ibis whose hands made her shake so hard that under no circumstances did Delta want her attempting to cut her free?

"Wait, no," Delta whispered back. "Who are you?"

"Robin. I'm so sorry," the girl said, trembling. "We didn't know, she promised to help us."

"Who? Ibis?"

"Yes. We hung out in the city, a couple of us stuck together to keep safe. And share whatever we could. It was safer that way."

Homeless. The girl had been homeless and was living in a city. Which city? Delta supposed it didn't matter and, most likely, Robin didn't know where she was now.

"She came to us. Gave us some food. She seemed nice enough. Said she was looking for a friend she'd lost track of. She called them a scryer. I didn't even know what that was. But one of the guys did. Said it seemed ironic trying to find a scryer when one could find her easy enough. Said that she must want to stay lost. That should have been our first clue not to go with her. But she seemed so nice, so safe. Obviously, if she was a man, we wouldn't have gone with her."

Not such obvious danger, but desperation made them ignore the signs. "You went with her?" Delta kept her voice light despite the anger that grew inside of her. They were children, desperate children.

Robin shook her head. "She looked at us all for a really long time. Sort of dismissed the guys right away. But she asked Sarah and me to come with her. Told us we were special and she had a job for us." The girl hiccupped as she fought back tears. "She killed Sarah. She was my friend. She'd been kicked out and I'd run away. I wish I'd never run away, things weren't that bad, but Sarah could make things happen to ward off people or distract them from what they were looking for. Little things, but sometimes those things helped."

The catalyst. Sarah was the catalyst—or rather, had been. Ibis had plucked her off the street after recognizing her gifts. Danger had come in the form of a middle-aged White lady driving a dusty old minivan. She must have seen something in Robin to collect her as well. Once she set her sights on them, they wouldn't have escaped her.

"She kept pushing Sarah further and harder. She wanted to know who was deterring, how many people, what direction they came from. Sarah couldn't do that even with… help. She burned out and died. And Ibis tossed her aside." Robin's words came in gasps. "I couldn't stop her. I was afraid."

"You couldn't have stopped her. She's very powerful," Delta offered, knowing they wouldn't erase the anguish and guilt Robin faced.

"You shouldn't stay here. I'm sorry I was a part of this. I can free you. At dawn, she plans to… I don't know her plan, but whatever it is, at dawn it's supposed to happen."

"No, don't free us. Take yourself and run away."

"Too late for me. She'll hunt me down like she did her scryer. I can't hide that well. I should die here." The broken-down girl seemed to accept her fate.

Malth broke in with an order. "Run. Can you remember this number?" He rattled off a number before ordering her to repeat it back to him, "Run. And when you get to a phone, call this number, no matter the hour, day or night. Tell them my name: Malthazar. They'll come and find you and keep you safe. Say the number again."

Robin hesitated, torn between the hope that somehow, she could leave the nightmare and knowing she couldn't leave others to the same fate. "One of the girls wants to kill you," she warned Delta. "I can see her heart, she's jealous. Ibis says she has enough power, but she's greedy. She knew she was a witch before all this." Robin stumbled over the word "witch." The world had been new to her. A fluke of a genetic cocktail and she'd inherited a bit of magic that had been enough to appeal to Ibis. This new world she'd been dumped in hadn't been kind, but there was still a chance to change it. A chance to nurture her baby power that had been forcibly enhanced by Ibis.

"I'll be fine," Delta promised the girl. "I'm a tough one to kill."

"She really hates you and wants you dead. She stands next to Ibis smiling and nodding, but I see what's in her heart. Given the chance, she'll kill you. No one else feels this strongly about any of this."

Reading between the lines, Delta realized that some of the others would fight for Ibis because they were afraid. The others would scatter if they saw Ibis falter.

"Will any leave with you?"

Robin softly snorted, before barely moving her head side to side.

"How many others?" Malth asked, keeping his voice low and calm.

"Five."

"All children?"

"We aren't kids."

The sharp words proved there was still a hint of backbone in the girl. But her words confirmed that they were, in fact, all youths.

"You need to go," Delta ordered the girl. "Do you remember the number?" A shimmer ran through her. It was time. Athena had been right; she did know when to use the mojo bag hanging around her neck. Only it wasn't for her. Whispering the words, she demanded Robin remove the bag. Without even knowing what was inside, she explained that the girl would need to mix the ingredients with water and a few drops of her own blood, enough to make a thick paste. Intuition told her the frightened teenager needed to apply it to her face to keep herself hidden.

Robin left as quietly as she'd appeared, this time not downtrodden, but filled with a kernel of hope.

"Damn, you're sexy when you're saving kids." Delta wasn't even joking after she'd watched Malth give the girl instructions to freedom and safety.

"Didn't do anything. Just told her a number to call."

"Agree to disagree," Delta whispered back, unable to believe he didn't see the things he did. That child had accepted death as her fate and with a few words, Malth had changed that.

"We end this today." If Delta had felt any sympathy for Ibis, it had disappeared when she learned that a reluctant witch had died from her abuse. How many other bodies lined the path for Ibis? Clearly, it hadn't only been the wendigo feasting on its victims.

"You have a plan." It wasn't a question that Malth asked, but reassurance.

"The magic within the seed, leaf, or root. I just

give it a little nudge with mine to activate it. The easiest, simplest way to utilize the magic around is without draining me. Magic never goes away or runs dry, but magic can try my body to the point I couldn't lift a finger. Rumors have told of those who have used magic until death, and that is a choice every magic user can make. Ibis forced that child's body to the brink of death and beyond without an ounce of remorse or danger to herself. That ends today."

CHAPTER TWENTY-TWO

*Vervain, which sprang from the tears of Isis, may help
you find what you search for.*

Robin wasn't wrong; they came for Delta and Malth
before dawn. Why not? Each time Ibis came up with
another grand scheme for immorality and power, she
picked a different time of day or event: full moon, new
moon, dusk, dawn. Like any of that made any sense,
but she was desperate.

Ibis's dark eyes narrowed suspiciously, as both of
them were prodded into a clearing. When she caught
Delta looking at her, she automatically smoothed her
face to a more pleasant, approachable countenance. No
wonder the homeless, desperate teens had followed
her; she could actually appear likable.

Delta was struck by how much she looked like an
older version of Ravyn. A version beaten down by
time, anger, and hate. A less-than version. Black eyes
that held no light and no joy, surrounded by deep lines.
Furrows lined her unsmiling mouth, hinting that a part
of her knew that she would always be less than the

girls who had become vampires; less than the witches and magic users. Bitterness oozed from her pores with the knowledge that she would never be what she'd once been.

After a long pause, Ibis made up her mind and reached out to Delta with a thin hand weighed down by multiple rings made of cheap medal and gaudy, over-sized jewels. The jewels were as worthless as Ibis's powers, and Delta mentally scoffed at the obsequious display.

"Take my hand, child, let me feel your power," she ordered, as if Delta were a mere fledgling.

Delta chafed at the slight, pulling her shoulders back. She was no one's child, least of all this wannabe witch. Still, she suppressed her urge to mouth off to the woman.

"Come closer, little fly," the spider invited the fly. Ibis mistakenly assumed Delta was the fly. Her groveling would be over soon, and Ibis would regret her patronizing tone. Delta lay a loose, timid hand into Ibis's grasp and tried to plaster a simpering expression on her face. She felt ridiculous, but apparently it was believable enough. The old witch gasped instantly, and then a true smile of joy—an evil joy—spread across her face.

"Oh, you… you are… so much more than…" A shiver passed through Ibis, and she greedily reached out with her other hand to firmly hold Delta's hand in both of hers, to feel the full force of what she thought was Delta's power.

Delta held herself in check as Ibis allowed the power to flow over and through her as she tasted and tested the magic. Ibis was attempting to learn the power she thought she could wield, Delta thought humorously.

Hold, she ordered herself as the witch's oily black magic ran over her, caressing every inch of her, inside and out, as it attempted to mold her magic. Delta nearly vomited as it sank deep in her stomach, searching out and attempting to access every part of her.

Ibis relaxed and leaned deeply into the magic. A profound sigh of satisfaction left her, as another shudder tore through her. She was turned on, Delta realized with horror and disgust as she fought to keep her face vacant. *Come, little fly.*

Then, in a moment, it happened. Ibis leaned a little too deeply into Delta's magic, giving of herself a little too freely. In the blink of an eye, and without even a change to her expression, Delta snapped her free hand over both of Ibis's hands that had so greedily gripped hers. Caught up in the feelings, Ibis didn't even recognize the shift for what it was. It wasn't until Delta freed her own magic and allowed it to wash over Ibis did the woman recognize what had happened.

But by then, it was too late. With a snap, Delta's magic locked down over Ibis's slick, oily mess of darkness. She held it into place with an ease that momentarily shocked the woman still. The black magic struggled, fighting back to free itself, emitting the odor that Delta had been tracking. Finally, Delta recognized what the scent reminded her of. It had been tickling her nose for days after she'd helped banish the wendigo.

Burnt popcorn. Who would have thought? Lifting a lip in amusement, Delta tightened her hands around the woman's now struggling hands as her eyes grew wide in panic.

"Ibis," Delta whispered. "You either forgot or you never knew. Curious. We had magic before we had words. Spells before the written word. There is no need for either."

The old women's eyes grew round in horror as she struggled against Delta's magic. Magic that needed no words or spells. It simply was.

Patiently, Delta examined the dark magic, slowly spreading her own magic over it, through it, and around it, attempting to discover where the magic began and ended within the woman.

The field which had moments ago been silent now lit up in a dim roar. Delta blocked the noises out as she focused on the task in front of her. She trusted Malth to have her back. By now, he would have snapped the zip tie from his wrists.

She kept the dark coven away from her as she examined their prisoner. In her mind's eye, she could see how it would play out in the field. He would protect her.

Staring deep into Ibis's hate-filled eyes, Delta recognized terror also reflecting back. It only took a few moments to examine and determine what Delta had suspected. There was nothing human about Ibis. Nothing demon either. There was nothing beyond magic, magic in its purest, undiluted form. No wonder Ibis couldn't wield it and needed to channel through magic users.

Even suspecting that Ibis wasn't a living being could prepare Delta for the magic mishmash. The woman simply didn't exist, not really.

When the hell gate had torn the magic from Anya, the magic hadn't known where to go or what to do. It chose to remake itself into its most recent form and call itself Ibis, its most recent name. Ibis didn't exist; she was the manifestation of magic and fear. The magic held the memories of the previous Ibis. It shared a link with Anya. It knew it was no longer an immortal vampire, so it made itself age based on the belief that it would or should age. Its greatest fear was ceasing to exist, but it didn't know how to exist. The magic believed it was a living creature and therefore it become one.

Sadly, Delta examined the binds that it had used to form itself. It wasn't human. It was actually amazing that it had managed to hold itself together for all these decades. Had the twins at Houska Castle's hell gate known what it was and simply held it captive to examine it? Or had they thought they were keeping the world safe while they held a demon? She supposed she would never know.

"You're going to be fine." Delta whispered

reassurances to the magic that struggled against her own magical grip. Unlike when she'd unraveled the magic that bound Eva to Ravyn, she didn't need to be careful of hurting the entity or a magical backlash. Ibis had opened herself up and invited her in, saving her from backlash. Despite her hating to do so, she knew a swift, brutal execution was the kindest. Then the magic could be free.

Taking a deep breath, Delta grasped the hands in front of her even tighter despite the fact that she didn't need to be touching the entity to do what needed to be done. Air whooshed behind her, blowing her hair briefly, before a grunt from Malth indicated that he'd removed whoever had gotten so close.

Letting her breath loose, slowly and with great control, Delta released her magic. Imagining her own magic like a long thick silver sword, she held it above Ibis before drawing it down and through the creation. The magic screeched as she tore it apart with a deep, brutal swipe from the top to the ground.

The air shimmered around the creature, which opened its mouth wide in horror as it split apart down its center. The air grew thick as Delta separated the magic, unraveling it from existence, denying it its desire to reform. Blackness sizzled as she revealed its true reality. Tearing apart piece by piece, it changed as the magic was ripped free. A sharp tang, nearly like lightning, snapped across the field as the magic fled its confines, accepting what its true form was.

It was brilliant and beautiful at the same time. The

magic caressed Delta's skin thanking her for setting it free, recognizing that Delta had given it a gift. It could see the truth now, and Delta found herself smiling at it as it flitted joyfully across her skin. Swirling around, it fluctuated in a splendor of vibrant colors, testing its newfound freedom. Dancing around her. It was a shame no one else could see the magic.

Looking down at her hands, Delta opened them. Hands that moments ago had held a terrified Ibis in place now released another sparkle of magic into the air. Magic that bounced happily along her hands in the dawning light.

Then a sharp pain jolted through Delta, beginning at her back and coming through her body. With horror, she watched the tip of a blade exit the front of her chest. Her hands, still lit with newly freed magic, went to her chest in shock, like they could stop the blades journey. A low grunt sounded behind her as the tip of the blade squelched itself forward and into her hands. The magic drew frantically around her, reacting to her panic.

An anguished howl sounded next to her, and the wind whirled around her as Malth's panicked face came into view. "Delta."

The fear in his voice scared her more than the shocking appearance of the blade. Delta opened her mouth to tell him she was fine. Reassure him that it didn't hurt. But words wouldn't come out. She couldn't draw a breath in to get a word out. Her chest grew tighter at her inability to draw a breath, and then the pain hit.

Malth held her face in his hands, looking down at her and speaking words she couldn't understand. The fear in his voice conveyed the message his words couldn't.

Gasping to draw breath, it hit Delta that she was dying. Then the magic whirled around her once again as Malth drew her against his chest.

The magic dancing on her skin.

The wind flying around her.

Falling. Falling.

Heat. Dry. Hot; no, scorching heat inching across her skin.

Too hot, too dry to draw a breath even if her lungs allowed it.

The beating of his heart against her. Too fast. Too fast.

Then darkness came. Blessed darkness.

CHAPTER TWENTY-THREE

White sage combined with desert sage can enhance clairvoyance and visions, as well as open the third eye.

*H*ell had always been filled with noise and chaos. The grunts and screams of battle. The soul wrenching shrieks of men's souls being tortured day in and day out. The clanging of metal, be it weapons or the heavy, grog-filled cups of the demon lords. Even the footsteps of boys scurrying about to fill chores and duties had added to the noise. Every noise meant something, and not hearing the noise meant you'd missed something.

For the first time in hell, Malthazar feared something other than hell itself. To the onlookers, it looked like Delta had violently split Ibis in half while Malth held off the coven. Before they could explain themselves, Delta had been run through. She'd trusted him to guard her back and he'd let her down.

Split second decisions had to be made. The fatal wound needed more care than he could offer, more than the ragtag coven of children could offer, even if he could make them understand.

Get her to safety, he demanded of the stone that was charged for only a few feet or, with luck, a few miles. *No matter the course, no matter the pathway.*

Before he could take a breath, the stone took them straight to hell. The boar-faced horned guard startled at his appearance but froze. For a second, Malth stood in his former prison and hell seemed to draw a quiet breath, shocked to its core by his sudden appearance.

Then they jumped again. Their landing sizzled as the wards they broke through snapped back into place. Not broken, stretched to accept them.

Delta would be safe, and hell knew he lived.

CHAPTER TWENTY-FOUR

Yerba Santa stimulates physic powers.

A shrill but quiet, persistent voice burrowed through the depths of the darkness that had pulled her under. Was Athena haunting her dreams? Hideous. How long had she been in the darkness? Her limbs felt heavy and impossible to lift. Her eyes struggled to open. Had they'd been sewn shut? *Damnation, what a thought.* Even her thoughts were heavy and black!

Fighting against the urge to be swept away back into the darkness, Delta focused on the tiny voice that seemed to urge her to swim upward.

Finally, her eyes cooperated and slowly opened before immediately closing against the assault of the light. So white and bright, it nearly blinded her after the darkness that had enveloped her. Definitely not her apartment with its tiny windows, and she would have closed her blackout curtains before she went to sleep. Wait. She didn't have an apartment anymore. All of her things had been packed away in storage and the lease had run out.

"We have to play quietly," a small voice instructed someone who didn't answer. "They'll make us leave if we don't." Whomever was being spoken to didn't answer. Or was the voice instructing her? She hadn't made a noise, had she?

Curiosity, rather than any since of wanting to wake up against the comforting darkness, forced her eyes to focus despite the blinding sunlight. Tucked in tightly up to her underarms, only her arms, so pale they might blend in, were free of the white covers. So much white. Mother's. She must be at her mother's home, but why? She couldn't remember the last time she'd willingly gone to sleep in Hecate's home.

Her blurry eyes focused on the one bit of color that lay before her. It was a… tiny car. A red car. A tiny, red convertible lay on her stomach, stark against all the white of the room. Odd.

Still, no one was directly in her line of sight. She could have sworn she heard a voice. Whose voice was that? A memory flitted, nearly on the tip of her tongue. Then a small boy's head popped up over the side of her bed.

Julian. Of course, it was Julian. Relief filled her as she recognized his young face. His hair was cut neater than the last time she'd seen him. Two small horns budded out the top of his head. Those weren't there before. Were they? His face looked fuller, more relaxed than before, and a smile stretched across his tiny face.

"I told them you were waking up soon," he

informed her with all the confidence a five-year-old could give.

Delta cleared her throat and croaked out, "Your tooth grew and you lost another."

Julian beamed, the tiny freckles moving across his face. "I did! 'Thena said it would grow in before you saw it."

What did Athena have to do with that? Why were she and Julian here? Here in her mother's home? Athena had seemed confident she would stay in Ohio with Julian until Malthazar returned to collect him. Panic filled her, pulling on her chest more painfully than it should. Julian shouldn't be here. If hell found him, that would be the end of him.

Another small head tentatively looked up over the edge of the bed at her. This one she didn't know. Delta was absolutely sure of that.

"We're playing cars with you," Julian explained. "That one's yours." That explained the red car, but not the other boy.

Gesturing toward the solemn set of eyes and forehead peering up at her, Julian casually explained, "This is my friend. He doesn't have a name, and he doesn't talk much. That's okay. I can talk for him. We're gonna let him pick it when he's ready. Malth says he'll know it when he knows it."

The words spilled quickly out of Julian. In Ohio, he'd warmed up to them and had been a little chatterbox, but now his voice carried a quiet confidence that sounded oddly similar to Malth's. And he had a new friend, apparently.

Another rescued child. Perhaps that was what had changed with the boy, the need to take care of someone who needed more help than he did.

Here? The rescued boys were here?

Twisting his fingers around, Julian added, "Malth didn't lie to me. He did come back even though I wasn't where he left me. He still hasn't said goodbye either."

The sound of soft footsteps outside had the boys looking quickly toward the door with wide eyes. Scooping up the cars, Julian promised, "We'll be back to see you. Gotta go before the witch finds us in here."

Which witch? Most likely, there was a household full of them here.

"Boys," her mother's voice sing-songed from outside the room, "I pray to the goddess you aren't disturbing Delta."

Wait. That cheerful tone came from her mother? *Mother Hecate?*

Memories flooded back. Tearing apart and freeing the magic. The knife through her body. Malth's face. Goddess, his face. That was it. She was dead. This was the afterlife. Heaven or hell; it had yet to be decided.

Was it her destiny to protect the boys from her mother? They didn't really sound scared of being caught, more like it was a game. What sort of hell had she woken up in? Despite being dead, Delta couldn't keep her eyes open and found herself falling back to sleep. Answers would have to wait.

Another voice broke through the darkness. *Weren't promises made that one could sleep when they were dead?* Delta thought irritably, refusing to open her eyes again. It could have been ten minutes since the boys had wakened her or ten hours, but still, couldn't a girl catch a break?

Of course she wasn't alone, but the female voice floating over the room was definitely not a child's. This time, the voice was closer to her head, speaking softly and pausing sounding like she held a one-sided conversation. Perhaps this visitor was on the phone? Couldn't people sit quietly at a bedside? But the more she listened, the more the melodious tone washed over her, calming and soothing, lulling her to release her irritation and open her eyes. But opening her eyes might break the spell… or was this a dream?

"Portaling out infused the wild magic into you. Magic, as you remember, exists no matter the state that it's formed or unraveled, it doesn't disappear or dissipate. It has to go somewhere, has to be used somehow. The demon magic formed the vampire. The gate took them apart, but the magic didn't cease to exist. Yes, it evolves and actually fights to continue its existence. Now it has settled into you, over you, or rather, more likely you both. But *he* doesn't want to be seen, let alone examined."

"I know you've tried to please me—a daughter does that. Tries to look up to her mother and win her approval. I liked that. It was different from the witches of the coven who adored me for my power or status. They can be frantic, almost draining, with their self-involved sucking up, but you glowed when I would smile at you. But it wasn't enough for you. I wasn't enough, and now, I suppose Athena has realized the same. Athena doesn't want the mantle. She claims she does, but in her heart she isn't ready. She would dutifully accept it, like she does her duty in all things, but it's not what she wants. She doesn't know what she wants. She's not like you."

It was her mother. She was in her mother's house, and her mother was sitting at her sick bed. She was dead or dying. No other option. A light clicking noise marked her words, the noise pausing on occasion, considering before beginning again. Was her mother knitting?

Knitting?

Hecate's voice continued, her voice soothing in a way it had never been before when she imparted knowledge to Delta. Lectures were stern, as if they needed the tone to impart the wisdom. This sounded… nice?

"Darling, you are all I could hope for. A wild, free-spirited witch not caught up in the stuffy politics and affairs. Pfft," she let out the sound in frustration, but her words still sounded affectionate. "Rubbing off on Athena, bringing—no, demanding—those boys come to live with us. Becoming a sanctuary. Can you imagine? My mother… well, let's just say my mother never would have allowed it. We must atone for what our sisters have done. We owe it to those children, to protect them."

Hecate was so quiet that Delta thought maybe she'd slipped from the room. Perhaps she'd fallen back to sleep and woken up to an empty room. Allowing her eyes to open a slit, she scanned the area the voice had come from.

Hecate was still there. Makeup-free and her hair pulled back off her face, but not the severe style she usually sported. She looked almost comfortable and relaxed, although it went against her nature and everything Delta knew about her. She was knitting. Poorly. It looked like a lumpy, endless knotting of yard balled up on her lap. Lifting the mess, she sighed as she examined it. Delta expected her to toss it on the floor, giving up on the endeavor. Surprisingly, she began clicking the needles together again, twisting the yarn into even more knots.

"Mama?" Delta whispered, her voice dry and unrecognizable even to herself.

Her mother's eyes shot toward her, and Delta thought she saw a hint of fear and then relief flash through them. Gone so quickly, perhaps she'd imagined it, because Mother Hecate didn't fear anything and relief would mean something worried her. But maybe…

Hecate didn't move as her stoic eyes examined Delta before settling onto her face. Then her entire demure relaxed… in relief? It was relief and happiness. Whatever had been done to her, her mother was *happy* to see her and hear her voice. Dropping the mess of yarn onto the floor beside her, Hecate leaned forward and reached out a trembling hand. She hesitated just before she might touch Delta's face, acting afraid that she might break a hidden spell.

Delta shifted her face enough for her cheek to brush her mother's fingertips. With that move, the wall broke and Hecate lay her hand fully on Delta's face.

"Child," she whispered, "you have given me—all of us—such a fright."

It was on the tip of Delta's tongue to automatically apologize for whatever transgression had occurred, just as she'd done for her entire lifetime. Apologizing, but never quite sure what she needed to be sorry for. But Hecate placed a soft finger over Delta's lips, cutting off the well-practiced words.

"No, I should be apologizing to you for putting you in such danger. I'm so happy you're awake. It's been days…" Her voice trailed off.

Days? Memories flashed of snapping her fingers and unraveling the magic that had taken the form of Ibis. Magic that had breathed a sigh of relief as it felt freedom for the first time in decades. It had sparkled and danced across the air and for a moment had caressed her face in thanks.

Then pain, so much fucking pain and the knife tip protruding from the front of her chest had shocked her, but it was the look on Malth's face as he bore down on her that had scared the shit out of her. His face. Fear.

So much fear. For her.

Delta lifted a weak hand to her chest, as if expecting the knife to still be in place. Not believing she could have survived a mortal wound. There was no way it had missed heart, lungs, everything. Days? If a wound like that didn't kill you, it would put you down for weeks or months, even.

"Maybe a few weeks," Hecate admitted, correctly reading Delta's expressions. When she was a child, Delta had thought her mother a mind reader but, in fact, she wasn't. Her years of living had simply made her astute to people's body language and thought patterns. She predicted what one was thinking but didn't quite read minds. "It's probably still tender."

It *was* still tender, a tug all the way through her chest. Or was that her heart wondering where Malth was?

"Your demon left you a gift." No judgment to her tone; factual, dry, but that was her usual manner.

"He's not my demon." Were these the first words she'd spoken in weeks? A lie?

"Nonetheless…" Gesturing toward the side table at Delta's head, Hecate pursed her lips; biting back words and questions.

A small bowl containing three purple passion fruits and an array of purple-and-white blossoms stared back at her. A silver-handled knife sat to the side on a small plate. For a moment, Delta's heart stuttered, but it wasn't the knife. This was a regular kitchen knife, not the dagger that was long enough to enter her back and exit her chest.

Malth had brought her passion fruit to try. He'd seemed appalled that she'd never tried it, and he obviously wanted to remedy that. The purple-and-white passion flowers were beautiful and delicate, with a soft, fragrant sweet scent. Delta had never been given flowers before, and she fought the urge to crush the blossoms to her chest. Malth had given her flowers and the fruit, sharing a part of himself with her, in a way she suspected he hadn't shared with anyone before.

"He's left a note."

A note? That wasn't good, not good at all.

Hecate waved a small single sheet of paper in the air; one she'd probably already read and tried to decipher and discover some hidden meaning. But Malth wouldn't have left great secrets in a note that anyone could read.

"Can you read it to me?" Delta croaked out the words, her throat suddenly dry. Despite not wanting to hear the words from her mother's mouth, she couldn't wait until her eyes could focus well enough to read them.

Everyone should try passion fruit.

I wish I'd told you more. How I remembered the fruit,

but not the face of the woman who fed it to me daily. You deserve more.

He'd said good bye.

"He loves you." Hecate stated this not as a question, but an observation.

Delta sat quietly, considering her mother's words. She *knew* her own feelings, but Malth's feelings were anyone's guess. "He never said those words," she finally admitted with certainty to her mother, who scoffed a most unladylike noise in response.

"Words." Hecate spat this out with a sharp laugh that was anything but amused. "Words mean nothing. Less than nothing. They can be a lie. But actions? Actions are clear, actions speak clearly and loudly, if you would only listen."

Biting her lip, Delta wondered for a moment who had been applying her beeswax lip balm to her still soft lips; the slight taste of strawberries and unmistakable hint of beeswax meant it had only been within the last few hours. Realization hit her, as she shot her eyes toward her mother, who began busying herself with an attempt at unraveling her knitting.

"If that's true, then where is he?" Delta questioned with a weak wave of her arm. "We barely know each other, really. Truly, who can fall in love this quickly? He's only seen me in, like, one set of clothes." Had their lust been fabricated just as easily as their anger and irritation? How could one trust, when such manipulations existed?

"Delta"—her mother tsked—"he had to take you through *hell* to get you here. He might as well have announced himself with a dinner bell, and you as well." Hecate sniffed, like it should all be clear to Delta. The same Delta who had been lying completely unaware in a coma for days, perhaps weeks. "The demon could only portal a short distance. Unless…"

Unless he skipped through hell, the fail-safe to keep tabs on the hunters who had the portal stone. For decades, Malthazar had controlled his use of the stone to ensure he wouldn't have to use hell as a go-through. He'd kept himself hidden, and as far as hell was concerned, dead. Malth had announced himself to hell to bring her to someone who could heal her.

The wound was fatal. Delta remembered the feeling of the metal sliding through her back, through her lung, and out the front of her. Closing her eyes, she could still see the blood-soaked steel pushing itself through the front of her chest. Had it hit her heart? Even a nick meant death was inevitable, so far from help. Delta's chest tightened as she relived her attempts to draw a breath, and Malth's panicked face bearing down on her as the newly released magic had danced around them. It had been beautiful and she'd wanted to reach out and touch his face, promise him that everything would be okay. But she hadn't been able to lift her arm.

"Malthazar," Delta whispered quietly as she rubbed the spot on her chest where the knife had protruded. There wasn't even a hint of tenderness now.

"What?" her mother questioned, looking up from the tangle of knitting.

"His name is Malthazar, and if you're lucky

enough to be called his friend, it's Malth. That's his name. You keep saying *him* and *his*, but his name is Malthazar."

"Of course it is, darling. I hadn't realized I hadn't said it."

"Well, I did," Delta snapped, knowing that she wasn't angry at her mother, but at herself or at Malth. Or maybe the witch who had stabbed her?

"He has come regularly. Malthazar, I mean. He has been here as often as he could even if it's for a few seconds to check on you, or at least that's what the boy has said."

Clearly, he hadn't shown himself again to her mother, and that irritated the woman.

"When he thought you might be ready to wake, he started showing up with this fruit. And every few days… Malth"—her mother stumbled slightly over the nickname—"would replace it. Even if we—well, the boy—didn't see him, it was replaced, along with the flowers."

Malth hadn't left her. In fact, he'd blown his entire cover, imploded the existence he'd carved out to get her to safety. Signed his own death warrant with hell, unless worse, they kept him alive as a slave. Malth would rather be dead than return; he'd been clear about that. And yet…

Hecate softened her voice. "You surprise me. You, of all people, should believe in love at first sight. You have the heart for it. Falling hard and falling fast, that is."

"Mother," Delta sniffed, "that sort of thing is for fairy tales. No one really believes it. There is no great love out there for most people. They get what they get and they settle into life."

Hecate glanced sharply at Delta. "Oh, my daughter." Looking back down at her lap, she fidgeted once again with her knitting knots. "I've been in love twice." She didn't seem to notice Delta's shocked expression. "My first marriage, to Athena's father, was arranged. I didn't know him at all. I didn't love him at all. But it grew. We started our marriage utter strangers, determined to find a life together. That grew into a tentative friendship of sorts. Then, little by little, things changed until one day I realized that I loved him deeply, and he loved me. We danced around it, but it happened. Until he broke my heart by dying. Fool, but I swore I wouldn't fall for folly again. I had my daughter; I had my title."

Delta couldn't breathe. Her mother had *loved* Athena's father? She never spoke of the man as far as Delta knew. Hecate never spoke of any man.

Hecate pulled the yarn up eye level, looking at it as it personally offended her. "Then I went to Europe for a grand tour. Years had passed, and I was content. Then I saw him." She looked up over Delta's head, seeming to stare into the past. "So good-looking. Such a flirt. He introduced himself to me and said I was the witch he would marry." She laughed at the memory. "He saw immediately who I was and what I was to him. It took me another two days of him following me around before I could admit he meant the same to me. When I saw him, it was like lightning struck, but after his bold pronouncement, I had to take him down a notch."

"You fell in love that fast?" Delta could scarcely believe this. Hecate did nothing without thought, considerations, weighing the pros and cons, a list. Spontaneity? No. Love at first sight? "Who is this man? Why aren't you with him now?" So many questions rapped at Delta's mind that she barely knew where to begin.

"Who was he?" Hecate parroted with a puzzled look and a head tilt. "Darling, that was your father."

Delta felt faint. Was she dead and this was the afterlife? Concussed and dreaming? "What? Who? Where?"

"Close your mouth, dear, flies will get in there. No, this love of mine went to war." She scoffed, "A human war in which he felt called to help. Said he was needed, and all the stuff young men say when they go off to do those things. We made plans to marry when he returned, when the war was over. He would meet me back in America. Europe wouldn't be safe for women or witches. Only he never made it back. He never even knew…" Hecate looked at Delta with tears in her eyes. "He never knew. If he'd known, I would like to think he wouldn't have gone.

"I sent someone to track down your sister and bring her home." Hecate was apparently finished with the subject and as was her way, abruptly changed the subject as Delta attempted to wrap her mind around her mother's confession. "She's not one to run away." A breath of silence followed those words. *"Like you are"* were the words that hung between them but were left unsaid.

"Angry as a wild cat, Athena was. I don't think I've ever seen her that angry. She's not you."

Guilt flashed through Delta now. Was she responsible for her older sister's behavior? Surely, Hecate had realized that Athena wasn't happy and hadn't been for quite some time. How could her mother bare her soul like that, and then turn around and be such a bitchy witch?

"She's not been out on her own like you have, and she doesn't know how the world works."

Delta found herself stifling a sharp bite of laughter. Duh. Her mother expected Athena to rule the coven someday, yet hid from her the realities of the world. Being an unwanted secondborn did have its advantages. No one really gave a shit what she did. Her mother had no one to blame but herself for sheltering Athena the way she had. It was decades beyond time for her older sister to revolt and live a little.

"I found her in bed with that friend of Eva's, Jackson." Her mother offered no infliction when she offered the information, but still Delta suspected her mother was disappointed. Had she honestly thought Athena some sort of virgin? The title of "Maiden" was mostly honorary and didn't really mean that she had to remain a maiden, especially when the Mother refused to relinquish her title.

After her initial surprise, Delta was happy for her sister. Goddess knew they all needed a little enjoyment in life or, you know, a few or several orgasms. "What? Who knew she had it in her? Go, girl—and a human, no less." Maybe Athena's visit hadn't been a mistake after all. Full on revolting against Hecate appeared more likely from her ambitious sister.

Hecate let out a very unladylike snort. Who was this woman sitting at her bedside? "Not a human. She didn't even check him before she bed him. His mother is a witch, and her grandmother before her. I suspect his father might have been as well, but they haven't been very forthcoming. They protected him from Eva's succubus side. He doesn't appear to or can't practice, but he carries the bloodline."

Delta could imagine her mother's annoyance at a group of witches refusing to answer her every question. And how had Jackson not lit up to her? She should have seen if he had any magic, and she definitely would have seen if he was covered in a protection spell. But then again, had she really even looked at him when he'd come around? She'd expected to see a human Jackson, so that's what she saw. Oliver would definitely be annoyed that all of his lessons had been forgotten the moment she assumed someone was a human.

"Now she imagines herself in love and wants to care for the half-breed… boy. Julian, she calls him, and the other nameless one, who appeared one day. Athena brought him out, bold as can be, and demanded breakfast for him. So now there are two of them."

"A boy. They're simply boys," Delta responded flatly. She couldn't figure her mother out; one moment she seemed different, and the next, not so much.

"Yes, you're right. It's time I learned and accepted new ways. She wants to care for the boys and boys like them. She's imagining some sort of sanctuary, I suppose. But she's destined for more as my successor."

"Goddess…" Delta cursed her shaky voice. Damnation, this woman would know how serious shit was if it was the last thing she could do. "Hecate—Mother—you aren't ready to accept the role of the Crone. Our coven has been without for decades. What does it hurt if their Maiden fulfills a few side quests while awaiting the role of Mother? Sounds like it might be good practice."

"You're right," Hecate conceded surprisingly quickly. "You're both right. It's our responsibility to right the wrongs that have been committed. Certainly, hell could do without."

It sounded like Hecate was simply parroting words that Athena had spoken to her, but it was a start. She still argued; that was her way, but perhaps Hecate was more open to change, especially when such suggestions came from her precious Maiden.

"Try your demon's fruit, dear. I think it's important to him you try it." Hecate took the silver knife and cut the fruit in half. A spoon appeared, and she scooped a small bit out, before urging it toward Delta's mouth. "Goddess knows he dropped enough of them off… passing my security." Pursing her lips at the inconceivable thought of anyone easily walking or portaling through her wards, as well as how ill-mannered the act was.

Seriously? Whatever magic Malth possessed had decided that here, with her mother, was the place to be healed? Something else to hold above her head for the rest of their lives.

Baby steps. *His name is Malthazar,* snipped through her mind, but already she was learning to hold her words for a breath.

The urge to argue with her mother about her ability to feed herself sat on the tip of her tongue. In the end, the desire to try the juicy spoonful of pulp won out as it tantalized her nose when her mother impatiently waved the spoon under it. The ripe scent of the fruit filled her senses. If it tasted half as good as it smelled, no wonder he'd dreamed of it in hell, especially if he'd eaten it during his brief childhood.

Delta felt like a baby bird as she dutifully opened her mouth to the spoon.

Wary of her stomach, as she'd lain sleeping for so long, Delta touched her tongue to the juicy fruit before nibbling it. He was right. Malth was right. It was an explosion of sweetness in her mouth. Holding it on her tongue, she savored the taste, carefully crunching the few seeds her mother had scooped as well. Her stomach growled as she savored the flavors. Who knew how long it had been since she'd eaten? Well, probably everyone but her.

"His name is Malthazar." Her mother knew that; she'd literally just told her. What was wrong with this woman? "Give me another bite. Please."

Silently, her mother scooped out another bit. *Still stingy*, Delta thought sourly. The fruit dripped down the spoon, leaving a small splatter on the white bedspread as Hecate brought the spoon to Delta's waiting mouth. Even as she ate it, Delta held out her hand in a "gimme" gesture. *Damnation, he wasn't wrong; it might be the best fruit in the world.*

Hecate shook her head. "That's enough for now. You can have more later, after you eat some broth. Now you need to sleep until it's brought to you." The air shimmered with her words, strumming through the air with the power behind it, hitting Delta straight on. No time to dissipate the purple tendrils of magic shooting toward her; all she could do was try to brace herself for its strike.

Even as her mind screamed against the order, the magic brushed over her skin, barely more noticeable than a soft breeze, but the power behind it hit hard. *Damnation, you witch.* Wait, what had her mother been talking about when she'd thought Delta asleep? Infused wild magic? *With whom?* It was too late to form words and within seconds, her eyes closed and she fell into darkness.

CHAPTER TWENTY-FIVE

The blood of a plant is simply the sap or juice.

Malth's unsanctioned foray into hell had alerted anyone or anything monitoring that sort of thing of his unauthorized presence. Not enough time had passed that they would forget the one who had gotten away. Death was the only escape, and now they knew that was a lie. Malthazar wouldn't have done anything differently, though—except, perhaps, kill the witch before she could have stabbed his Delta. The smallest and youngest-looking of the group had been the most dangerous, the most corrupted by Ibis. He'd underestimated both her devotion to Ibis and her viciousness. Power corrupted, even the youngest. He regretted not seeing her as a threat like he did the others, but Malthazar didn't regret opening a portal through hell to remedy his misstep. Decisions had to be made within a second.

Hopping through hell was the only choice. If hell hunted him to his true death, then so be it. At least Delta was safe. Malth wouldn't go back to the prison without a fight. Freedom or death were his only options.

Something had happened in that portal. The magic that Delta released hadn't dissipated yet, its fate not yet decided. It had all happened so fast—swooping Delta into his arms, wildly opening a portal with the lone intention of getting her to safety, with no regard to the magic floating around them. He hadn't only portaled the two of them. He'd brought the wild magic with them into the portal, the same newly released magic that would look for a place to settle.

Instincts took him through hell. A hell jump ensured he could get her to safety. Ensure that he could jump them more than a dozen feet. Malth had once thought he would never forget how his prison had felt, but the hot, dry air sucked the shocked breath from him. How had he survived this? How did the others? The heat rippled across his skin, reddening it within seconds, going as far as to singeing the fine hairs on his arms. He wrapped his arms around Delta as tightly as he dared in the hope of warding away death as well as protect her from the heat of hell.

From hell, the portal stone transported them hundreds of miles away from the northern Minnesota forest, dropping the two of them in a room with yet another shocked, redheaded witch—clearly Delta's mother, and just as clearly, her private quarters. To her credit, the level-headed witch hadn't even questioned how he'd managed to bypass her wards. Perhaps having Delta with him helped, or perhaps there was something else.

Fueled by fear, he spat out orders to take care of her daughter. His attempts to explain the situation and why he needed to leave immediately left him tongue-tied as Delta's blood dripped from the both of them onto the pristine floor.

Carefully, he placed her on the bed, not caring that her injuries would soak the white bedding. Gently he laid her on her side, not sure how else he could place her without causing more pain or injury. Her face was as white as the sheets, her red hair not nearly as bright as the blood flowing from her wounds. Malth had allowed himself a moment to smooth the wild curls away from her still face, laying a gentle kiss on her forehead, followed by a prayer for any god or goddess who might be listening.

"Help her," he pleaded.

In a manner befitting the woman who had created Delta, Hecate hadn't panicked. She immediately and calmly assessed the urgency of the situation even as Malth turned again to tell her he needed to leave.

Touching a hand to her daughter's head, Hecate had turned a look toward him that would have killed a lesser demon. "Why is my daughter infected with demon magic?"

Malth drew back from the venom in her voice. Demon magic was her concern? Not the knife jutting from her small frame? Tilting his head, he looked at the older woman. How could one simultaneously be so wise and so stupid? Opening his palms, he informed her softly, "Magic is magic. There is no ours and theirs. It's how it's wielded that makes it what it is."

She'd waved him off. "Go," she'd whispered before laying both hands on her child.

And so, he'd left.

It killed him to leave, but he couldn't leave a trail leading straight from hell to her home. He would die rather than put her in danger… more danger. Bouncing back into hell, he headbutted the now alert demon, before snapping as far from the spot Delta lay as the stone would allow.

The stone surged and seared his hand, as if it had awakened for the first time in centuries. Math didn't dare open his palm to see what it was doing. *Keep her safe.* The words repeated over and over in his head, the mantra bouncing around as it became his sole focus. But after his portaling, the stone portaled him again and again and again. Maybe hell had recharged it in same strange way after all these years. Instead of each entry into hell boosting it, maybe it had sucked up some strange hell energy, like a dried sponge hitting water for the first time. Malthazar wasn't about to question it, though, and he continued jumping into cities, into the countryside, forests, jungles, a river, faster and faster, until he fell to his knees in exhaustion even as the stone hummed happily in the palm of his hand, clearly still energized.

Finally, after catching his breath, he'd dared to open his palm. The stone was… gone. Gone? He stared in exhaustion at his palm in disbelief. Perhaps he'd missed the small stone that always returned to him. Frantically looking at the ground to see if it had fallen free into the lush vegetation. Despite not seeing the stone, it felt like it was still in his hand, warm and humming happily. Using his left hand, he traced the area of his palm where it should have been. A slight bump and a pulse of colors under his skin proved that he hadn't lost the stone. Instead, it had infused itself under his skin and if he looked closely enough, he could see the outline of it even when he didn't touch it.

After all these years, the stone had fused itself to him.

After more days of endless jumping, he made his way to Oliver's compound in the hope that his friend was there. Thank the gods he was. Both he and his mate Eva were in residence. And finally, for a moment, Malth dared to rest within Oliver's security. He slept for twenty-four hours and when he shot awake, he immediately asked the couple if they'd heard from Delta's mother, before opening a portal to her side to check on her. She was sleeping and had been for days, at least according to Julian, who was less surprised to see him than he was. He'd forgotten the boy, he realized with guilt. Of course, he always forgot about the boys once he got them to safety, but Julian's wasn't a closed case yet.

Delta's face was still pale, but not as gray. Julian sat with her, playing cars on the side of her bed, racing them along her unmoving arm even as he informed Malth that he was living here from now on. Malth didn't dare allow himself to stay long. She lived. Thank the gods, she lived.

It felt like the weight of the world had been thrust on his shoulders, and he was tired, so damn tired. He'd portaled once, twice, and then rapidly in succession until he'd lost count. It had nearly killed him when the acolyte had stabbed Delta, gutting her with the dagger. Rendering the witch's head from her body had brought no satisfaction, his fear for Delta too great. Her face had been frozen in a smile as she dissolved the magic creating Ibis and it had slowly faded, her face going gray in shock.

Returning to Oliver's place, he shaved and showered, before finally feeling a semblance of humanity again. Eva's hellhound was in residence, lying by the roaring gas fireplace, looking fully relaxed and at home. The three of them sat quietly, watching the beast sleep, perhaps waiting for the others to talk, to ask questions, or to bask in the silence.

The hellhound woke with a stretch, blinking his giant eyes that fluctuated between dark brown, blood red, and a strange crystal blue, before settling into their usual brown shade. His eyes had changed, and he continued to grow rapidly despite his less than stellar beginnings. None on this plane even recognized the changes in the creature. What was his name? Baby Boy or Big Boy. When would the creature reveal his true name? Did Eva and Oliver know he should do that?

Casually sniffing the air, the hound narrowed in on Malth before sauntering to him and laying his massive head on Malth's knee. Malth casually scratched the creature's head as he let out a deep sigh of contentment. Without thinking, he moved on to his ears, giving them a solid rub as the hellhound moaned and leaned deeper into the pets. The hound was more earth bound then hell bound, a feral creature walking among them like a golden retriever. What had the world come to? The hellhound couldn't survive forever on earth's plane, but had Eva's energy and the magic of the house altered him enough that he couldn't survive without it as well?

"He has gotten ridiculously spoiled," Oliver complained from the sofa across from the two. "Not that he doesn't deserve it," he amended with a hasty glance toward his mate, who was bringing coffee for herself and their guest.

"You're one lucky vampire," Malthazar mumbled lowly, knowing his friend's supernatural hearing would pick up his words as well as his meaning.

Malth could feel the pleased energy emanating from his old friend, and he didn't have to look at him to know that a smile that must be crossing his face.

"Déjà Bloody Brew for my beloved," Eva announced while delivering the coffee to Oliver, and if Malth's nose didn't deceive him, the black coffee actually contained a shot or two of blood. His sister was taking to the supernatural life with ease. One could almost believe she'd been born into it and not been hidden away from it as well as from her own lineage.

He still couldn't believe he had a sister. Malth had to refrain himself from openly staring at her; even being Oliver's oldest, closest friend wouldn't stop the vampire's instincts kicking in. And they were siblings in the most general sense. Both of them were demon spawn, although not from the same demon, of course. They each had their own mothers, one a witch and one a human, and they'd been loved by their mothers. That last bit was a rarity among demon offspring. Eva was mostly untouched by the taint of her sperm donor. Living unaware but hidden away on earth had its own set of problems, but it seemed to Malth the better of the options. Her adopted grandmother had meant well, even if Eva couldn't understand it completely. She'd saved the girl from an eternity worse than death.

"And an extra hot, extra-large Mocha Loca for you, Malth." As always, Eva knew exactly what to brew or whip up for guests. Definitely had to do with her succubus side, although Malth didn't want to spell it out for her. He was sure Oliver must suspect the reason his mate knew others' desires before they themselves knew them.

"Perfect," he said gently to the awaiting Eva, who smiled in appreciation. She enjoyed taking care of people, and if anyone claimed her care was less than perfect, they would have Oliver to answer to.

Sinking into the sofa next to Oliver, she sipped on her own iced coffee. Malth shivered at the thought. Iced coffee. In this weather?

"Are you safe, my friend?" Oliver asked, but Malth suspected he was asking in a roundabout way if his Eva was safe. Malth would never bring trouble to their doorstep, and Oliver knew that, but now that he had a mate…

"Oliver," Eva's low, sharp voice gently warned him. "Malth is only in the situation he's in because he was helping us. Us and Ravyn," she reminded him. "He never would have had to make the choices he did if we hadn't put him in this situation."

She was right, but Malth wouldn't shift the blame or responsibility to anyone else. He'd made the decision to pop through hell. He would do it all again if it meant Delta would be saved. The only thing he would have changed was never putting Delta in that situation in the first place. Gods, she must hate him. Still, he couldn't keep from checking on her.

"Hecate says someone keeps leaving passion fruit and flowers by her daughter's sickbed," Eva said carefully.

"She will wake soon." That was the mantra that Malth kept chanting to himself, at all hours, like he could make it happen by belief and prayer. Delta looked like a redheaded Sleeping Beauty, and at any moment her eyes would open.

When no one else spoke, Malth found himself continuing, "She, Delta, has never eaten a passion fruit." Pausing and swallowing another gulp of the hot drink, he added, "I… I… told her she needed to try one, and I wanted her to."

Every few days, the stone took him to a remote spot in Brazil where he picked a few fresh fruits, as well as the flowers, from trees deep in the jungle. Malth refused to have her first fruits be commercially grown, store-bought crap. Something about that spot drew him to it, and Malth refused to imagine what that might mean.

"Thanks, Tommy," Eva chirped as a human sat down an array of small breads and muffins in front of them.

"You're welcome, ma'am." The tall, thin human seemed pleased with her words and smiled at her acknowledgment.

"Yes, thank you, Tommy," Oliver added dryly and abruptly, as if he had more words to add but opted not to.

"Sir." Tommy shortly nodded more solemnly, before backing out of the room to well-trained to turn his back on the group.

"What's that about? Feels awkward," Malth noted, matching Oliver's dry tone.

"Eva says we should thank the staff more," Oliver grunted. "It makes them uncomfortable when I speak directly to them, though."

Eva poked Oliver with a foot. "Eva also says we shouldn't call them 'the staff.' " Apparently, this was an ongoing discussion. This felt so *normal*. Sitting around drinking coffee, teasing friends and mates, so different from his usual daily life. Would he ever get this? Or would he forever be making retribution on a crime that had an impossible value?

"Don't they get paid?" Malth offered, not understanding the issue, or why Eva and for that matter, Delta, insisted on so many unnecessary conversations and words. Although he admitted he did miss what he'd once considered a never-ending stream of prattle, her voice had become comforting.

"That's what I said." Oliver softened his words with a smile.

"Thanking them is more than a paycheck. It's about knowing they're appreciated for the work they do." Eva sounded well-rehearsed in this argument.

"Doesn't a paycheck do that?" Oliver offered back. "Maybe I'll give Tommy a raise and quit saying thank you."

"Oliver."

"What? You want me to tell Tommy he's not getting a raise because you want me to say thank you?"

"Can't it be both?"

"I would quite rather give him the raise, and you can continue thanking him. It scares the staff when I thank them."

Eva turned the full force of her smile on him, before turning back to Malth. "Malth, why are you bringing Delta vine-ripened passion fruit straight from South America?" This one didn't mince words, and those words were like a knife to the heart.

Something about her knowing look tore away Malth's ability to lie and downplay the fruit. He didn't dare ask her how she knew.

"I... I… told her what they meant to me, but I didn't tell her everything." Malth wanted to tell Delta these things, but Delta wasn't here. "I wanted to share it with her, but not by telling her everything…" His words trailed off as he considered his truths.

"I think my mother gave it to me when I was a boy, before… well, before. I think I grew up eating it fresh from the vine. But what does it say about me when I remember the taste of it better than I can remember my own damn mother's face? What kind of monster does that make me?" Malth looked at the two of them, pleading for understanding, hopeful that if they understood, then maybe Delta would understand why he'd downplayed something so, so simple, yet not.

He began to rub the hellhound's head again. The beast seemed glued to his knee today and looked up at him with his eyes flashing blue again, acting as though he understood Malth's dilemma. Damn, his eyes were uncanny and a bit disturbing.

Malth expected Eva to respond, and he was surprised when Oliver spoke to him instead.

"A hungry child whose mother and the passion fruit both represented love, hope, dreams, desires… freedom. But only one was within your reach and that's what you focused on, that's what kept you going. For decades, perhaps centuries, you had to live with the knowledge that the life you should have led was stolen from you. The mother who loved you was killed protecting you, and the demons enslaved you. Of course, you would focus on the one thing that you could regain, the one clear memory you had that didn't bring you pain. A memory that you could someday recreate when all else was lost."

Oliver paused, but he wasn't done yet. "What do you want from life? Not what do you think you deserve. We don't get to choose that. But the things we want, we can go after"—he pulled Eva closer to him—"and we're never too old and it's never too late to get that happiness."

What did he want? A place to lay his head. A porch. A dog or maybe a cat to start with. Delta. Shaking his head, Malth explained, "The things I want can't—shouldn't—be brought into this life. I've built a life on a house of cards. I can't bring a cat into this life, let alone Delta." There, he'd admitted he wanted her, but even then, he couldn't offer her more.

Eva lay her head on Oliver's shoulder as she examined Malth closely, leaving him shifting uneasily in his seat. Could she see deep inside him? No one should be that vulnerable. While she stared at him well past the point of comfort, Malth fought to not drop his eyes. Even if Eva were unaware, in their world—a world of predators, of monsters—one didn't simply drop his or her eyes. You might as well sign your own death warrant.

Tilting her head, a soft smile lifting one side of her mouth, she made him feel even more vulnerable than her quiet yet through examination. "You love Delta, don't you." The knowing tone in her voice made this less of a question and more of an observation.

"Eva…" Oliver's tone held a hint of warning, as if he might expect Malth to attack her for such words.

But Malth considered the statement. He'd only spent a few days with her, and they'd butted heads most of that time. It seemed ridiculous, impossible to fall in love with someone that quickly. But the feeling in his gut, the ripping out of his chest when Ibis had trapped the two of them, and then the stopping of his heart when Delta had a blade run through her said otherwise.

The hellhound shifted his position, forcing Malth to rub the back of his neck now, as the words lay heavy in the air around them. Pausing his petting, Malth finally admitted, "Yes. But that's why I need to stay away from her."

A home, a kitten, Delta—all of that was further from reach than it had been a week ago.

Eva nodded shortly and tightly, relieving a bit of the tightness in his chest. She understood. Even if she didn't agree with it. But of course, she wasn't done. "So, have you guys played *Hide and Shriek*?"

The seriousness of her tone had Malth wondering if he'd misheard her. What was she talking about?

"Eva." This time Oliver groaned.

Ahhhh, hide and seek, but… ohhhhh.

"Clever one, aren't you?" His tone was a hint lighter, before he added to Oliver, "That's what you get for mating a book flea."

"A what?" Eva sat up with a shriek, but Oliver caught on quickly, wrapping his arms around her and holding her in place to their teasing.

"Yes, my little library mouse likes her play on words."

Malth scoffed, "More like a reading rat, or a reading horse, even."

"I don't even know what you all are talking about!" Eva quit struggling, acting as though her ignoring them might shut them up.

Not before Oliver got one last one in. "Really, though, being a writer, I suppose you're more of an ink drinker."

Eva's mock indignation and squirming free from Oliver had Malth smiling ear to ear as he sipped his now cool coffee. She did make a good cuppa. And even if he wasn't permitted love, he had some sort of family now, at least for another few days. He selfishly wanted to spend his time with those he loved, and since he couldn't be with Delta...

They watched for different reasons as Eva flounced from the room, Oliver smiling in happiness at his mate, and Malth thankful that his friend had been granted the happiness Eva claimed they all should receive. With a sigh, Malth released the feeling of reprieve he'd been granted. He needed to bounce again. It had been nice to finally rest at Oliver's home, but who knew how much of hell might be following him, and if they had a tracker as good as him they would eventually find him, no matter where he hid.

Oliver leaned forward, his elbows on his knees. "Hold up one more minute, if you would." Glancing toward the doorway where Eva had left, he admitted, "I'm marrying Eva. She wants a wedding. I want to give her a wedding," he amended.

Malth didn't follow, and he felt his face wrinkle in confusion. "But you're mates," he finally offered. "That's more than marriage or a wedding."

"I know that and you know that. But Eva, well, she was born and raised in the human world."

"Does she understand? Do you want me to talk to her?" Malth asked hesitantly, despite having no idea what he would say to her, but he felt he should offer.

Oliver waved him off. "No, Malth, I don't need you to talk to my mate for me. I want to do this with her. She says she doesn't care about this stuff, but she also hasn't stopped planning since I proposed. Eva lived in the human world, and she's been a human her entire life. I want to give this to her. Something that ties her old beliefs in with the new."

"She's not a human…"

"As far as she knew she was. You can't shut that off. A wedding is a reflection of love, and that's what she knows. I want to give her flowers and a dress, so expensive it makes her cry. Friends to celebrate with."

Unusual, but Malth couldn't judge the way anyone expressed their love, even if the concept seemed foreign to him.

Dropping his voice a note, as if his home weren't the most secure place in or out of the city, Oliver admitted, "But I think we can, as they say, kill two birds with one stone. A highly publicized wedding of one of Chicago's most sought after, secretive bachelors."

Malth grinned at that assessment, but Oliver wasn't done.

"A best-selling, secretive author whose real identity is finally made public. A wedding attended by secretive societies and wealthy folks, as well as one of Hollywood's beloved actresses, who will come out of hiding for the occasion."

Clearly, he was speaking of Ravyn, and a wedding like he was describing would be all of the news, not the low-key existence they usually led. Lowering his voice again, Oliver added, "And I want you to be my best man."

Sitting back, Oliver grinned, clearly pleased with this series of announcements. "I won't take no for an answer," he added.

Malth shook his head. "That's insanity. Do you understand *hell* wants me back? I tracked down and brought in more issue the years I was active than all the others combined. Nothing will stop them from trying to get to me. You're literally inviting hellfire down on you. Besides," he scoffed, pointing out the obvious, "I'm barely a man. I'm more demon than man."

Oliver flashed his fangs at the self-loathing words. "You're the best man I know. I can't think of anyone more worthy to stand beside me while I tell the world I love Eva and want to spend my forever with her."

Malth still shook his head, yet he found himself hesitantly agreeing. "If you're sure."

"More than sure, brother." Oliver's smile was full of fang. There was nothing the vampire loved better than executing a good plan. "Now, I want you to listen to this two birds, one stone plan I have."

CHAPTER TWENTY-SIX

Thankfully, no one need be beheaded when asked for a head, simply a flower or seed head.

Sitting cross-legged on the floor, Delta snapped her fingers sharply in the air, watching as the colorful sparks sprang from her finger tips. Narrowing her eyes, she studied the bits of magic for several seconds, before snapping again a few times, adding more to the kaleidoscope of colors floating around her.

She held out her hands to either side of her. Each of the two boys placed a small hand in hers before grasping their own hands together, creating a small circle. The boys stared at the area in the middle of the circle, quietly, expectantly, before a smile broke across the nameless one's face, causing Delta to smile in return. Then Julian's eyes lit up, and she knew they could see the magic floating and dancing in the air above and around them. If someone entered the room, the trio would appear to be laughing and watching some unseen entity dance in front of them.

This was a new trick. Since she woke, Delta had

discovered slight alterations of her magic. Now not only could she see magic, but she could share those connections, at least for a few minutes, with anyone she was touching. Combine this with controlling it to dance or sparkle like fireworks, and she was super popular with the boys.

It went beyond that: Delta could see bits of free magic that floated in the air, not belonging to anyone. When no one was around, she tested it, drawing it to her with a thought, inviting it to join her own magic. If she pulled enough from the air around her, she could utilize the magic without touching her own. Turn the lights off? Done. Snap a fire into existence to ward off the cold? Done and done.

The second boy Malth had dropped off still wasn't speaking, but so far, Julian spoke enough for both of them and interpreted his needs well enough. No name had been picked out or given to him, but Athena said his name would come when he was ready. Same as what Julian had told her, but Delta wasn't sure who had made the decision first.

But he was smiling. Sometimes anyway. The first few days, his expression had remained somber all day long, but as time went by, small smiles flitted across his face. It made Delta happy, when she could be the cause of that.

She hadn't seen Malth. After she awoke and tried the succulent, fleshy passion fruit, none had appeared again. Either he'd popped in and discovered her recovering or someone had told him that she was getting back to her normal, sassy self. Either way, she hadn't laid eyes on him. The few fruits he'd left were long gone, and Delta couldn't bring herself to ask anyone to buy any as a pathetic replacement.

"Delta." Her mother's strangely soft voice interrupted their play, still startling Delta. She wasn't used to seeing this softer side of her mother, and she wasn't sure if she ever would be. "You have a guest, if you're up for it."

For a moment, Delta's heart leaped out her chest. Could it be?

"It's not Malth," Julian whisper-shouted in the way only a child could, immediately crashing her hope that her demon was walking through her doorway. Still, the boys stood and wordlessly offered a hand each to Delta to help pull her off the floor. With an exaggerated grunt, she stood and smiled her thanks at them. She hadn't needed their help for a few days, but they insisted, so she accepted their pampering a bit longer.

Then, to her surprise, the quiet youth—the unnamed one—wrapped his arms around her waist and then released so quickly she might have thought she'd imagined his small, warm hug.

"He's excited that our sister is here to see you," Julian explained matter-of-factly, as if the smaller of the two hadn't sought out physical contact with her for the first time.

"I'll let her know you would both like to meet her after she meets with Delta," Hecate offered the two, "assuming Delta agrees to see her."

"Let's practice our moves." Julian never seemed to run out of energy, and the quieter boy seemed content to keep up as he smiled his agreement. "Can we play *Legends and Legends*?" He couldn't remember the correct name, but he knew they enjoyed playing it. Probably enjoyed it more when Delta didn't join them.

"Don't play my account," Delta warned the boys. Once she'd felt like sitting up more, she'd been kicking the children's asses in and teaching them life lessons on the gaming console that had been collecting dust at her mother's place. They had their own logins, but Julian kept hinting that if he could log in using Delta's account, he would be a better player. But generosity only went so far. Playing with complete toddler newbies was generous; letting them use her well-honed account was insanity.

"I can set her up in the sitting room," her mother offered.

"No, it's fine. Let her in here."

"If you're sure," her mother said with a sniff, as if the mere thought of sitting Eva in a guest bedroom with a newly-healed Delta was more than she could bear. The guest room was probably bigger than Delta's old apartment, and it certainly held more furniture. Extending an invitation for visiting in it was hardly the hardship her mother presumed.

Delta had been turning away visitors. Polite people who called were denied. More aggressive ones who showed up at the door were forced to visit with

Hecate and Athena before being turned away. This was the first time Eva had shown up in person. Mentally, Delta sighed; she should meet with her. It wasn't her fault… well, none of it was her fault. Eva wasn't one to stop and stare at Delta like a zoo animal and then return home to gossip about her. Sincere concern brought Eva to Delta's home away from home. Damnation, she needed to get out of the busyness of her mother's home and return to… where? Her apartment was gone. Her rooms at Oliver's place seemed so foreign, and she didn't think she could bear to live with the newly mated happy couple. Eva's cottage no longer seemed to be the same sanctuary she'd drifted to weeks—months—ago. *Soon*, she promised herself. She would find herself a spot again.

"I need you to be my bridesmaid." Eva jumped right into the reason for her visit, thankfully not pointing out Delta's greasy hair or asking the mundane questions about how she was feeling or what she'd gone through. "I want you to be, and technically, since you're the only one, you would also be my maid of honor."

That was *not* what Delta had expected. In fact, it was the last thing in the world she'd expected. "You and Oliver are getting *married*?" She couldn't stop the disbelief as well as the happiness for her friends from her squealing voice.

"Yes!" Eva confirmed with an ear-to-ear smile as she held out the large rock on her left hand. "I know we're mates and that's supposed to be even better, but dammit, a wedding! How can I say no to an unlimited budget and a chance to fulfill every princess dream I never knew I had?"

"But, like"—shaking her head, Delta tried to understand—"in a church or what? Is that even possible?

"A wedding doesn't have to take place in a church," Eva admonished, "and just because Oliver is a vampire doesn't mean we can't celebrate with everyone. To be honest, I'm not sure about the church thing. I mean, we went into churches in Europe during the tours and he didn't burst into flames, so I don't think that's a thing. Another misconception circulated to make people feel safe."

"Right," Delta agreed, not completely understanding. "And yes, yes, I will, even though I have no idea what any of that means. I'll be your maid."

Eva laughed. "It means you stand up next to the two of us in a beautiful dress and witness our union, then you dance and party the night away, because we're going all out."

Caught up in Eva's excitement, Delta felt lighter for the first time in several weeks. Her mother was actually right: she shouldn't have been shutting people out. A wedding! It had been years since she'd attended a human wedding. Supernaturals and witches didn't tend to celebrate the same. But if Eva was having a wedding… "I'm in. Obviously, as long as boss man is okay with me being a part of it. I'm honored to…"

Delta found herself inexplicably choking on her words. "…to be a part of your ceremony."

Eva caught Delta's hand and drew her down to sit on the bed. "Before you agree, I do want you to know that Oliver asked Malth to be his best man. And I know something happened… between the two of you."

"You've seen Malth?" Delta interrupted the mood from moments before, plummeting. He'd been that close to her.

"A bit," Eva said cautiously. "He's been on the run since he portaled to hell. They want him back, and since he rescued the other child, they also want to stop him from that. They know now, he's the one who's been wreaking havoc on their collections. One of the ones anyway, as I understand."

He'd been to see Eva and Oliver, but not her. Hurt shot through Delta's stomach, but this was Eva's moment, and she refused to be the reason the smile was wiped off her face.

"I'm still in," Delta said firmly, adding a nod, but she wanted to ask was it safe for Malth? Why hadn't he been back to see her now that she was awake?

"He asks about you," Eva admitted, her words stabbing Delta right in the heart. "He's so used to being alone, he doesn't know any other way. You won't believe what Big Boy did to him."

Delta forced a smile. "Sure." She waved her hand, blinking back tears that threatened to fall. "What did your hound do? Big Boy seemed a little obsessed with him."

"He brought Malth a kitten!" Eva shouted out the words to a shocked Delta. "Literally showed up with this tiny ball of fur in his mouth and dropped it in his lap, then poofed off like he does. We're all sitting there shaken as hell. Malth has this wet ball about this big on his lap"—Eva held her hands a few inches apart—"then it meows, like a crazy shriek."

Malth had a kitten. Delta should feel happy for him, but instead, she felt jealous of some little kitten that a hellhound had found for him.

"That's nice for him to have," Delta garbled out nonsense. "But your wedding! How exciting, we have so much to look forward to." She couldn't focus on what Malth had and didn't have; it would only make the crushing feeling in her chest that much stronger.

"Glad you're a-veil-able," Eva enunciated with a rise of her eyebrows.

Delta groaned, thoughts of Malth fleeing momentarily, most likely as Eva planned.

"Good. I was worried that one was only good on paper. Although I guess I'm supposed to say, 'I can't say I do without you,' or something cheesy like that."

Shaking her head, Delta groaned. "Keep that up and you'll be… doing it without me, that is," she promised with a smile to ensure that Eva knew she could toss out all the word play she wanted, and it wouldn't keep her away from the wedding.

Biting her lip, Eva crinkled up her forehead. Did she had more news that might deter Delta from agreeing?

"Spit it out, girl," Delta ordered, as if knowing that she would see Malth again wasn't news enough to shake her to her core. At this point, there wasn't anything Eva could throw at her that would shock her.

"Well, a lot has been going on and you've been… sick…."

Delta raised an eyebrow and gestured to keep going with her hand.

"Remember, you've already said you're in, no matter what." Eva let out a deep breath before spitting out her words without taking another breath. "Our-wedding-will-be-in-four-days-so-you-need-to-get-a-dress-like-yesterday-but-today-is-the-next-best-time."

So, it looked like today's order of business would be a shower and shopping.

CHAPTER TWENTY-SEVEN

An earth apple is simple to find, just dig up a potato.

The longest night of the year—a perfect evening for a vampire wedding. A spectacular wedding put together in days, and his sister deserved nothing less. Malth wasn't a fool; money could ensure anything could get done. Money, power, and more than likely a few thinly veiled threats. If anyone had hesitated putting Eva's dream wedding together on a tight timeline, Oliver had quickly ensured it wasn't a problem before Eva could even get a whiff of it. Who would have imagined his old friend planning a human-type wedding for a group of paranormals?

Malth found himself shifting from side to side slightly as he stood next to a beaming Oliver. Nonchalantly, he attempted to smooth down the sides of his crisp black tuxedo jacket while drying his nervous hands at the same time. Heart pounding, he ordered himself to relax. He'd faced demons, dammit.

Now, standing in front of a crowd, dressed in unfamiliar clothes, he was sweating as if he faced the fire demon all over again. How did Oliver manage to look so calm while he was next to him having heart palpitations? Was his upper lip sweating?

Calm down, he ordered himself, as if such a sentiment was so easy to force. More than aware that everyone could see him wiping his hands on his pants, he crossed them behind his back to cease any chance of fidgeting with the unfamiliar clothing any more than he had. Eva had sworn he looked handsome as hell, and he didn't think that was meant to be offensive. Oliver had patted him hard on the back and declared him a makeover success. Someone had tamed his wild curls with some sort of gel, and now they lay plastered against his head. That same someone had offered to cut some of the curls and "clean up the back," but she'd thankfully backed away when he snarled at her. Perhaps if she hadn't let her fingers linger on the back of his neck when she offered, he wouldn't have responded so rudely.

Malth wished he could have convinced them to let him don his black stocking cap. Despite nearly all of the wedding guests being paranormals, he still felt vulnerable without it. Oliver's eyes had narrowed when Malth brought it up to Eva, and he stared pointedly at him when Eva had asked why on earth he would want to wear it.

As guests entered, no one seemed to notice or care about him. They were murmuring about the paparazzi at the gate, as well as the surprisingly highly publicized guest list. A few acted aghast at the overwhelming flash of cameras, but Malth knew they secretly were enjoying their brush with fame, even if it was secondhand. Oliver had already arranged for photos of himself and Malth to be released at the start of the ceremony. A very public announcement had already been made that Oliver's good friend would be standing up as a witness, but pictures couldn't hurt on making sure the right people—i.e., demons—knew of his attendance.

The soft murmurs of the crowd faded as a cello began to play, signaling the start of the ceremony. Even the air changed as the guests turned toward the entryway, and the few stragglers quickly moved to available seats. Malthazar's breath caught in his chest, and he found he couldn't draw another. If that was so, he would die happy.

Delta was breathtaking. She literally took his breath away, and he happily gave it. The woman walking down the aisle was always beautiful, but he'd spent days with her in the same travel outfit, alternated with tossing on one of his tees. Her hair—always long, wild, and beautiful—had been coaxed and crisscrossed into an intricate crown around her glorious curls. Curls that had been tamed for the day, but he knew it would only take an instant to free them from whatever magic kept them under control. The lavender satin dress, simple by many standards, emphasized her slender frame. He wondered if her bare arms were slathered in sunscreen. Despite it being the shortest day of the year, she would take precautions to save herself from being burned by any sunlight, even if most of the day was spent indoors. A fine silver chain held a small lavender teardrop pendant that lay between her breasts. The V neck showed just enough that he longed to pull the silky strap from her shoulder and see what else she might have hidden below the dress. Silk? Lace? The satin dress clung gently to her hips and widened slightly at her knees down to her ankles to allow her small, steady steps down the aisle. Silver shoes occasionally peeked out from below the fabric.

Malth didn't even try to hold himself in check as he drank her in like a dying man. This might be his last chance to really look at her. He took in this vision as she slowly walked down the aisle holding a small bouquet of white-and-purple flowers. As she walked closer, he could see the tiny white flowers adorning her crown of hair. Delta's eyes glistened with excitement, but her small, practiced smile not once landed on him. She was avoiding him.

He didn't care. This vision of her would be filed away with the few other memories of her to sustain him for a lifetime. The last few rays of that day's sun flickered through the windows, reflecting on her copper hair, making her glow even brighter, if that were possible.

Delta smiled at Oliver and mouthed something toward him that Malth didn't catch, but Oliver stifled a laugh. Probably something snarky to help him relax.

When Oliver had told him of his plan to marry Eva, he hadn't really understood it. After all, they were mates; no ceremony announced it or changed that. But seeing Delta walk down the aisle toward him helped Malth understand that this ceremony meant something to the lovers. He would never have this. A spark of sadness and regret attempted to wash through him, but today wasn't about him. Not yet anyway.

Malth didn't see when Eva starting her own trek down the aisle. He had his head turned, trying to see Delta on the other side of Oliver. But when Oliver's entire face lit up, Malth knew Eva had come into view. Focus. He needed to focus. Giving Oliver a strong pat on the arm, he forced a smile on to his face.

"Your love comes."

Oliver nodded in agreement with a smile unlike any Malth had ever seen on his old friend's face. Jealousy punched him in the gut. He was happy for his friend. He deserved this like no other, but still…

Eva had wanted a wedding, and Oliver had given it to her. Malth knew that for as long as they lived, Oliver would do his best to give her everything she ever wanted. What a gift to have.

Oliver and Eva had begun the dance, swishing and dipping around the dance floor while their guests watched. After the band requested the wedding party join them on the dance floor, it had only taken Malth a beat to silently hold out a hand to Delta. His heart nearly stopped when it took her several long moments before she grasped his hand and joined him.

"You look beautiful." Malth bent down low to whisper in Delta's ear. One dance. He could do one dance. One last chance to hold her in his arms. Even with her heels on, she still barely reached the top of his chest. Adjusting his grip, he pulled her tighter against him. It took a moment, but Delta relaxed against him, molding her body against his as they swayed to the music. He rested his lips on the top of her head, briefly breathing in her scent. If he could stop time at that moment with his lips on her, enveloped in her clean earthy scent, he would.

Requesting that the wedding party join them was a sneaky little trick that Eva had probably decided on, hoping that pushing Delta into his arms might change things. She didn't understand that Malth was certain of his feelings for Delta; so certain that he was leaving her to keep her safe. A fact he knew without a doubt that Oliver had shared with his mate. Secrets between the two would be impossible, and Malth knew that anything he told Oliver could be told to Eva, especially if it impacted her in any way. Even Oliver wasn't insane enough to implode his own wedding without making certain his mate would be fine with it.

Others slowly trickled onto the floor but as far as Malth was concerned, he and Delta were the only two beings in the world. Already the sun had dipped low enough in the sky that the windows no longer allowed in the filtered light. Eva had planned the day so that as soon as Oliver was at full strength, they could recite their vows and then party the rest of the long, dark night away.

"Thank you," Delta responded, moving her head against Malth's chest, but avoiding looking up at him. "You clean up pretty well yourself."

Magic-conjured butterflies flitted around them, dancing to the music, landing on flowers, as if they could really sample the sweet nectar. One landed on the side of Delta's head, its wings slowly opening and closing. Another one joined the first, then another landed on her shoulder, and yet another made its way down her arm. Their wings slowly flexed, as if resting or perhaps waiting for her to notice.

"Dammit," she muttered before freeing an arm to brush off the ones tickling her skin. "This magic…" She trailed off, shaking her head, knowing that more had attached themselves to her. The displaced magic flitted around her for several more beats before meandering off to perhaps entertain more guests. Her body trembled in Malth's arms, as if fighting back an emotion.

"What?" he asked, drawing back a hint to look down at her. Was that laughter or tears? He didn't want the last time he held her in his arms to be tearful. Without knowing it, Oliver and Eva were giving him the chance to replace the last time she'd been in his arms, when she was pale as death and less than a breath away from the afterlife. *This* memory would supersede the last without denying or replacing what had happened, but knowing this specific moment existed would nourish him for years.

"Magic seems to like me lately." Delta's voice sounded strained as she brushed off his concern. "I do feel like a princess tonight. In this dress. Here." She looked up at him with eyes shining brightly, her thick lashes framing them. Glitter and gold surrounded them, enhancing the color as he fell into them. He never understood women who painted their faces, but right now he understood the appeal of the practice. It could take something extraordinary and make it explosive.

"Of course you do." He smiled down at her, pulling her close against him as he closed his own eyes. Another moment in time he would remember forever and replay again and again.

"Thank you for the passion fruit. You were right, it was delicious and definitely something worth dreaming of." Delta's voice was low and barely over a whisper. "And the flowers helped me sleep."

Wordlessly, he nodded over her head, knowing he held her too tightly for her to see, but he didn't trust his voice for a breath. "I wanted you to know that I messed up. You asked me tell you something real, but it was only partially real," he finally admitted, letting out the breath he held. "My mother fed them to me when I was a child, before… well… before." Trailing off, he felt her nod against his chest. He needed her to understand. "It felt so wrong to admit I could remember how badly I missed the fresh fruit, but I couldn't even remember my mother's face."

"I do… well, I think I do understand," Delta assured him. "Being vulnerable is hard."

They continued swaying together with the music building around them, everything elsc background noise. "Thank you for sharing both… I mean the truth of it as well.

"Why didn't you come back?" she questioned quietly. "I mean, I know you did, and thanks for saving my life and everything, but I thought you might… come… back to see me."

The sharp, uncomfortable pain in Malth's chest returned. "I wanted to. I want to, but it's not… It's not what's best for you. What's best is if I leave." The song which at first had felt like it wouldn't be long enough now seemed like it would never end.

"Why do you get to decide this? Why does everyone get to decide things for me except me?" Delta ran her hand down Malth's jacket, her fingers gripping the lapels momentarily before releasing them.

"Delta, Princess," Malth pleaded softly, "some things aren't meant to be. Can't be. Sometimes, we have to grab hold of the moments we have and for some of us, those moments are all we get. Not all of us get a lifetime, but it doesn't make those moments any less precious. That jump with you, well, hell knows I'm out here now. And I can't ask you to… things are different now."

The jumble of words barely seemed coherent, but still Delta understood. She had to understand. The hurt

337

in her eyes nearly broke him, before he tore his gaze away to avoid seeing her anguish, the same anguish he felt. Malth looked out around the dance floor, avoiding the woman in his arms. More couples had filtered out onto the floor to join the happy couple. Even Jackson and Athena swayed to the music under the twinkling lights and floating butterflies.

"Damn, I wish I could hate you," Delta hissed to Malth, probably aware that in a roomful of supernatural creatures any of them might hear her. Moving in his arms, she clutched his jacket—forcefully, this time—demanding his attention back on her. "Why can't I hate you?"

Stepping back and looking up at him with a tilt of her head, she added, "That would make things easy, I suppose, and we can't get easy, can we? Seems like the gods don't want us to have it easy."

Cold guilt spread through Malth's limbs as she left his arms. He didn't deserve easy. Spinning away from him in a splash of silver and pale purple, Delta rushed from the dance floor toward a flashing exit sign, leaving the intoxicating scent of her in her wake.

Malthazar hesitated. Hating him might be easier, might be kinder to her, in fact. Unfortunately, he knew all too well that hate was the polar opposite of love. To hate, one must have loved at some point. Love. How could love feel so perfect and hurt so much at the same time?

Chapter Twenty-Eight

Buttons may sound easy enough to procure, but if you aren't using tansy, your spell will certainly fail.

The wedding was perfect, as if it dared be anything but, for the two most wonderful people she knew. It was beautiful and everything that Oliver and Eva deserved. Lavender, white, and silver spun across the ballroom, and waiters kept the guests plied with the drinks of their choice, be that red wine or a darker red drink created to satiate the deepest of hungers. Delta was lucky that Eva's favorite lavender color complemented her so much as well. Knowing she looked as beautiful as she felt helped her face the evening—and Malth. It was easier to be well-armored when feeling beautiful versus wearing a color that clashed with your very being. But she hadn't counted on her feelings of loss belying her courage. With a glance at the couple on the dance floor, Delta knew they wouldn't be aware if she left the wedding for a bit, or even completely.

She couldn't be on the dance floor another second longer, so close to him and yet so far away. She couldn't pretend that she didn't want to climb up Math, demanding sex and answers simultaneously. She thought that maybe…

The lights were too bright, and she blinked back tears that threatened to give away her emotions. Where were the damn exits? Shouldn't they have them every ten feet or so for fire codes or something? She took a few steps one way and then another, searching for a door, any door. A flurry of butterflies circled around her head once again. Delta waved them off, knowing that even hitting them wouldn't flatten or injure them. In theory, magical dancing butterflies sounded marvelous, but that was before she knew they would be so attracted to her. No one else seemed to be fighting the insects off.

Dammit, she'd entered through a door not too long ago. The lights reflected in her unshed tears, making it difficult to see. Determined, Delta headed straight ahead. She had to reach a wall and then she would follow it around until she found a door. A door to anywhere outside of this room. Then she could breathe, away from Malth and away from the infernal butterflies. Surely the expensive magic would keep the illusions tied to the ballroom.

Too impatient. In too much of a hurry. The accusations rushed through her head. Always something and never enough. Would she ever be enough? Would she ever be someone's first choice?

Before she could reach the wall, a hand lightly touched her lower arm, pausing her in her determination to get anywhere that wasn't near Malth. Biting her tongue, she plastered on a large, toothy smile before turning toward the offender, prepared to give her regards and continue on her way.

Ravyn.

Ravyn Sinclair held lightly onto her arm, as if Delta could choose to shake off the ancient vampire and walk away. Despite Ravyn being Oliver's maker and one of his closest friends, she was also elusive in the way that famous people were. Delta wasn't sure if her perceived distance was due to her being a vampire or a famous actress; either option seemed possible. Nonetheless, she'd spent little to no time in the woman's presence. In fact, the most time she'd spent was during the time Eva had met Oliver and needed some serious magical healing. Despite the fact that Ravyn had been present most of the time, Delta had either been focused on Eva or wiped out. Of course, there was more recently when they'd taken down the wendigo together. But it still wasn't like they'd focused much on each other. Ravyn's imprisonment, escape-slash-rescue, and subsequent destruction of the wendigo hadn't left much time for bonding. Plus, she'd been a little hot for her supposed bodyguard, Sebastian. He currently stood much closer than a bodyguard should to Ravyn's backside, glaring down at Delta, as if she might refuse the woman who was basically the queen of vampires an audience.

"Good evening, Ms. Sinclair, it's lovely to see you again." A neutral greeting seemed appropriate. Referring specifically to any previous meetings might be ill-mannered.

Half the time in the California wilderness, Ravyn had been out of her mind and near feral and the rest of the time, she'd spent devising and implementing a plan to destroy the wendigo. Did that move them past casual acquaintance or were they supposed to ignore the events?

"You look beautiful tonight." That wasn't a lie. Not a hair on Ravyn's head was out of place, and her long, navy dress fit her like she'd been sewn into it, while it puddled to the ground as if someone had run after her to fan it out. Her gold jewelry was simple and understated, as if she'd read a book on how to dress perfectly for a formal wedding event without outshining the bride.

Delta suddenly felt like a child trying on her mother's dress, while Ravyn was, well, Ravyn. Impossible to feel anything but inadequate standing beside the ancient vampire.

The tiny beauty closed the small gap between them, tightening her grip slightly, as if she knew every self-deprecating thought flying through Delta's mind.

"Darling, that is too kind. It's wonderful to see you again under these joyous circumstances. You look beautiful, Delta, absolutely beautiful. Doesn't she, love?" The last question was tossed over her shoulder to the large wolf shifter, who seemed to have worked out the issues he'd been having with Ravyn the last time they were all together. Awkward stuff that had been.

Sebastian stopped his predatorial perusal of the room to briefly glance down at Delta, appearing to consider the question before responding, "Yes, she does look quite lovely as well."

This beast had certainly been tamed. The wolf almost sounded like he meant it, and a good five more words than he'd spoken to her in the past—the wendigo situation aside, and that had been more like barking orders. Delta nearly snickered aloud; Eva would appreciate that thought. Although, Delta suspected, Sebastian wouldn't find it nearly as amusing. Hell, he might even snarl at her.

She needed to get out of here before she completely lost her mind and said something stupid aloud.

Diplomatically, Delta smiled her appreciation, at the same time attempting to extract her arm from Ravyn's grip. Only the vampire wasn't quite done with her yet.

"Bash and I wanted to thank you for all you've done."

When Delta would have shrugged off the thanks, Ravyn insisted, "Darling, you're better than that. Don't underestimate your worth and contributions. You dropped everything and flew across the country to take down a… well, you know. Then you faced what remained of my sister and you nearly *died.* Died doing what I couldn't."

Delta could feel the tremble in Ravyn's grip and the sincerity of her words. Did Ravyn feel guilty or responsible for what happened? Ravyn hadn't placed anyone in danger. She bore no responsibility for what the magic had done nor the actions of a deranged follower.

She leaned in closer to Ravyn, her nose just brushing the vampire's dark hair. Despite knowing that Sebastian would hear, and possibly anyone else who dared to eavesdrop, she lowered her voice even more as she shared, "No, you need to understand. The magic that remained was absolutely not your sister. It had tricked itself into believing it was. It misunderstood and then manipulated the bond with your sister. Then it blamed, lashed out, and killed, not knowing what it was, not understanding. It was truly not your sister," Delta promised, knowing this knowledge was important to Ravyn.

The tension Ravyn had been holding in her shoulders melted a bit as she searched Delta's eyes for truth. It was the truth. Ravyn couldn't have stopped the magic, even with a familial bond. Seeing, controlling, and then pulling apart the magic was what Delta had been born to do.

Wordlessly and swiftly, Ravyn pulled Delta into a hug, her arms squeezing her a tad tighter than what was comfortable.

Clearing his throat, Sebastian reminded Ravyn

before Delta needed to, or before she passed out. She still hadn't decided if she would tell the woman it was too tight. "Ravyn, let the witch catch her breath." His deadpanned tone sounded as if he needed to remind her of this very thing all too often.

It was all too much. Delta found she couldn't have uttered another word and thankfully, Bash took Ravyn by the arm and led her away, but not without a sympathetic glance back at her. The breath hitched in her throat as she followed the wall down until she reached a door with a large red exit sign above it.

Relief temporarily pushed down the rising panic, and she pushed the door open and ran the steps out of the room. *Damnation.* The fucking door had led her straight outside into the cold night air. In her hurry, she hadn't paid attention, and the heavy gray door slammed shut behind her, effectively blocking off the bit of light that had pierced the temporary darkness.

Immediately, she turned to pull the door open and bit back another curse, realizing the outer door didn't have a handle because it was a damn *emergency* exit. Now she was stuck outside in a slinky lavender gown that did nothing against the cold, in heels, and with no idea where the actual entrance to the building was.

Why did Oliver need to rent such an obsequious ballroom? Everyone already knew he was richer than Midas. Did he really need to flaunt it like this?

Banging on the thick door did no good. Mostly likely, the hum of conversation and music faded out her futile attempts. Plus, it hurt her hand. Running her hands down the seams of the door, let her know it had been covered in security magic. Not only did the door only open one way, she would set off a plethora of magical wards, and alarms. That was only if she were lucky. Dismantling it to allow her entry, might have even more dire consequences. Closing her eyes briefly in frustration, Delta recognized that despite her own discomfort, she couldn't chance ruining this night for Oliver and Eva.

Apparently, she was in for a walk along the dark edge of the building. She would either find the entrance or the car park and simply leave. Except that her purse was safely in a changing room with her keys inside it, and her phone. Delta groaned. She was stuck here, unless she wanted to walk miles in her heels and dress, or find someone to let her inside.

Walking wasn't so bad, was it? Goosebumps moved down her arms and she held herself like that alone could ward off the cold. Couldn't the longest night of the year be a clear night that allowed the stars and moon to light up the area? It could also be warmer, she mentally amended with a shiver.

She'd only rounded one corner of the building before realizing that yes, walking would be that bad. The building blocked any lights from trickling over, and upon turning the corner, she found that only a hint more glow filled the area. She continued running her hand along the building to both guide her and let her know if another door, one perhaps with a handle, was on the wall. Her hand should feel the difference before her eyesight would adjust to the dimness.

A driver had brought them to the event, but her car had been shuttled there, available for when she left. She barely remembered the entrance to the building and knew it was a maze of event rooms, overnight rooms, and whatever else the building owners had felt inclined to add. Unfortunately for her, enhanced sight wasn't a benefit of being a witch.

The hand on the wall felt the difference seconds before her eyes could focus enough to see that it had changed to glass. Peering as closely through the windows as she could, she could barely see plants inside the frosty windows. Maybe?

Damnation, had the temperature dropped more? Delta wouldn't be surprised if it began to snow, the damp, heavy air silent, as if considering that as an option. Finally, her stiff fingers brushed a door handle in the darkness. Twisting and pulling on it didn't budge the door, and Delta nearly screamed in frustration. Dammit, she was a witch! She refused to freeze to death outside a party. Her mother would die from the shame of it.

Fuuuck. She was a witch. The cold had done a number on her—that and the turmoil of being in Malth's arms—but she refused to ponder that thought too long. She snapped her cold fingers, once, twice, and then a false snap as her fingers refused to cooperate. Blowing on her hands while she rubbed them together temporary warmed the digits. She snapped again, this time one, two, three, and drew a small circle in the air, starting at her head and trailing down. The chill subsided immediately, at least a bit. By no means was she warm, but she was no longer in danger of freezing to death.

Focusing on the door handle, she drew a not-freezing finger over the lock, feeling the mechanisms beneath her touch as she puffed a breath of air over them. She imagined she could feel them moving, feel the click of the mechanism beneath her finger, warming to her touch. Victory! Her lip curled upward in satisfaction. Since her attack, her control over magic was better than ever before. Her mother hadn't been wrong: something had happened when they'd portaled with the freed magic. Delta had been practicing, and it was becoming easier to manipulate any bits of magic she found. She wasn't unlocking the door herself; she was using the magic to push the mechanisms and once she let go of the bits of wild magic, it flitted off. Her biggest problem had been to remember that she could use the magic. Years of habits and constraints were difficult to break.

Pulling the door open, she scurried into the room, surprised it wasn't warmer, but still thankful to be indoors, after a fashion. The ground rolled under her heels like bits of… gravel? Wiggling her toes, she wished that it had been appropriate to change into socks and comfortable shoes for the reception. With a hand in front of her, she walked forward a few steps, to where a warm glow of light filtered through the darkness. Ah-ha! She touched the next glass door, which was warmer under her fingers. As she suspected, she'd found the solarium connected to the main building. It would definitely be warmer inside, and if the hints of light were anything to go by, it promised to be better lit than outside, with possibly a door back into the party or at the very least the main building.

She wasn't wrong. The solarium wasn't as warm as a tropical jungle, but it was an acceptable temperature and the tinted windows hit the low lights of the pathway, ideally leading to a way out. Concrete blocks and pea gravel marked the way in various directions in the greenhouse, and tall plants as well as the dark a few feet above hid the view in all directions. As her feet followed the pea gravel path deeper amid the plants, she briefly considered magicking herself a light but quickly dispelled the idea. The idea would have been helpful when she was stumbling through the darkness outside. Now, however, she could see well enough, and when she remained still, perhaps no one would see her either. Turning sharply into the maze that towered above her head, her feet picked up speed. She willed herself to go deeper into the year-round greenery that would give her a moment to collect herself. The lush plants were thick and healthy, and the yellow floor lights did little to hint at the colors of the flowers or leaves, but if she got out of here, she promised herself she would come back and enjoy the greenery during the day.

Behind her, the doors she'd fought to enter banged

loudly one after another, as if someone had run through, opening them and entering the same as her. She wasn't alone. Delta had been through enough recently that she couldn't assume it was a friend. There was a pause before the crunching of the pea gravel began. Whoever it was wasn't trying to hide their steps.

"Delta?" The frantic hiss of Math's voice cut through her, thank the goddess. Of course, Malthazar would follow her. Damnation. Of course, now wouldn't be the time he would leave her alone, when she stumbled around in the dark and cold due to walking out the wrong door. Embarrassment at her predicament fought with the relief of being found.

"Delta," he whispered through the humid garden as though his heart were the one breaking. "I'm sorry. I didn't realize. You were gone so long."

Malth moved closer out of the shadows so she could see him. The anguish on his face proved that, strangely, he seemed to be hurting as much as she was. "I didn't know that door led outside. I'm so sorry, and then I came to apologize…"

"You have nothing to apologize for." The steadiness of her voice surprised her. "I'm the one who keeps walking into messes."

"Don't do that." Malth's tone changed with the low, husky order. "That's your mother's voice telling you that. You fix things. You make things better. You make the world better."

His words were her undoing. While her mind

screamed to keep a distance, her body demanded otherwise. She found herself moving toward him, as if her feet had a mind of their own focused solely on him.

Malth closed the difference as well, but he didn't touch her even though barely a whisper separated their bodies. Delta could feel the heat rising from his body, and she grew frantic with the thought of touching him. Maybe feeling him against her would quench the desire she had for him. Maybe she could prove to herself that this infatuation simply needed reality to burn itself out.

"I want you one more time," she whispered, lying, knowing that one more time would never be enough, but she would take whatever crumbs he might give her. If that was what she was given, though, she would greedily take it.

At her words, the mental restraints of the man in front of her broke. Delta could see the fire light his eyes at her words, the instant he accepted what she offered.

The air itself seemed to change as his lustful eyes stared heatedly at her, warmer and deeper than her spell. Clasping her face in his hands, Malth pulled her closer to lay a kiss lightly on her head. That was the last of the gentleness as urgency took over. He ran his hands down her bare shoulders, down her hips, then back up, drawing the satin dress up her thighs. With a growl, he lifted her up, nudging her legs to open and drape themselves around him.

Wrapping her arms around his neck, Delta found herself greedily urging him closer as the warmth of his body surrounded her. Then releasing her grip, she trusted him to hold her in place as she began unraveling the bow tie around his neck and franticly unbuttoning the incandescent buttons of his crisp white shirt.

Malth released one of his hands and held her with the other arm as he pulled off first one jacket sleeve, then the other. He pulled out his shirt from his pants, tearing the final buttons free from their stitching. His skin still goosebumped from the cold.

"I hope that's not a rental." Delta smiled as she matched his urgency, running her hands down his chest as far as she could reach, her own body blocking her from reaching into his pants. Instead, she reached up to grab his head, running her fingers along his horns as he ground against her.

"Calor bulla, calor bulla," she commanded the air around them in Latin, alongside a slight gesture between her forefinger and thumb to encase and warm them in a bubble of magic. The air snapped into place around them, instantly warming her bare skin… or was that the fire in his touch?

"Wouldn't. Matter," he ground out, pulling the top of her dress to the side as he exposed her to the warmer air. "Beautiful." Pulling her upward enough that his mouth could encase the pebbled nipple, he gasped out, "You taste…"

His wet mouth covered her nipple, and Delta gave

a soft gasp as the sensation spread straight to her feverish core. Shameless, she ground herself against him, knowing he had to feel the heat of her.

Pulling himself back, he released her nipple, immediately leaving her feeling cold and missing the feel of his mouth. Confidently, he walked a few steps farther into the solarium; thankfully, he could see well in any amount of darkness. Setting her on her feet he demanded, "Hold on," before placing his tuxedo jacket on a bench off the pathway.

Taking her hand, he urged her to a narrow bench and into a sitting position before having her lie back. Confused, Delta complied, but not before rising up on her elbows to look at him.

With lust thick in his eyes, he stared down at her. She already knew her hair was a mess, and her lips were swollen from the few moments between them. Her dress was hiked to her waist; Delta knew she looked as wanton as she felt.

"Gods and goddesses, you're beautiful." Malth knelt between her legs, nudging her knees apart with his hands. "Lace and satin," he murmured, "of course, both." Pushing her dress up higher, he ran a finger down the lace of her panties, through the wet warmth between her legs.

Delta squirmed, embarrassed by the instantaneous moan, and attempted to push his hand away. "I…" He was burning her up, and happily she would burn alive.

"No, don't ever hide this from me. You don't need to hide anything from me."

He slid the panties down her legs, allowing his hands to linger on every part of her, as if he was memorizing the feeling of her body as Delta whimpered from his exploration. Lifting each heeled foot, he placed the leg over his shoulder, before sliding her closer to the edge. Without taking his eyes off her, Malth placed his mouth on her and slowly licked upward before devouring her like a dying man.

Tilting her head back, Delta allowed herself to be swept away, reaching down only to grab his head with her thumbs placed on his horns as she held on and allowed him to pull her over the edge.

CHAPTER TWENTY-NINE

Wolf's foot is the bud or leaf of the bugleweed. No wolves need be harmed.

Being in Malthazar's arms as he sat on the ground with his back against the bench where he'd done wicked, wicked things to her, felt like home. He didn't even seem to notice the cold, and he'd carefully adjusted her dress, smoothing it downward before wrapping her in his jacket and pulling her back against him.

Leaning down to lay a kiss on her neck, he noted tentatively, "You don't even seem to have a scar." Running a finger down her collarbone, he traced the spot where the knife had exited her chest. "Did your back scar?" He lay another kiss on the side of her head, as if he couldn't bear to keep his lips off her.

"As if," Delta scoffed, immediately feeling a trace of guilt over her dismissive attitude toward her mother. They'd made great strides, but they had years of bad habits to overcome. "Mother doesn't exactly allow for imperfections; a healer's job is to fix the outside as well as the inside. It still twinges inside, but muscles and sinews are more difficult to stitch back together than skin."

She didn't want to tell him she'd scarred lightly; the low lights hid things even from his superior eyesight. Despite her mother's best efforts, the skin was faded and stretched thinner. Perhaps with time the marks would disappear completely, but if this was her last time with Malth, she didn't want to leave him with anything but perfection.

"Even with scars, you're still perfect."

Delta knew he wasn't talking about physical scars, but she didn't press him to spell out her faults and shortcomings. Goddess knew, she did enough of that herself.

Delta allowed herself to melt against his body, relaxing against him, enveloping herself in the warmth and feelings of home he offered.

Slowly and seeming to carefully chose his words, Malth informed Delta quietly, "I have to leave. Tonight. Tonight, I'm going away for a time. A very long time. I don't think we'll see each other again." His body tensed as he amended firmly, as if reminding himself as well, "We will not see each other again."

Delta tore herself away from his comforting body, as if he'd slapped her. "What do you mean?" Her voice was sharp as she searched his face for answers. Always one step forward with him and two steps back.

He came to me. He followed me. Yet immediately he's telling me he's walking away once again?

"It means, my precious, that I'm a danger to everyone here. Hell knows I'm alive and they know I still portal. They will want me back. They want me back and they want the portal stone." Sighing, Malth tried to pull Delta back into his tight grasp, as if he could hold onto the moment longer, but she refused to give an inch. He'd broken this moment as well as her heart, and now he wanted to hold her?

Staring up at the sky, Malth continued, "Already they've been searching for me. Enough years had passed, hell probably assumed I was dead and gone. But now, after my big return to hell, they know. So tonight, the only thing I can do is disappear in a very big way. Know that you've been the best thing that's ever happened to me. The best for me, but the best thing for you is to never see me again."

"For me to never see you again?" Delta asked incredulously, surprised at how fast the mood could change with a few words. "Malth," she asked sharply, "what are your plans? Hide away and then sneak around to spy on *me*? Catch a glimpse of me while I think you're gone forever, while I pretend you don't exist? That *we* didn't exist?"

When he didn't answer right away, Delta closed her eyes, letting out another sigh. *That's exactly what he plans to do.*

The silence lay thick in the air between them while she waited his confirmation. She wasn't going to let him off easy.

Finally, he softly admitted, "Yes. Not right away, but maybe in a few years, after things have cooled off. Knowing that maybe I could see you from even afar, someday, makes it easier to go. If I thought I'd never see you again, I don't know how I could bear to go."

Dammit!

"Goddess, no!" Pulling herself off him, she pummeled his chest in frustration with both fists, but annoyingly enough, he didn't even flinch. "I'm not okay with this. I don't get to see you? How is that fair? How do you even know that hell is trying to find you?" Delta was peppering questions at him faster than he could answer, but she couldn't stop herself.

"Babe, they've been following me since our visit. It took multiple jumps to hide a trail. Even tonight, there are three trackers outside the gates, outside the boundary's protection, waiting for me to leave. I don't want to leave you. But to keep you safe, I will. If they knew what you meant to me…" Malth trailed off, clearly not wanting to spell out the alternative.

"But how, if you laid out a fake trail? How do they know you're here tonight?"

Hesitating, Malth admitted, "I jumped into hell before I jumped here. I needed them to follow me here tonight. They're assuming that I went through hell because my stone can't—couldn't—portal me on its own, before. So, they're laying a trap now, waiting until I drive through the gates."

The hands Delta had used to hit Malth covered her

face. "Malth." Her voice wavered as she fought back what he was giving up.

"I'm not going back to hell. I'm disappearing tonight." Malth's words were meant to be reassuring, but Delta found she couldn't quite believe him.

"If you're disappearing, take me with you," she demanded, fighting back tears as she twisted herself completely around to face him. "I want to go with you."

He shook his head. She knew his answer before he even said the words. "You don't want to go where I go and live the life I do. You deserve so much more."

Poking him in the chest, Delta insisted, "Why do you get to decide that? Why don't you understand that without you, I have no life? For the first time in my life, I feel everything. I feel wanted, needed, loved, and I feel the same about you. *I want you and need you.*"

Poking him repeatedly in the chest finally caused him to reach down and hold her hand still.

Frustrated, she added, "I finally know how Rose Tyler felt with the Doctor in *Doctor Who*. Being separated from him was worse than… than anything. Saying a permanent goodbye? Saying I'll never see you again? Why would you *choose* that for me? For you? A life together is what I want. I don't care if I never play another video game or role-playing game again in my life. A life with you is all the adventure I need."

Closing his eyes, Malth asked, "Who is this doctor

you keep talking about?"

Despite how close she was to tears, Delta barked out a hint of laughter. "Sometimes it's impossible to believe that you and Oliver are such close friends if he hasn't introduced you to some of his favorites. Take me with you and I'll show you the Doctor. You can learn all about him." Futilely, she dangled the offering at him. Oliver had been the one to introduce her to the Doctor and his companions years ago. His love of television wasn't a new thing; only since he'd met Eva had he begun to actually read more books.

Closing his eyes for a long second, then opening them, Malth pleaded with Delta to understand. "I can't ask you to give up—"

"Give up what?" Delta's tone wasn't sharp. It was pleading and she hated herself for begging him to understand, but damnation, the thick-headed fool couldn't or wouldn't get it. "Give up what? I'm on a hamster wheel, spinning in circles, finding ways to wear myself out without actually doing anything. Keeping out of the coven's sight. Making sure not to remind anyone I exist. Dropping whatever nothingness that occupies me to do a job for Oliver and then returning to my nothingness."

Malth brushed Delta's hair back from her face as she blinked back the tears that threatened to erupt. She didn't want his pity. She thought they were past that, more than that. "Malth, I…"

Holding her face tenderly in his rough hands, Malth gently kissed her forehead, moving down to her eyes, a quick kiss to her nose. "Delta, I'm leaving because I *love* you. I do this to keep you safe."

Delta scoffed but couldn't bring herself to pull away. "Safety isn't living. What you're suggesting is that I slowly die alone, without you." Closing her eyes, she pleaded, "What can I do to make you understand? I love you too. I love you more than the half-life I'm living. I don't want to live knowing you're out there somewhere without me. If you love me like you say you do, you won't leave me. I want to face whatever you're facing together with you. Side by side." Delta enunciated the words, hoping the half-demon would understand.

"I almost lost you. Delta, do you understand what it felt like seeing you with that knife running through you? I almost lost you and I was helpless. I nearly got you killed."

"Malthazar." Delta softened her tone in shock, touching his face, forcing him to meet her eyes. "You didn't put me in danger. You *saved* me. I would have bled out right there on the ground in Minnesota. No one there would have lifted a finger to help me. You were the one who risked everything to save my life. How could I not trust you more than anyone else in my life?"

Delta could see Malth begin to soften, begin to believe that her love was greater than the half-life she led. That his love was better than the half-life he led. Together, they could be whole. Holding her breath, she waited while he considered, emotions flitting across his face before he wiped them away. All that remained was a resolute frown, and Delta's heart dropped. He'd locked it all away.

"It's time for me to go." Using the bench at his back, he bent his elbows, hoisting himself up with it, at the last second wrapping an arm around her, bringing her to a standing position as well.

He left her there. Not right there, of course; he led her through the solarium and through the maze of hallways to deposit her directly inside the doorway of the wedding reception. Malth held her hand the entire way and lingered long enough to squeeze her hand against his chest before kissing it one last time. The lavender scent hanging heavy in the air from the plethora of flowers that lined the entryway would now forever remind her of her broken heart.

Delta tried to draw a breath, but her chest rebelled against the very air it needed.

He may well have ripped her heart out and thrown it on the floor of the ballroom for all to see. How could Malth hold her and say the things he'd said to her and then leave so easily? Had she imagined him holding her and loving her? Delta cursed her weakness but knew he suffered the same as her. He wasn't lying to her, but he did see this as the only option.

"Damn you, Malthazar. Damn you to the hell you're hiding from," she muttered, shivering as her body adjusted to the temperature and despite Malth's tuxedo jacket still wrapped around her. Closing her eyes, she rubbed the jacket against her face, breathing in the scent of him.

Is this this how our story will end? The thought echoed through her head, bouncing around as she considered. Delta didn't deny for a second that Malth's heart was breaking too. He couldn't fathom that someone would choose him. Choose him over anything or anyone else. He'd made the decision not to allow anyone a choice to save himself from the hurt. Then dropped the bombshell that he loved her, as if that wouldn't rip her heart out.

Fuck that, Delta thought. *Fuck all that. The Witch Who Wasn't Supposed to Be.* That's what they whispered about her, but maybe, just maybe, she was. And this was what she was supposed to do. Had everything in her life led up to this moment, this choice? Malth and her against hell itself?

If Malth planned to portal out, he would have done it right there, but instead he'd walked away. He must have driven here and planned to drive away, more than likely making certain that whoever followed him knew he'd left the party and didn't go after the wrong person.

The room had fallen silent. Oliver and Eva were making speeches, obviously skipping the scheduled best man and maid of honor speeches. Delta felt a twinge of guilt, but it wasn't like she'd prepared anything anyway.

"Thank you all for coming." Oliver's voice

boomed across the room, echoing before he cursed at the microphone, drawing laughter from the guests. It wasn't often one got to see a vampire such as Oliver Patrick make a misstep.

Despite not seeing them, Delta knew Eva would be smiling gently at the man she loved.

Eva's voice filled the room, not quite as booming as Oliver's; she held the microphone farther from her mouth. "Yes, thank you all for coming. It means a latte to us"—she paused, allowing the crowd the chance to laugh—"that you've all come to celebrate with us during this solstice. It shouldn't come as any surprise, but the coffee bar will be opening up along the south side of the ballroom, for anyone who needs a jolt of caffeine to stay up all night with us, or to simply enjoy. And it's a looonnnggg shot."

She paused. "Okay, espresso jokes might go over everyone's heads. But I thank the gods and goddesses for bringing Oliver and me together. Not everyone gets a chance to love and be loved like this and for that, I'm eternally thankful. Because we're the perfect blend." More laughter and polite applause, before Oliver began speaking again, but Delta wasn't listening. It was as if Eva was solidifying Delta's choice. If you were given this chance at love, you didn't walk away from it.

Firm in the resolution that leaving was the right thing to do for her as well as him, Delta began to turn away from the entryway. Eva and Oliver would understand why she didn't say goodbye, and if Oliver didn't, then Eva would explain it. To her surprise, her mother stood in the hallway, looking at her with her well-schooled expression once again. Delta wondered if Hecate could hold off on lectures on appropriate behavior and actions one time.

Just as Delta would have walked around her to avoid collision, Hecate stepped closer to her, holding up a single hand as if requesting a moment. "Delta?"

Sighing, Delta stopped but didn't turn completely toward her. "Yes, Hecate?" She didn't have the time nor the patience for this right now.

Her mother stepped closer, but still not close enough to touch. "Delta, where are you going? I've been… worried."

Delta turned to face her. Hecate's face did, in fact, show a mixture of worry and relief. Had she actually been worried about her?

"Hecate, I'm going with him, and I don't know when I'll be back." Delta spoke the words out loud, the finality of them settling over her and releasing the anxious energy she felt. Relief. This was the right thing to do.

"I thought you would," Hecate admitted. "You should follow your heart. I'm… happy for you. I'm so proud of you. I wish I'd done things differently, daughter. But know that I love you. I've loved you since the moment you came screaming into the world. I… I wasn't strong enough or good enough to be the mother I should have been."

Looking at her mother in surprise, Delta saw her.

Really saw her, a powerful witch who had been told since the beginning of her life that she was destined to lead and that she was permitted a single child. A single female child who would inherit all of her power and the leadership mantle. A momentary indiscretion or a forbidden love—it didn't matter which—had toppled the world as she knew it to be. Her mother was looking old, she realized. The set of her shoulders wasn't quite as tall as it once was. Her vivid green eyes didn't hold the same shine, and the wrinkles framing them were deeper than they once were. Even under the dim lighting, worry lines creased her forehead and around her mouth, lines that surely hadn't been there before. With a jolt, Delta realized the next time she saw her mother she would be the coven's Crone. The mantel of leadership that she'd clung to so strongly would be given to her daughter. Her only living daughter.

For the first time in her adulthood, Delta hugged her mother tightly.

Hecate's body went rigid for a second before she relaxed and returned the hug with a ferociousness that surprised Delta. "I love you, my beautiful, precious child. May the goddess guide and protect you both on your journey."

She released the hug just as quickly, pulling her shoulders upright and once again embracing the mantel of the coven's Mother. "Go. Hurry and go, don't let him get away." She urged her daughter forward. "Follow the green arrows in the low corners of the hallway," she suggested.

Delta blinked back a few shocked tears, wiping away a stray one that somehow had made its way down her face. "I love you too, Mama," she whispered before turning toward the lot, knowing the clock was ticking down to find Malthazar before he left forever. Looking down, she realized her mother was right. Barely discernible light green arrows inches above the floor pointed the way. Maybe she did have a chance of reaching him.

Her heart beat faster and faster in her chest and the ache in her lung reminded her how severely she'd been injured a few weeks before. She paused only to pull her heels off. Once free from the confines of the shoes, she could run faster and the ache in her lungs grew tighter. Shoes in hand, she ran so fast her hair loosened from the hair pins so strategically placed hours earlier. Giggles peeled uncontrollably at the thought of her leaving a trail of hairpins so no others would get lost leaving the ballroom.

A snap decision had her heading for the gatehouse. The only exit from the compound, better to stop him there than to try to catch up to him on the grounds or in the parking lot.

Cutting through the nearly dead outdoor gardens, she stepped between the rising gate in front of the oncoming headlights. Hand to chest, she gasped, trying to catch her pained breath, and prayed that he would see her.

The brakes squealed as the car stopped abruptly,

blinding her with the headlights.

CHAPTER THIRTY

Hairs of a hamadryas baboon sounds very difficult to obtain, unless you know it's dill seed.

*M*omentarily, Malth had idled the flashy sports car, waiting to switch gears and tear out of the lot in a screech of tires. With enough noise and flash, he ensured the squad of demons who sat approximately half a mile down the drive, outside the protective magic, would know he was coming. They truly believed he had no idea they were this close or had laid a trap to capture him. For one moment, had any one of them considered how he'd stayed alive and out of sight for decades? Clearly, hell's smartest minions hadn't been sent to retrieve him. Between their brains and their egos, they were going to be fairly easy to trick. Again.

The goal was to have them think he was attempting to race away from them, but the truth was much more. He and Oliver had timed out how fast he needed to be going when he reached them as well as how fast he needed to exit the gate to line up the speeds perfectly. Timing was everything. They needed to see him and know he was coming.

Entering had been through a barrage of checkpoints held by Sebastian's wolf shifter employees from the physical security side of Oliver's business. Leaving was as simple as driving out the automated gates. Security inside and outside the gates would resume after his exit. But for now, it appeared that sloppy oversight had left the only way out unguarded. As if.

Shifting gears roughly, he shot forward with a deep breath, ready for what was next. If by chance it all fell apart, at least those he loved would be safe. *She* would be safe.

A dark shadow launched itself in front of the car. With instincts honed in hell, Malth stomped the brakes with both feet. Heart in his chest, he squinted through the headlines, attempting to determine what or who had been foolish enough to step in front of a speeding car. It should be impossible for a demon to enter the grounds, but he himself had done enough impossible things to know anything was possible.

It took a moment for the angry redhead who stood blocking his escape to come into view. Her once smooth lavender gown was hiked up to her hips and her hair had escaped its confines, either due to their earlier escapades or her hoofing it across the grounds to catch up with him. His headlights lighting her up surely blinded her, but walking with a slight limp, she confidently approached the passenger side of the car.

What was she doing? She shouldn't be running, even if she didn't hate it. Less than a week ago, she'd been bedbound. Acting like he'd chosen to stop and pick her up before he left the party, Delta wrenched the passenger side door open. It nearly slammed back closed before she stopped it with her hip. Sliding in, she slammed the door behind her, suggesting she had no intention of getting out again. Wordlessly, she turned with her strappy shoes in one hand, preparing to launch them in the back seat.

Before she released the shoes, Delta froze as she looked in the back seat. Her mouth opened and closed slightly, as if she were choosing her next words carefully or, perhaps, she'd been made speechless again. He seemed to do that to her; the thought warmed him.

Tilting her head back at him as the shoes continued to dangle from her fingers, she casually asked, "Do I want to know why there is a body in the back seat charmed to look like you? And is it going the whole way with us?"

Malth couldn't stop the half-grin from forming on his face. "I thought it was a pretty good charm. And no, no, it's not. We're going different directions."

Using the hand still holding her shoes, Delta gestured to herself, "Witch sees magic, takes apart magic. I see right through those things. It is 'we,' correct?"

"I mean, it could be if you want it to be," Malth finally admitted the words. What if giving her the choice meant she didn't choose him? This time, hope made his heart speed up.

"Who else could 'we' be then?"

A tiny meow answered her question before Malth could. Both their heads dropped toward his lap—hers in surprise, his in concern. The hellcat was young to be away from its real mother, but he'd been left no other choice.

The witch he'd hired to babysit the kitten during the event had assured him it would be fine under her care for a few hours. Apparently, hellcats fell under a different set of rules then hellhounds and could be seen by witches. She'd been set up in a private room after being vetted by Oliver and apparently Hecate as well, as a witch with a strong affinity to animals. The baby had been fed mere moments before his arrival, and the witch assured him that the kitten's deep sleep was natural for her age. Still, he'd cupped her carefully in his hands as he took her to his car, before deciding that his lap would be the best place for her during their short drive.

"You have a kitten? Eva wasn't making that up?" Delta voice cracked when she asked the question, lowering her tone as she stared in surprise at the tiny orange, gray, and white piece of patchwork burrowing its way into the warmth of his lap.

"I have a hellcat," Malth corrected, waiting for her response. Why did he want her approval on this now that she knew? Did she sound surprised because he couldn't take care of such a thing or surprised that he added full-time responsibility for a life?

"Baby-Big Boy?" Understanding flashed through her eyes as she glanced up at him before her eyes flitted back between the dead demon in the back seat wearing his face and the hellcat in his lap in an attempt to piece together the puzzle before her.

Malth nodded. "The hellhound decided I needed her or she needed me. Not sure which, but we're stuck with each other now." His hand brushed the tiny bits of white and gray fur down on the sleeping kitten's head. "None of us have any idea how to send her back and the hellhound doesn't seem inclined to do so."

Delta nodding again, still glancing between the man, the hellcat, and the body. "As are we—stuck with each other, that is." After another glance at the back seat, she opted to drop her shoes in front of her. "Seatbelt or no seatbelt?" she asked as her hand hovered over the shoulder strap.

"Are you sure?" Did she understand what he was asking of her? There would be no going back.

"More than anything."

"Do you trust me?" Malth repeated her words back to her, the same question she'd asked him, and the moment he knew he did trust her inexplicably.

Her smile filled his soul. "More than anything," she promised. "Pinkie promise." She wiggled her little finger at him with a very Delta-like giggle.

This, this moment here, was what absolute joy felt like. "No seatbelt. Just hold my hand. Hold on tight, and hold onto the little one."

And she did.

Chapter Thirty-One

Sometimes graveyard dust is just graveyard dust.

Simple and with little fanfare, the funerals were held.

Delta's event was open to only her coven members under the full moon, but a memorial service open to friends and family was well attended. Friends she'd gamed with in real life and online, a few dignitaries who knew her relationship to Hecate, while vampires and shifters alike paid their respects to the family. Her old college roommate even flew in from Utah, wailing that so many years had passed and she hadn't made the journey. All of them were in disbelief that someone so vibrate, so full of life, could be gone in a flash. The world would be duller without her and her frankness. Flowers filled the memorial, huge bouquets that bespoke of the void she would leave behind, their cloying scent filling the room like her personality once had. No one whispered of her unusual birth or existence. They only spoke of loss. No one complained about her wild hair and over-the-top personality. They admired her beauty and her excitement for life.

Malthazar's funeral had less fanfare.

No memorial marked the loss, no one spoke, just a service in which his good friend Oliver called for the great beyond to welcome his friend. Hecate and Athena, the Mother and the Maiden, attended out of respect and diplomacy. A few of Oliver's employees who had worked with Malth in the line of duty saw his send-off. When it was finished, no one sang his accolades. No one really knew what he'd done during his missions or what he'd done in his free time or even what his favorite snack had been. He couldn't be considered heroic or even that caring or personable. Everyone agreed that he appeared fair, and after the service was over, they carried on with their day.

There were no bodies for either. The explosion and flames that engulfed the car had ensured that every bit of it as well as them was incinerated to a smallish pile of ash and unrecognizable molten chunks of metal. Whatever trap had been set had been poorly done and reacted with whatever magic had been laid on the car, causing a chain reaction that ensured no one would walk away from the accident.

If he'd known the explosion would be that grand, he wouldn't have bothered with the decoy body. But it did take care of the remains of the low-level demon who had thought he could overtake Malthazar on his own. By the time anyone noticed him missing, no one would be able to add two and two together.

At least, that was how Malthazar imagined the

scenes to play out. He couldn't be sure. He wasn't there, and it would be years before he could ask anyone in attendance.

Malth would never forget the completeness that settled into his chest as Delta seated herself snuggly into the seat next to him that night. "Are you sure?"

"More than anything."

"Do you trust me?"

Still holding her hand, he shifted the gear of the car, smoothly moving through the gates. Revving it, he shifted to second gear and, with a side glance added, "Soon."

As the long driveway opened up before them, he slid it into third and at the same time, he released the steering wheel, holding it for a split second with his left knee. In one smooth motion, he pulled a surprised Delta toward him with the hand holding her. Laying his mouth on hers as his left arm wrapped around her, he pulled her and the hell kitten close.

Delta's shock of surprise against his mouth didn't surprise him, the careening of the car didn't surprise him, and neither did the implosion around him.

In a blink, the heat of the flames surrounded them, and just as quickly, Delta and Malth blinked out of existence as the car burned away any proof of their existence as well as any magical trails left behind. Later, Malthazar liked to imagine the surprise on the demon trackers' faces when their well-laid plan imploded in front of them, fueled by other magics set upon the car, as well as a better set counter plan. One that ended with flames so hot the pavement couldn't be touched for days, melting and warping it so deeply that several dozen yards needed replaced in either direction.

No, what surprised him was Delta pulling him closer to her as they portaled from one place to the next. After the second jump, with the hellcat tucked in her elbow, she pressed herself so deeply against him, he wasn't sure where one of them ended and the other began. Then they fell… and fell… and fell.

For two days, they portaled from one spot to another, stopping only to eat, rest, and feed the kitten before beginning again. The magic infused when Ibis had disintegrated had to go somewhere. As Delta had explained, magic didn't cease to exist, and when it exploded at her unraveling and Malth had portaled, the magic had gone with them, into them, changing them both. The portal stone had infused itself into his body. Even if the demons caught up with him, they would never be able to take ownership of the stone. It was a part of him now. Remove it from his body and it would be nothing, and when he died it would die with him. Although after Delta's very thorough examination, she'd announced it would be eons before that happened, sealing it with a kiss.

Delta hadn't escaped the magic unscathed, although it was weeks before she realized the magnitude of her own changes. The very magic that had been used to enhance other witches' powers now magnified her own. Magic effortlessly unraveled under her glance. Powerful spells that had once taken days to break apart now took hours. Those that had taken hours now took minutes. And a weaker spell or potion? As if it didn't exist in the first place. They never recovered the stone he wore around his neck. That night, when Delta had almost died, it had been lost in the shuffle, buried under leaves or in the dirt. The stone used to enhance and hone his magical tracking was no longer needed due to the magic he'd taken into himself.

They finally stopped at a beach. Delta wasn't sure if they were on an island or the shore of a larger spot. She didn't care. She smiled at Malth, a glorious smile that made him think he was the most, the most everything in the world, and told him, "As long as I'm with you."

They settled in to relax and nurse a growing hellcat. It was a beach day, every day. Delta sat under the shade of an umbrella the beach house had provided. She slathered sunscreen on every inch of her body, while Malth lay next to her in full sun, soaking up the sunshine he never seemed to get enough of. He found he couldn't stop looking at her with a smile on his face.

Pulling her sunglasses down, Delta examined her drink, frowning. Sticking a finger in the glass, she stirred in circles until the outside was white with chill. She sucked the droplets of the now cold drink on her finger while Malth watched. Everything about her made him hard with desire.

"Stop it," she demanded after she popped her finger out of her mouth. "You can't possibly."

A deep chuckle escaped Malthazar before he could stop it. Damn, he laughed around her more than he had the rest of his entire life. "Yes, yes, I could. But you need your rest." He swiped her drink for his own warm drink. With an exaggerated sigh buffered by a small smile, she again swirled her finger around, chilling the drink. This time, before she could stick it in her mouth, he caught her finger and slowly licked the sweet, ice-cold droplets from her finger. Her well of magic was now so deep that she could chill drink after drink and never run low. He knew on her morning walks, where she insisted she go alone for meditation, she'd been tentatively testing the limits on her magic—if there were any, and he doubted there was. He hadn't asked her the results and knew Delta would share when she was ready.

"My hair still smells burnt." Every few days like clockwork, the same observation, not a complaint so much as an observation. She'd experimented with the plants and herbs she'd found in the jungle surrounding the cottage and on the beach, but within a few days, the smell came back. "Maybe if you hadn't gone out with such a bang," she teased as she pulled a curl around, sniffing it questioningly, as if trying to determine the exact smell.

Soon Malth would explain that it wasn't a leftover lingering scent from the car explosion and magical burning. It was brimstone and the scent of her, part of him and part of her, a combination of the two of them. A pairing brought about through each of their heritages and their trip through hell as well as their mating. They were forever entwined.

"Do my back," Delta ordered, tossing him the industrial-size sunscreen she'd made as one of her first purchases when he declared this was where they would settle… for a while anyway.

Rolling over, she settled her head down on her arms, knowing he wouldn't hesitate to rub the skin protection all over her body. Of course, he thought with a slight grin, her backside needed extra layers.

After the third time of applying the lotion to the hint of cheek that snuck out from her emerald-green bikini bottoms—that had been one of his first purchases—Delta popped up on her elbows and twisted around to look at him over her gold sunglasses. "Any regrets yet?"

She asked him this every day.

Malth had none, but he knew she needed the reassurance. The day would come where she didn't but for now, he lay a kiss on her hip, then peppered kisses up her back and nuzzled her neck as she giggled. "Not a one," he promised in her ear before sucking on it and letting loose with a loud pop that caused her to laugh loudly as she wiped away the remaining wetness.

"And you?" He only asked because she expected him to. But he knew in his heart that she had none.

"Never." Delta smiled. "Although starting an online gamer profile from zero is sort of a bitch, and if one more dude calls me newbie or newb I may drop a curse into their system."

She was serious, one of the many things he loved about her. "Of course you will. Anyone who provokes W1tchb1tch123 deserves a curse or two. That's why I love you."

Delta rolled back over to her back with a serious look that nearly had Malth ready to take a step back. Were the online gamers really that bothersome? He could get an encrypted message to Oliver and have them taken care of. Not *taken care of*, of course, but maybe some drained bank accounts or shady background stuff.

"Malthazar, seriously, if—"

"No," he interrupted firmly. "Don't borrow trouble from tomorrow. Today we drink, we soak up the sunshine—well, some of us do—make love, and enjoy the life we're given." Looking at Delta, he reminded himself that she still wasn't as sure of herself as she projected.

"Tomorrow or next week or next month, when the magic beckons, *we* will return to the mission. For now, the boys are safe with Athena and the coven, hell thinks I'm dead, and I have my beautiful, wild redheaded witch keeping me on my toes."

For the first time in his life, Malth meant it. He could live for today, and whatever tomorrow brought, he wouldn't face it alone.

"What do you think Hecate and Athena are doing right now?" Delta asked pensively.

Did she have regrets about how things had been left? Questions, asked and unasked, had been answered. The women had come to some sort of truce or acceptance. While they were never going to be a picture-perfect family, after decades, they'd come to an unusual acceptance of the family they were. Delta claimed that in itself had made it the perfect time for her to leave, split before the walls went back up and the mistrust and unease returned.

"Still publicly mourning you, but secretly jealous that you're the princess who got her happily ever after." Hecate had been in on his plan from the beginning—Oliver and Hecate both. Oliver had the firepower and Hecate the magic. Hecate knew when she encouraged Delta to follow her heart that it would take her daughter away for a long time. Surely, she'd told Athena that her sister lived, but it might be decades before they could contact one another. Malthazar would miss the time he'd spent with Oliver, but he'd lived without the friendship before and he would again until they could meet again.

Meow, chirped their tiny hell kitten, who had slept nestled up against the warmth of Malth's leg, enjoying the extra body heat as well as the sunshine. She stretched deeply, before kneading her paws against the seat of the chair.

"Big stretches," Delta told the tiny kitten. "I wonder what makes a hellcat different from a regular cat? Just that she likes the heat more?" She waved a hand around her head in irritation as a large, buzzing fly flew between them. The fly caught the kitten's attention and her head whipped back and forth, watching the annoying insect. "I should make a spell…" Delta began.

The gift of the hellcat hadn't come with instructions, apparently, only orders. Between the two of them, they were sharing the often-time-consuming task of nursing the kitten. What it would eat after kitten formula was anyone's guess, and Delta really hoped it would take to eating regular kitten food soon.

The flying bug landed a few inches from the now still kitten, whose ears laid back at her attempt to flatten herself into Malth's chair. Delta prepared to zap the bug with a finger, but the tiny predator beat her to it. With a hiss, she pounced forward, easily covering the short distance before the fly could react. Smacking both paws on top of the insect, she hissed again, this time with a small amount of gray smoke billowing out of her mouth. Opening her mouth impossibly wide, the kitten caught the bug as it tried to wiggle free of her paws, eating it with three chomps before swallowing exaggeratedly.

"Widget, your first kill?!" Delta excitedly exclaimed as the kitten's tiny pink tongue darted out, trying to lick every bit of the bug off her face.

"Not Widget," Malthazar deadpanned. Delta wouldn't give up trying out names for the kitten. "She'll know her name when she knows it." He rubbed two fingers on the kitten's head, smiling proudly at the little one, who responded with a tiny purr. "Plus, she won't be this size forever; we can't have a hellcat with a cutesy little name."

"What if she wants a cutesy little name?"

"She won't."

"But what if she does?"

"Then it will be like having a nine-hundred-pound hellhound named Baby Boy," Malth answered with a shudder.

Delta's eyes grew wide. "Is that how big he's going to get?"

Shaking his head, Malth responded, "We can only hope he stops growing then. The magic that feeds him could make him enormous." Scooping up the kitten, he snuggled the fuzzy little creature to his chest. "Thankfully, our little Fatal Fury won't get that big."

"No, absolutely not. We are *not* naming that sweet little girl Fatal Fury."

"Why not? She made her first kill. She's quite young for that. She's probably advanced," Malth teased. "She's almost ready to go on rescues with me."

"Yeah, no. We'll keep trying names, and she's not nearly old enough to go on rescues. She still trips over her own feet and goes to sleep when she falls down."

Malthazar waited a beat before asking with a whisper, "How about you? Have you thought about going on rescues with me?" The kitten had stopped moving against his chest, and if her slow breathing was any indication, she'd already settled against him, falling asleep as she listened to his heartbeat.

Delta took off her sunglasses and squinted up at

him to examine his face. She seemed to consider, before choosing her next words carefully. "Is it time again?"

Malth nodded once. "Not yet, but soon."

Shaking her head in the affirmative, the corner of Delta's mouth quirked upward. "I can't imagine doing anything else with anyone else."

Malth heart paused for a moment. She was his and he was hers, now and forever.

"Good. I'm glad to hear that, because I think it might be somewhere cold."

"Nooooo," Delta groaned, the noise startling the kitten awake. Her eyes flashed red before she slowly blinked and her normal dark color returned. "Oh my gosh, snap! I wonder if her name could be any of the spirits that guide cats?"

Malth stroked the kitten again before shrugging. "Your guess is as good as mine. Actually, probably better, since I don't know the names. You're the scholar. List them out and see if she responds."

Delta turned on her side to gain a better view of the kitten, who let out a tiny yawn, her pink tongue darting around white teeth. Most of the time, it was hard to imagine she was anything other than a regular cat.

"All right, our little hellcat, how about Lilith?"

Nothing.

"Bastet?" Maybe it was an obvious choice.

Another yawn, and the hell kitten tilted her head, as if daring Delta to continue guessing.

"Greta." It was a stretch, but maybe?

"Pekhat?"

No. The kitten closed her eyes, as if the entire thing was too exhausting to stay awake through. Delta frantically racked her brain for more options, before the moment was lost. "Hecate? Artemis?"

The tiny calico hellcat's eyes shot open, flickering between red and black before burning red. Her ears pointed forward, following the sound of…

"Oh shit," Delta moaned, as Malth began laughing so deeply that he rattled the kitten attempting to relax on his chest. She hissed, letting out another soft stream of sulfur before digging her claws into his chest to balance herself. "Which one was it?"

Delta's hand flew over her mouth and she shook her head. "No, no, no." Slapping a hand against Malth's leg, she demanded, "You have to stop laughing. Which one was her name? Did she choose a name?"

"I think she did."

Delta groaned, "On the bright side, if it's Hecate it will be decades before Mother knows she shares her name with a hellcat. Or centuries even."

Drawing Malth's hand to her mouth, Delta lightly kissed his knuckles. "I love you, my demon. Today, tomorrow and forever." Delta reminded him of that fact daily on the beach.

Holding her jaw, Malth leaned in closer, "I never knew what I was missing until I met you. Love isn't a strong enough word."

Delta smiled as she nuzzled against his hand, "I mean I did die for you, so you're going to have to come up with some words or something."

Malth's smile nearly broke his face, "For now then, know that I love you with all of my heart, and I will spend an eternity finding a way to match your sacrifice."

That was the truth of it. Malth would thank the gods daily for giving him the gift of a smart-mouth fiery witch to love and be loved by. Leaning in closer, he caught her mouth for a kiss. A kiss that promised he would spend all his days, showing her how much he loved her.